THE ULTIMATE EXIT STRATEGY

A VIRGINIA KELLY MYSTERY

BY

NIKKI BAKER

Bella
BOOKS

Ferndale, Michigan
2001

Bella Books, Inc.
P.O. Box 201007
Ferndale, MI 48220

Printed in the United States of America on acid-free paper
First Edition

Editor: Lila Empson
Cover designer: Bonnie Liss (Phoenix Graphics)

ISBN 1-931513-03-1

Baker is back.
Thanks to Kelly, Bella, and Juliet.

Acknowledgments

The quote on page 134 is from *The Lover* by Marguerite Duras, translated by Barbara Bray, Pantheon Books, New York, translation copyright 1985 by Random House, Inc. The passage used is from pages 4–5.

I

I went down not so hard, really. Gently enough that it felt almost peaceful — the way they say it feels to drown. I remembered considering exactly this in those few slow-moving seconds it took for my body to crumple, an oddly unhurried, unharried thought as I dropped the short distance of my height to the cool, hard floor. It was as if my mind were a prism, perfectly focusing a million coursing streams of time through the blink of an eye, like tons of water in the narrowing nozzle of a fire hose. My thoughts came intensely, a flood, carrying the sordid debris of events that had led to this unfortunate position. I imagined for a moment it was the force of all that sudden clarity that held me helplessly pressed against the floor. But really, I had just fallen — the way people are always falling, with every step, a whole lifetime of lurching forward and handily regaining our balance, just seconds before we crash chin first. I'd stepped away from Wesley Winslow's bathroom sink, and this time I couldn't stop myself. On this occasion, my timing was off in so many ways.

Queen of the road. Oddly the last thought I'd had was of Naomi singing, the memory of a few days before, Columbus Day. She had been sitting Indian-style, crooning hoarsely, *No girls, no pool, no pets*, reinventing this musical list of misfortunes in a way she clearly believed was very clever.

Ain't got no cigarettes. This, Naomi caterwauled most ruefully as she had planned the next day to embark on the difficult regimen of smoking cessation her internist had demanded.

I was reading aloud the cautionary selections from the Nicoderm patient information — a flimsy paper pamphlet folded about a million times to accommodate its inclusion in the Nicoderm packaging — by way of homemade aversion therapy: *It is possible to get too much Nicotine (an overdose), especially if you use the Nicoderm Patch and smoke at the same time* — The threats of various dangers continued for a good many more scary paragraphs, rendered in tiny black print, and illustrated with diagrams of complicated organic chemicals.

Still, that evening Naomi was smoking through her remaining carton of Marlboro Lights and managing her separation trauma with Xanax. She shook out a palm full of pills from the orange prescription bottle and offered me one, two, three, some for now, some for later, extolling their virtues. *Don't you need a little peace of mind? A good night's sleep?*

"You'll thank me; you'll feel better. You'll *be* better." Naomi promised as if I were sick, an end to the angst I wasn't even aware I needed to subdue in the single white pill deftly extricated from its brothers. She tucked the lonely pharmacological soldier in the change purse of my billfold. "Trust me;

2

you need it." I supposed she was right; it had been a rough few months that promised to get rougher.

Which was Naomi's point; she'd had her troubles too and she had emerged from their crucible burnished into a better person with the help of Xanax and psycho-therapy, and, of course, a stiff upper lip, which was not to be discounted. In July her girlfriend, Maria Sacchi, a twenty-six year old "spin" aerobics instructor at the East Bank Athletic Club had left her stumbling around six bedrooms, four baths and a formal library, filled with mass-market paperbacks which Naomi had expressly created and furnished to suit Maria, as if a particularly fussy issue of Martha Stewart's Living had exploded.

"But the point is," Naomi gave a rattle of her Xanax for emphasis. "I've grown from my mistakes."

Not the least of these had been completely remodeling the two flats of her historic, gray stone apartment building in De Paul at Maria Sacchi's gold digging insistence. In little more than a month and a half, Maria had transformed Naomi's long-time digs from comfortable bachelorette quarters with rental income into a small single-family mansion painted in rag-rolled celadon and taupe, which, according to Maria's decorator, Falko, were the colors for the next millennium. I could agree that taupe certainly had been a mistake. Not that the whole ugly mess wasn't something anyone, Naomi included, had not seen coming, but breakups are a lot like head-on collisions — even in anticipation there's not very much you can do.

I had been watching the end of my own relationship come at me like telltale high beams glowing over the crest of a hill. So, at nearly ten o'clock at the close of a very long weekend, Naomi and I were drinking fatalistically to the ends of our respective love affairs — Naomi's with nicotine and mine with Spike McMann. We'd enjoyed a companionable evening since early on I had conceded that Naomi's suffering was far worse than my own as she was not to be outdone — least of all in the quality of her misery.

3

As for my misery, Naomi had been my friend long enough for me to know she had the emotional depth of a two-speed blender: hard and harder with no setting at all for empathy. Whatever changed in my life, I took a measure of comfort that Naomi's high marks for hard-hearted consistency would never waver.

Through the drapeless floor to ceiling glass, the Chicago skyline sparkled into Naomi's living room. Looking south, there was the Field Museum. East there was the lake and beyond that Saugatuck, the gay summer Mecca where Naomi's ex-lover, Maria Sacchi, was now living with a woman who designed same-sex commitment jewelry.

After Maria moved out, Naomi sold her place in De Paul, which, filled with memories and decorated as aggressively taupe as it was, no longer felt like home. She had fled to this corner unit at the Park Shore, a new, upscale apartment building where we were lounging on the floor beside a bottle of fancy scotch, Bowmore Clariet, in the huge and nearly empty living room. Empty because, after a week on Xanax, Naomi had found the energy to rid herself of the Maria-related furniture at a two-day garage sale. All that remained was Maria's low-slung, Italian sofa, which in the big white-walled space seemed to be afloat all by itself on a vast, plush expanse of champagne-colored carpeting. This was sufficient; Naomi was listening to herself these days, listening to what the room told her about how it should be furnished. Listening, she insisted, took time.

While we were waiting for the walls to talk, I continued to cite the Nicoderm pamphlet: 'Signs of an overdose include bad headaches, dizziness, drooling, vomiting, weakness, cold sweats.' Naomi blew a dissolute line of smoke at her vaulted ceiling as if simply hearing this litany of overdose symptoms had brought about the promised weakness. Had she been an equity investment, you could have called Naomi Wolf a "pure play." She was the oil company that limits itself to the business of drilling, the electric company that only delivers

4

electricity. If for me, mongrelized emotions ran together like too many servings of bad, smorgasbord food on a cramped buffet plate, Naomi knew exactly what she wanted. I envied the crystalline quality of her emotions, all cordoned off into the appropriate compartments — no spillover — neat and homogenized like the artificially-colored portions of salt and preservatives offered up in the TV dinners of my youth.

Growing up, my sister Adeline and I had begged for them, *Please, please, please Swanson's fried chicken,* ogling the frost-covered, open freezers at the IGA grocery store, and wheedling shamelessly because my mother considered this fast food to be heretical, palpable evidence of the movement of upstanding Black folks towards a lifestyle indistinguishable from the ways of white trash. A fried chicken back, carrots and peas in their own little private soup of melted butter, heated for twenty short minutes in an oven — no flour-sticky-on-the-counter, all-day-frying smell — to be served to two little, pig-tailed Negro princesses on TV trays in the TV room of our tri-level, suburban, nearly TV-family house. That picture epitomized what I had wanted from my life — present and future: the bland, prepackage, *Anglo* control that seemed to elude my parents — two adults who raised their voices not only at their children, but at each other as well. Ours were volatile temperaments, patently unsuitable for a Midwestern, Wonderbread existence.

This obsession with the neat, tidy corners of The Good Life had driven me to business school, to a crass, tiny-brained curriculum devoted to the acquisition, care and feeding of capital. But somehow I'd missed the boat. I'd spent the long bull market of the 1990s watching for the next great scam, jealously eyeing the lucky few who'd come upon independent means the old fashion way — inheriting it.

My father was a steelworker's son made good enough to attend his regionally prestigious college, upgrade to his nationally prestigious graduate school, and plateau in a comfortable, even affluent, home and a job in upper middle management. His position, troublingly, was the mirror of my own (as if, as I had often suspected in so many other personal venues, I was doomed to repeat the lives of my parents), a comfortable situation with all the trappings of power, if none of the kick. Dad had managed just a nice enough living to educate me on what I was missing. If I lasted, like my old man, for thirty-plus years of mediocre employment, this girl could look forward with sweaty satisfaction to nothing more than the rewards of time-in-grade, nothing beyond the expectation of a gold-plated watch and a handshake lunch in twenty or so more years — that is until lately.

Lately, there was the offer by Gold Rush Investments, a big Kansas City money manager. They wanted to buy Whytebread, Greese, Winslow and Sloat — lock, stock and barrel. That meant that Whytebread stock, which junior partners like me had bought mostly for the sake of job security — that in the past had been traded nowhere except back to the company at retirements for pennies more than what had been paid for it — would be exchanged for shares of NYSE-traded Gold Rush stock and cash.

Still, that afternoon, by the time I'd deposited my soon to be ex-girlfriend, Spike McMann, at the United Airlines departures curb of Chicago O'Hare Airport I needed a drink the way a Peter Pan collar needs some nice pearl earrings and a matching necklace. Our weekend rendezvous had deteriorated rapidly from terrific to tense. It was two months and counting since Spike and I had last had sex and two weeks more since I had ceased to care, proving that even in the face of my Lottery Jackpot-sized good fortune, money couldn't reliably purchase marital bliss.

"Listen, honey," Naomi fortified our glasses with another slosh of scotch from the handsome bottle. "All that proves is that you just don't know where to shop." I'd resisted the temptation to revisit her financial arrangements with Maria Sacchi. Even in her peculiar dyke grudge, Spike was at least economically self-sufficient, even upwardly mobile in her ambitions as a restaurateur.

Spike, nee Mary Ellen McMann, and I had been reunited four years before at my ten year high school reunion, back in Blue River, a Midwestern town so completely mired in the archetype of Sinclair Lewis Americana that I had found my growing up years impossible to explain to the procession of city girls I had been fucking. Blue River was a *village*, a town so small that you had to drive to the next biggest one twenty miles away to buy underwear. No, I'd told the citified and suburban girlfriends alike, there was no mall. Aside from the desire to escape, my small town upbringing had left me with certain antiquated, stiff-backed sensibilities I couldn't seem to shake no matter how far I ran from my origins: honor, duty, guilt, a lack of surprise at the highway billboards reading, *Got problems? Read the Bible.*

"Oh honey," Naomi pronounced, "you are a rube," appalled at the notion that in this day and age there could be somewhere in America without a Victoria's Secret Outlet. She'd chalked up my sticky involvement with Spike as just another unfortunate symptom of my lack of exposure.

But there it was. Spike and I had grown up together in the same provincial, little enclave where my parents still lived, oblivious of the social and technological shopping advances that the rest of the world had come to take for granted, and where Spike had returned after cooking school in New York City to open a restaurant, Spike's, perhaps, because for all of its narrowness Blue River was still her home.

Somehow, though, in the intervening years between high school and the present, Spike-Mary Ellen had evolved into something a little less straight forward than the girl next door; and predictably, our uncomplicated one-night stand had devolved into a monogamous, committed, long-distance nightmare due in part to the presumption that being from the same tiny spot in a great big world, we understood each other's secret hearts and in larger part to the congenial disability of lesbians to discern the difference between sex and marriage. At first that was all just fine, as if Spike and I had escaped from the same place to meet in similar emotional places. Certainly both of us wanted companionship. And there was the convenience.

With a long-distance girlfriend I had my evenings to myself, and the cache of wanting, missing and longing for, which always seems to be more attractive than having. Now the absence wasn't working so well, or maybe it was working too well at least for me. Really ever since Spike had had her tongue pierced, I'd felt we'd been moving in irreconcilably different directions.

Not that her name hadn't been an early tip-off to the woman's unsettling penchant for self-reinvention. At twenty-five she'd had it changed legally from Mary Ellen. At twenty-nine, only months into our romance, she had dyed her previously copperish hair a deeply unambiguous purple — not all at once, but in progressively larger patches and streaks until I looked up one day and her whole head was a totally different color than it had been when we'd met — lavender. It was not what I would have elected for my girlfriend's hair. And it was messy. The semi-permanent dye washed out over time in rivers of grape juice-looking water; and after we made love in the shower spray, occasionally I would be disturbed to discover a peculiar cast in my own hair as if to suggest that Spike's creeping tendency towards unorthodoxy might be catching.

A year later, in honor of her new restaurant in Cincinnati, Spike colored her flat top platinum and had both nipples pierced with heavy gauge, stainless steel rings. The nose and the eyebrow jewelry followed that summer, and I began to feel as if people were staring at us, at her. Spike assured me that she liked for people to notice her, but anonymity would have been my own lifestyle choice, the discreet, assmilationist darkness of the closet with the occasional out-and-proud summer trip to Provincetown or San Francisco. Through all of this, I continued to envision a bland middle-class existence, sweetened to perfection by the lovely extra disposable income my Gold Rush deal money would bring — another Kate Spade bag, a few more pairs of Via Spigia shoes.

Until now it had been easier to file away my objections to Spike's evolving persona with the rest of the somewhat unsatisfying circumstances of my life than to proactively court the drama of change. Now, a fair proximity to wealth gave me a little tickle that my life ought to be much better than it was and soon. The Gold Rush deal was the trust fund fate had denied me — not nearly enough to retire, but a little nest-egg to fall back on — at least one more collar button blown wide open in my stiflingly buttoned-up existence.

To my ever increasing horror, all Spike had been able to see in this good fortune was investment capital for her restaurant chain. She'd fantasized about Spike's New-Style Cafes sprinkled with my money, growing into a regional franchise, her up-scale answer to Big Boy's poised for an haute cuisine boom in the farm belt. Now, after years of hemming and hawing, weekend rendezvous and airport reunions, I had spent that past few days explaining why when the buyout went through, I didn't want to move back to Blue River and be Spike's wife and business partner. Spike maintained sullenly that what this really meant was that I didn't want to be her partner at all, and I was beginning to recognize she was absolutely right.

What I wanted to believe was that there was a new, better girlfriend out there to replace the increasingly unsatisfactory Spike. But standing at my not quite middle-aged crossroads, all the good ones really did seem to be either married or straight.

Naomi's most recent cigarette bobbed and dipped as she counseled me, "Women are just like CTA busses — miss one and another will be along shortly," giggling, "one where you can get a seat." It was easy for Naomi to say — she always drove to work.

Since I'd left (or been left depending on who told it) by my long-term lover, Emily Karnowski, years ago now, you could have populated two or three lesbian support groups with my embittered ex's. I was staring down an endless procession of Friday evenings spent with Curve magazine in self-abuse. And over and over again, I blinked — petrified at how easy it had become to imagine that having someone (namely Spike) was better than having no one at all.

Time was running out and the laws of gravity seemed incontrovertible. Women's bodies have the asset lives of cars — Lexus to Geo — it's all depreciation once you've left puberty. So, here I was, the bulletproof quality of my twenties replaced by an eerie comfort in discussing elective cosmetic surgeries. The lines in my forehead and at the edges of my eyes were coalescing into the ugly inevitability of looking every second of my age, thirty-five in only a few short years.

Sure, I'd watched Naomi mature into the best middle age had to offer: that crisp, impeccable, self-assurance of the forty-ish dyke matrons you passed slouched in Business Class on your way to Coach — the gray in her hair colored agelessly away and the three-hundred dollar, Jill Sander slacks hanging tastefully off of her gym-tight haunches. I was looking at the future and I didn't want to go there — at least not alone.

"My God, you know, you can't have everything," Naomi was saying of my troubles with Spike, I thought a little too facilely, "but, Virginia, I just don't think you're getting enough here."

She was promising in true Naomi Wolf form, that with sufficient commitment to what I wanted, life really could be like Burger King — my way. Freed by Xanax from any anxiety about her behavior whatsoever, these days Naomi was Naomi squared. "Why don't you just cut the bitch loose? Anyone could see you'd be much happier."

But happier, in my book, was still a long way from happy.

"Do you want to hear some real troubles, Virginia?" Waiting two beats for effect, Naomi puffed a long exasperated breath. "Chief of Criminal Prosecutions. I've been circling that old man's carcass for years now, smelling retirement and when he goes I think they're going to give that job, MY job, to Luther Payton." She was looking vaguely ill, "Oh, yeah; you know him," murderously rolling the tip of her cigarette against the side of the big round ashtray in her lap.

I recalled having met the good-looking, machine-liberal, Black man. A Cook County State's Attorney like Naomi, from a well-connected family, ironically much like Naomi's, Luther Payton was frequently photographed along side the Mayor — Washington, Sawyer, Daley whichever mayor happened to need photographing for the Sun Times with an upstanding citizen at some African-American community fund-raiser.

"Old, lucky Luther," Naomi was bitching, "right place, right time, right color — just dark smoke really," blowing out her acrimony. "There's nothing to him. I'm getting way too old for this," she announced as if it were a recent decision.

I was watching myself in her picture windows: the short coarse hair still mostly black, my laugh lines forgiven in the blur of the faintly reflected image. Maybe Naomi was right about Spike and making the happiness I deserved in my life; and maybe, certainly, with the help of the Gold Rush deal, I still had plenty of time to get every little thing I wanted.

"Let's face it," Naomi had fallen into a kind of rhythm of complaint, "we're just plain getting old."

"Who cares?" I said, "Honey, we look great." I thought there were worse things than being who we were. *I* still looked great. "You look fine," I told Naomi, "honestly."

"A minute ago I looked *great*," she allowed. "That's just how it goes — every year the praise gets fainter."

Grant Park fountain was all lit up below us, a lovely view. I tipped the bottle in Naomi's direction, but she wagged her finger churlishly, "I'm not having anymore," considering her glass with reproach. "It makes me puffy."

"You know," I said, "you're as young as you feel."

"Well, I *feel* puffy." Naomi's laugh had brittle edges. "You know, the Dems'll probably want to run *him* for Circuit Court judge next year. HA. He probably doesn't even want to be Chief if he can be a judge." She tipped up her glass at that cheerful thought. "Waste not, want not. Who knows if I'll *ever* get Chief? With my luck they'll decide it ought to be a Black slot or something."

I was thinking you never know about people. Even people you think you know.

"Fuck you," I offered, which Naomi found not even in the least off putting.

"Which brings me to Spike — " she was saying. "I mean, God knows, there are enough real problems in the world, and if this were one of them I'd be the first one to say, go on and worry yourself to death. I'd *encourage* you but as it is, you know, chop chop, time to move on, girl." She looked at me with expectant self-satisfaction. "So, am I always right or what?"

II

I began that week by stepping into the puddle of puke my cat, Sweet Potato, had hacked up onto the rug beside my bed. My head on crooked and my gut still brimming with unmetabolized designer scotch, it was shaping up to be a terrific morning.

From the top of the refrigerator, Sweet Potato slow-blinked his love, as I sauntered down the hall, stepped in and trailed another sticky pile of his leavings from the bathroom threshold to the lavatory. I had overslept, among other disasters, and so, was about an hour and a half late for work, a habitual tardiness that had dogged me for most of my tenure at the third-tier investment firm of Whytebread, Greese,

Winslow and Sloat where I was employed (at least for the moment) as a stock analyst.

It had been a romantic kind of notion just out of business school to sell advice for a living — expert advice I would hasten to add when explaining my career to single women at cocktail parties — an almost glamorous way to pay the rent. Now, on a bad day Whytebread was my albatross, the last shiny, six-inch, finishing nail in my red, velvet-lined, bourgeois coffin; and short week or no, that Tuesday had all the makings of a very bad day.

I'd arrived at work, three burnt pieces of raisin toast and a sardine-style bus ride later, crawling from the elevator into Whytebread's gracious wood-paneled lobby. The heavy oak and gold-tone clock behind the receptionist's console warned that the time was well after ten, and the veins in the marble floor seemed to dance sadistically in the east light that roared through the big, lobby windows. My hangover headache still an integral part of my physical experience, I felt ungently spit out by the Chicago public transportation system like a gristly piece of meat. Still, I'd had the wit to duck my head as I skirted past the child receptionist, Pamela, who had, today, gotten herself dressed so as to suggest aspirations towards kiddy porn. Pamela with her sharp, little black-lined eyes and convenient position by the door was the worst kind of company informer on tardiness or early departure.

Being a repeat offender on both fronts, I had learned to fear her notice. More so these days, because with the Whytebread-Gold Rush merger, layoffs were looming. It was only prudent to cut a conscientious figure while management was still shuffling around the names on the body bags. Failing prudence, that morning I had chosen stealth, as Pamela was fairly autistic in her examination of her pink telephone message forms. Nearly home free, around her desk and through the side entrance door, I was stopped in my slippery tracks by the sight of some unfamiliar suits — plain-clothes

14

police officers. I could tell because one of them, Cassandra Hope, was a long lost trick from my uniform and authority fetish period. She and the other one, a forty-something looking white man, whom I had never seen before were taking turns talking at Herb Symon.

Herb was Whytebread's administrative VP, a title designed to dress up the fact that despite his impressive tenure at the firm, he had been passed over for genuine laurels of leadership so many times that management didn't know quite how to blunt the slight of it anymore — and still, he wouldn't leave. There was nothing to do but dress him up.

Herb was a "lifer", the kind of company man who is destined to find himself working for people he's hired as trainees once upon a time. Stoop-shouldered and spreading at the gut, with each sally from the cops, Herb's body language seemed to droop incrementally. But it was the sight of Cassandra that held me with my hand on the door handle, gawking for who could say how long — too long as the time allowed by the cipher lock combination expired and the rattle of my pull on the secure door roused Pamela from the intricacies of her message pad.

She eyed me, frowning, and paused momentarily in her telephone mantra of: "Whytebread, Greese, Winslow and Sloat" to push aside the Madonna-esque headset microphone at her chin conveying, with only the ominous expression in her narrowly-set pig eyes that I was now swimming neck-deep in shit.

"He's been looking for you, Virginia." Pamela indulged just enough of a smile to let me know she was enjoying this gambit.

He was my boss, Tom Zemluski, aka The Irishman, who couldn't have cared less really when I arrived. Rather, The Irishman, so nicknamed for his love of a lunchtime Martini, was completely the kind of guy who liked to keep note of the odd infraction, a club to wield at bonus time when you were arguing how you were paid too little and he was arguing how you were lucky to be paid at all.

On my very first day of employment, The Irishman — Zemluski as I respectfully called him then — invited me to a welcome lunch at The Berghoff Restaurant near Whytebread's offices. He had laid out the old-world practice of the Berghoff waiters who literally bought their orders from the kitchen, reselling the meals at menu prices to the dining room patrons. The double-book rigors of this financial arrangement, with exacting Germanness, kept even a single veal chop or strudel from going unaccounted for.

The Irishman, who had started in the mailroom about a million years ago, saw himself as Whytebread's bulwark against the tendency of cocky, young, MBAs to cost the firm money and prestige. "I'm here," he assured me, "to make sure you don't screw up." *You*, being punctuated with a signature poke of his index finger at the air just in front of my chest. In the time I had worked at Whytebread, The Irishman had shown himself to revel in the errors of his juniors as if chewing our asses was his singular life purpose.

He took these pleasures catch as catch can, so I could only imagine what was in store if The Irishman had expended the energy to be *looking for me* in particular on the emotional equivalent of a Monday morning — just like those scenes in the horror films where you cover your eyes to no avail because it is clear to anyone over the age of five what bloody pictures accompany the flesh-slashing sounds of the knife-fingered killer.

"I'll tell him you're just now in. Ten thirty six, my . . ." Pamela tossed her head as she turned to consult the clock. "Late night?" Before I could answer she was throatily back at her headset: "Mr. Rostow, I'll have to give you voice mail."

During my apprehension by Pamela, Cassandra Hope and her colleague continued in hush-voiced assignation with Herb on the opposite side of the lobby. The interaction was serious enough to make three deep unattractive lines in Cassie's forehead.

Aside from this minor blemish, however, Cassandra Hope looked miraculously pulled together, especially if my own appearance was any sort of barometer for what "fashion don'ts" were possible after a long weekend in the middle of transitional wardrobe weather.

Since she'd left me, someone had taught Cassandra how to dress — someone with very good taste indeed. Under her crisp, pale trench coat, I could see she was as nicely turned out as anyone who might normally frequent Whytebread's lobby; and she had straightened and coifed her hair into an attitude achievable only by a Black salon and six hours on a Saturday afternoon — the confluence of lye, water, and some really excellent auburn highlighting, a Dutch boy bob. Even her jewelry looked real — at least from a distance.

Herb Symon by contrast, was less attractively composed. He was practically painted over with that sweaty-pitted look, a Yeoman who doesn't want any trouble on his watch. Herb had a good bit to feel sweaty about. His dubious distinction as the head man's Girl Friday was at risk now owing to Wesley Winslow's recent rise to president of the firm. Wes had his own favorite lap dogs and whipping boys. Included nowhere on Winslow's radar screen was the pot-bellied, balding Symon, Mr. Quick-As-Anything to explain to a new acquaintance that his name was spelled with a y (rather than "the Jewish way"). Rupert Dean, Justin Collier, and other younger Turks, not Herb, could be expected to rise with Winslow's ascent — or as Ellen Borgia called it, his coronation.

Two years ago, Wes had stepped over Herb and a pack of other hopefuls to the top of the firm where his uncle, August Madsen had been Chairman for as many years as I had been alive. Wes brought his own special cronies, a certain peculiar obsession with physical fitness and a free-floating contempt for women as reported by Ellen Borgia who kept an ear to the ground for such things.

Her diary chronicled the abuse she'd endured: inadequate bonuses, missed promotions, untoward remarks by her male co-workers, but had, to date, surprisingly failed to mention that men at the firm called her "The Popsicle," reportedly "cold as ice with a stick up her ass," possibly the only actionable one of her allegations. When I had started at Whytebread she suggested by way of sisterly advice that I maintain the same procedure, reporting complaints in a weekly letter to management, which August Madsen had addressed by taking Ellen out to a nice lunch every couple of months and letting her vent, making occasional special bonus payments to recognize her work. He had, in short, patronized her like a small-town doctor proscribing Valium to a slightly hysterical spinster who in his opinion needed nothing more pharmacological than a good lay. *My door is always open, dear.* To me the prescription seemed worse than the disease.

Madsen's dubious attentions, however, had served to keep Ellen on a fairly even keel — knowing and apparently believing that Maddy was always prepared as he said, "to discuss the reasonable concerns of the firm's ladies." Uncle Madsen, at least, had taken the time and energy to patronize her. But his nephew, Winslow, had ignored her notes. And anyone who ignored *her*, Ellen advised, could be no good news to the odd Negro associate, destined in her mind's obvious order of things to be in all worlds less than herself.

Even fresh out of business school, I hadn't been green enough to harbor hopes of race and gender inclusiveness in financial services. This, presumably, was why banking paid so much better than social work.

Pamela was singing with cheerful enthusiasm into her headset, performing, "Whytebread, Greese, Winslow and Sloat," like the jingle for a new improved brand of laundry detergent. Herb twisted at the ends of his hair. Thin and white, it hung in a longish fringe below his ears, as if he were trying to make up at the bottom for what was missing on top. The longer the cops kept talking, the more Herb looked like worry would take what little fuzz remained on his pink melon head.

I'd have given even odds as to which of the two of us was more discomfited by Cassie Hope's visit. For me it had the makings of a cringingly uncomfortable meeting, as once from deep in the marching throng of the Gay Pride Parade, I had heard someone call out my name, "Virginia." Amid the homemade bar floats covered with dancing men in falsies and bad party dresses, the voice was unmistakably familiar: "Virginia Kelly?" an old college girlfriend came at me from across the barricade at Fullerton Street. Far less attractive than I would have liked to remember her, buck-toothed, buck naked, she was painted green. The rest of the raucous crowd rolled past as she stepped, like from a horror movie, out of her contingent — Fairies? Friends of fairies? Elves? Who could tell?

All I knew was that she had hailed me loudly in a way that was impossible to slip away from, "It's been ages," and I could only agree politely that of course we should get together soon, writing her phone number on a day-glow pink paper flyer advertising a dance — something that I wouldn't mind losing just as soon as she in all her freaky, naked greenness had retreated back into the frightening Mardi Gras-like mass.

That morning, I was reading Cassandra's expression for any sign of social terror, as if I might be a bit of naked, green history she wanted to forget. Dressed in a pilling, navy suit and a dingy silk blouse overdue for the cleaners, I'd hardly put my best foot forward that day. There was a wide, long ladder of a run, climbing up my calf from my commuter's tennis shoes to my kneecap, in the panty hose that seemed fine when I'd left the house, but now were inescapably black. And I was having a bad hair day. Even so, after a moment of apparent disorientation, Cassandra had not dodged my gaze.

She'd recognized me even in my dark glasses and, in the course of her nodding sagely with Herb Symon at the floor, distinctly smiled, sliding her eyes briefly up to mine, and mouthing, "Later," as I'd passed through the side door into Whytebread's offices.

The rusty cogs in my brain were grinding slowly, so I had pressed my combination into the cipher lock and proceeded halfway down the blue-gray pastel maze of fabric-covered associate's cubicles towards my office before I had begun to wonder what Cassandra's "Protect and Serve" ensemble might want with Herb. It seemed best to puzzle this out in the lunchroom where I felt I could hide until I had marshaled sufficient emotional resources for a meeting with The Irishman.

III

Justin Collier barely grunted back when I good morn-inged him on my way to a suitably quiet corner of the lunchroom. He was squatting caveman-style, surveying the open refrigerator. I watched as his hand moved thoughtfully through his blond hair, from the fridge, to the hair, to the fridge. Justin absently groomed himself like a handsome, yellow cat as he peered at the metal shelves.

One of Winslow's chosen, I owed my favored relationship with Justin to gayness — his, which was secret and apolitical, his sexuality a discrete tattoo that he could display, or not, depending on the audience, and mine, which though hardly obvious could not have been impossible to guess.

Justin had come out to me unexpectedly after a company-wide golf outing the year before, the intimacy of his disclosure feeling like a weird reward for playing so passably in our foursome, a fact that surprised nearly everyone including me. My 18 holes of serially serendipitous shots were almost as shocking as his admission — the fact of it, not so much the content as I supposed I'd already known in some unconscious way about Justin. It was a sense I couldn't pinpoint and sought to rationalize in little ways. Hadn't I sometimes heard a sing-song cadence in his straight man's voice, a fey undercurrent that gave him away to me, the way you might get the idea that a voice on the phone is Black, apropos of nothing that has been said, a persistent conviction of inconclusive origin?

He'd confirmed it and in coming clean, Justin cautioned, "I'd prefer it that this not become a subject for shared discussion," somehow negating the reality of what he was telling me, even as he said it. It was a smiling threat, I imagined, lest I begin to think his admission leveled our positions at the firm.

"So you're passing then?" I made a nervous joke.

"Aren't you? Isn't everybody in some way or another? This can be our special club." Somehow I'd known that Justin liked clubs — the more limited the membership the better. He'd laughed.

I'd laughed then too, eager in whatever affiliation he might propose, hungry in my own way for his proximity to Winslow's ear.

Justin had woven a tireless, ass-licking willingness to stroke authority into success. If his rapid (and maybe undeserved) rise through the sales ranks to his present post of Marketing Director rankled some of our less generous colleagues, to me he was holding open the door of an exclusive club — and all I wanted was to go inside.

"Any excitement this morning?" I was asking to tell,

aching to show the inside track promised by Cassandra's whispered *later*. Disappointingly, Justin could not be interested. He remained fully engaged in removing every item from the open refrigerator and laying them out on the floor behind him. "Fuck," said Justin, "Fuck, fuck, fuck." He'd lost his bagels, the information conveyed on a steady draft of frigid air.

"Is it cold in here?" Ellen Borgia glared her way past Justin to the little faux butcher-block table where I sat imagining what could have brought Cassandra Hope to Whytebread's lobby, and visoring my hand above my forehead to reduce the million or so foot candles of overhead florescent lunchroom illumination to an environment nearly approximating normal daylight. I considered with relish it would be a sexy crime that engaged her, something sordid — drug possession, spousal abuse, or best yet, incest.

"Are you cold?" Ellen was hugging a Wall Street Journal in her armpit. She might have arranged to be warmer, but she was barefoot — rather, stocking foot — what she called her "toes-free" look. This was the latest in a series of strange pronouncements, a battery of herb potions and the elimination of all wheat and potatoes from her diet postured craziness, another bizarre attempt to provoke management to rashness. I didn't say anything. No display by Ellen Borgia could surprise me.

Management, too, had held to stony silence on shoeless Ellen's wardrobe peculiarities — never mind the battered pair of Tretorn tennis shoes she kept in her desk for the walk to the El. Ellen's sex discrimination suit filed over a year ago with no resolution in sight — litigious or settled — would need to be resolved as a condition of the Gold Rush deal. It had them all biting their tongues on advice of counsel, although I'd seen Herb dropping thumbtacks in the hall.

"Are you cold?" Her voice was steeped in irritation. Justin

was ignoring the comment she obliquely directed at him. Ellen rubbed the arms of her shirt-dress in emphasis. A thin, yellow silk affair, it was printed with black, spiral doodads that were doing their own special part in making my eyes hurt. The sheer, navy hose gave an enviable blue sheen to her chalky legs.

My own stockings were still regrettably black, at odds with the blue of my suit and the brown of my shoes — and a little bit thick as well. I was promising myself that as soon as I could bear the full light of day I would venture out to Marshall Field's. Somewhere beyond the low grade pounding in my head, the refrigerator motor began to work, softly humming.

"What's with that?" Ellen jerked her head at Justin and I repeated that he'd lost his bagels, though lost was not likely the word.

Whytebread had an on-going problem with theft, mostly big-ticket items — newly ordered laptop computers, telephones, but it wasn't all together unusual for food to go missing from the communal refrigerator — bagels, Lean Cuisine frozen dinners, Le Croix sparkling water brought from home. For months, someone had been raiding the stash of Hostess Snowball cakes that Herb Symon had cached in the crisper.

"Well, does it have to be so cold?" Ellen was marching towards the refrigerator as if her purpose was to make it warmer. When she was nearly standing over him, Justin rose, turning as she reached past his nose to slam the refrigerator door and open the freezer in one rapid, hostile motion. "Maybe these are yours." Ellen dropped the bag of frozen bagels she'd produced on the floor near Justin's wingtip shoe. Her lips were pursed in a tight red line across her face that might or might not have been a smile, but under no circumstances a well-meaning one.

"Oh?" Justin round-eyed the frost-covered bag in stupid surprise as Ellen poked at the plastic with her toe, the nails of which showed magenta through her sandal-foot hose. "Shit."

"Nice mouth, Collier," Ellen chirped.

"Nice mouth?" His voice had recovered to sophomore irony and his face formed an identical expression of dislike. Stooping to pick up the bag, Justin narrowly avoided being kicked. "Funny, I think I've heard the same about you, Ms. Borgia. It *is* cold in here?" He had belled his cheeks maliciously, blowing hard into big, cupped hands, and rubbing them together. "You're right, I feel just like a Popsicle."

"This big," Ellen curled a pejorative pinky finger at the wall of his chest, stepping back unsteadily from his advancing bulk — a big, wide, salmon-patina, brick wall in an attractively contrasting power tie.

"Brrrrr." Justin blew into his hands again, the sound of which seemed to push Ellen back the remaining distance, across the room where she made herself conspicuously busy at the coffee machine and in the cupboard above the sink.

"Asshole," Ellen hissed to me as Justin left the room, a loser's request for commiseration I wasn't inclined to give. I thought to myself, mean and practical, what did Justin always say? *Why side with the losers?* Besides, Ellen had started it, unnecessarily. Why side with the stupid against the powerful?

Ellen had special venom for Winslow and it seemed, by extension his cronies, old grudges brought from past professional lives, for which I could never seem to get satisfactory explanation. I'd asked Justin once what it was with Ellen and Wes. He'd laughed and leered. "Where there's smoke, there's fire."

"Do you want some tea?" Ellen asked, her voice a little too bright in the attempt to resuscitate conversation. "It's herbal." She had made a production of bringing the box to me at my table, straining cheerfulness.

But I pretended I didn't notice, gamely reading the

festively decorated cardboard box aloud. It said: *Diet Daily*, with advertising copy proclaiming: ALL NATURAL, ORGANIC. *Ingredients: Garcinia combogia extract, choline and inositol, L-carnitine and chromium picolinate.* Except for rosehips, cayenne pepper and "natural flavors," *Diet Daily* sounded like a chemistry experiment.

"It'll drop your weight just like that." Ellen made prophetic snap of her fingers. She was twiggy enough herself to do testimonials for eating disorders. But I was just declining the miracle beverage when Herb Symon's shiny head appeared in the doorway — just his head at first, which he turned, very quickly, to the right and left as if he were intending to cross a busy street.

He walked in, rubbing the pink skin on the back of his neck, and just stood for a few moments when he'd reached the center of the room before he even registered that he was not alone there scratching himself.

Noticing Ellen and me, Herb frowned, announcing "All hands meeting," as if to say that was precisely what he had come here to tell us, "half an hour in the big conference room." Herb made to go, but then he didn't, frowning harder, as he peered past Ellen and me at the refrigerator door. "What's that?" He was walking and looking squinty-eyed at what I then saw was a newspaper clipping. It was attached to the refrigerator in among the homemade fliers offering used boats, cars and vacation homes for sale, held to the smooth white metal by souvenir magnets that colleagues brought back in business triumph from such exotic parts as Cleveland, Ohio and Appleton, Wisconsin to signify we now had clients in these thriving metropolises.

There was a picture above the bold, block type of the Tribune obituary, a picture of Winslow, a tan and natty sailor, dressed for what might have been the Mackinac race, his thin, fair hair fluffed up by some unseen wind. The text below began simply:

Chicago financier, Wesley Winslow, (45) dies unexpectedly of flu . . .

At the bottom of the article there was a neatly typed yellow Post-it Note, which read: "I will repay."

IV

Ellen Borgia was gasping beside me — a shock I shared inaudibly, unsure of whether the writer was promising Winslow vengeance or taking it, and stupidly trying to remember how to breathe. I was not especially incapacitated by sadness, rather I felt a strange *whump* of realization that left me teary and winded as if I'd been punched in the stomach, the shock resolving after a few moments into a disbelieving swell of nostalgia. Wes was a fixture on my professional landscape, which like my lovers and my hometown I expected to deliver no surprises. Wes was a tree that had stood for a long time and was suddenly gone, leaving a conspicuous emptiness where the eye anticipates it, reminding your mind of the memory.

I could still recall Winslow at the podium in the share-holder's meeting, a fuzzy dreamlike image, but maybe not so much due to the shock of his death, but rather to my own condition. A lot had gone on that afternoon and I was not at my most observant.

In the close thick air of the meeting room I had felt as if Mr. Sandman were mugging me with a baseball bat, this courtesy of a long, well-lubricated lunch. My head lolled first onto one shoulder and then the other; and my chin flopped down against the boat neck of my red *silk de chin* blouse, encouraging drool.

There in the plush First Chicago conference room Whytebread had rented for the occasion, Wesley Winslow was going to talk about my future — about everyone's future really. Laying out, in glorious detail, Gold Rush Investments' offer to buy Whytebread, all blue sky and easy long green. Rupert Dean had taken a front row seat, predictably close to the action. He had sandwiched himself between Herb Symon and Jon Patel, a guy who sat cross-legged on the toilet in the men's room so he could listen to conversations that were none of his business. Among the fifty-odd heads, Rupert was twisting his around as if he couldn't bear to miss even one meaningful eye contact.

Ellen Borgia pretended to shoot at him from across the room, her hand bent into the figure of a gun. Allison Price was tittering girlishly. As Ellen took aim again at the back vent of Wesley Winslow's charcoal-gray suit jacket, she caught my eye and winked. Allison tittered some more.

The firm's first female analyst, Price was minted before investment research was fashionable. Now she was a kind of a historical exhibit, a reference point for a certain time and sensibility. In her broadcloth shirts and silk ties, she seemed to acknowledge, if not happily, then willingly, that her engage-ment with change had ended in 1985. Her life was static and her life was Whytebread. Twenty-odd years at the firm had gotten Allison close to fifty years old with nothing to show for her efforts, but a bowl-shaped, graying hairdo, a wardrobe of mannishly-cut, tropical-weight woolen suits and a starter house in Winnetka, which she shared with six elderly Siamese cats. I was hoping that life would deal me a better hand. At least I only had the one cat.

"Tell yourself a joke, girlfriend?" Justin Collier slid into the empty seat next to mine, leaning close to dish Wesley Winslow's outfit. He let his arm relax across the back of my chair. "Can you believe it? All the money on the planet and the man still looks like he came off the rack at Sears." Justin's breath was warm in my ear. "My God, do you think his wife knows he goes out looking like that?"

I said didn't think Trisha Winslow was the type to lay out his clothes. More likely Winslow dressed *her*. His blond wife looked as if he had all but thought her up in the image of a society matron. But even perfectly draped in her snake-hipped, designer knits, somehow Trisha Winslow made an uncomfortable caricature of leisure class grace, a pale anxious figure carried along awkwardly in Wes's splashy professional wake. On her own she was definitely lacking something, not class, but contentment, a noblesse oblige that wasn't for sale at St. John. No. Winslow'd had better luck grooming Starr D'nofrio with whom he had replaced his old secretary, Camille Guiterrez, about four months ago. Gone was the baby blue eye shadow, gone the hair of three separate colors — platinum, yellow and ragged, dark brown roots growing in. Starr was dignified — reborn as an ash blond, the continuous open-mouthed crack of her Juicy Fruit gum forever silenced. Starr had even put down her cigarettes, I thought imagining herself very nearly suitable in the lore of the 1950s movie to be the executive secretary who marries her older, richer, daddy of a boss. Because whether or not Trisha was the type to lay out Winslow's clothes, we all knew that Wes was hardly the type to spend much time at home waiting for her attention. He'd proven that at the last Christmas party.

Wes was smoothing his hair and neatening the lapels of

his full cut suit on his way up the aisle that divided the chairs in the meeting room, apparently unaware of the dilapidated state of his wardrobe. The wide yellow stripes of his tie were broken up by thinner ones of blue and red, a pattern likely named by its catalogue merchant for some long forgotten British army regiment.

"I'll bet that's not the only thing Miss Trish has stopped laying." Justin snorted a laugh. "I mean, it's tragic, really, just look at that tie."

Wesley Winslow made long strides towards the podium, an entrance rendered only a little less impressive by the slight stoop to his shoulders. What I thought Justin didn't quite understand was that Winslow didn't have anything to prove to the likes of us — his financial presence was large and pedigreed enough that it didn't much matter what he wore. He was Whytebread's walking billboard sign, a founder's great-grandson, peddling trust and dependability to clients in the Heartland where pink shirts were still a little suspect, balm to the double-chinned bank and trust officers in Rockford, Illinois that, even if he was a little peculiar in his diet and tighter-stomached than most, amid the crush of racy, Italiante investment bankers, Wes Winslow was still one of them. Whytebread was still their kind of firm.

I had been watching Starr D'nofrio let her eyes follow and fix; her gaze stroked Justin covetously as he took his seat. He was a fine looking man, if you liked that sort of thing — tall, solid, blond and mostly retaining his hair at thirty-five or whatever he was (I thought maybe older around the eyes). Since her promotion and makeover, Starr had frequented attention on Justin who, beside me, continued to shudder at Winslow's unfortunate choice of tie — his own sense of style unassailable in a shiny, moss green, double breasted suit, and crocodile embossed loafers thin enough to be confused in some less sophisticated venues with house slippers.

That afternoon the new, improved Starr had been tasked with taking meeting notes on a steno pad, but on the occasions that her eyes left Justin, it was to cast a green-eyed glare at me — either for sitting next to him or for throwing water on her dress during that afternoon's dispute with Camille.

They fought daily over one thing or another since Camille's demotion to work for me. This time, it was ostensibly Starr's dismantlement of Camille's beloved filing system. I'd discovered them, body slamming each other off the white, metal stalls of the 25th floor powder room, while an ever expanding crowd of middle-aged ladies hung back by the sinks egging them on. A cup of cold water down the back of Starr's dress had been enough to redirect the hostilities. So, whether because of Justin or Camille, Starr kept up her malevolent staring at me until Winslow made a sign for her to dim the lights.

As the first slide appeared on a large projection screen behind him, Wes was clearing his throat and pulling the microphone stand upward to accommodate his height. Whytebread had been on a downward slide since the crash of 1987, nothing really precipitous, but our earnings were undeniably sluggish during a period when the money management industry was exploding. No one could deny that Whytebread needed something. Gold Rush Investments would bring new blood — and, not the least, much needed equity capital, since Winslow's Uncle Maddy had leveraged the business to the hilt, so high that the money he'd borrowed in the junk bond boom was starting to hurt the bottom line, the interest payments cutting into the cash freebies for the Winslows and Madsens.

Wes's Monteblanc pen cast a fat, authoritative shadow across the screen, outlining the downward slope of Whytebread's profitability line. "Well, I'm sure our past performance isn't news to anyone here. The question is, what are we going to do about our futures and our security?"

In the rented conference room that afternoon, the air seemed to throb with the thrill of greed and possibility.

Winslow went on: "At Whytebread and Greese we've been

managing other people's money since 1893, I think it's about time we start managing our own." An appreciative murmur rose from the room.

"Where did he get that accent?" Justin was whispering much too loudly for my comfort as Wes nattered on in that just-us-folks way that played so well in Peoria, about "Us" and "Our" and "We" when even if I got the pile of money he was promising me, I couldn't buy a house in his exclusively WASPy neighborhood, which I imaged was just the way he liked it. "It sounds like he ought to be shoveling manure somewhere downstate."

"Why should he," said Price who was seated behind us, "when it's so darn convenient to shovel it right here."

"Shush." I said and Price tittered.

Marty Goodman turned in his seat. "Do you folks mind? I've got two kids in college."

In the front of the room, Hal Hobert was growling, "Come on. You want to keep it down, people," as if someone had suddenly elected him Sergeant at Arms.

The next slide showed the value of Whytebread under different scenarios in two thick blocks — one black, one red. The smaller, red one was the current valuation of our shares in Whytebread. The much bigger, black rectangle showed our value in Gold Rush shares. The difference between them was the benefit of the buy-out, a huge positive number that laid down a blanket of silent awe across the room. We were, all of us, counting.

Who knew what a bag full of bucks from the corporate lottery could buy?

Justin had laughed when I'd asked him what he would do with the money. "I'm going to cancel my Journal subscription — check out for a while," he said, "enjoy life," although I didn't believe that story for a minute.

He loved the thrill of the game too much to sit by the sidelines — the self-important print of your name on the business card, the dizzying proximity to other people's money. I was hooked as well — on Whytebread and my genteel marginalization. Sure, my nose was bloody from all that bumping up against the hard, glass ceiling, but all the time I was loving the view.

Like Justin had said, "You'd be surprised what people really want when it comes right down to it."

Before Wes could even finish asking for questions, Cal Fraiser threw a hand up in the air. "Where exactly is Gold Rush stock trading these days?" Cal was the shill in the Winslow traveling medicine show, teeing up a question for the answer Wes was just dying to give.

"I believe Gold Rush was at thirty-five and a quarter as of the close of market today." It slid out of Winslow's mouth like a pat of warm butter; and if the P.T. Barnum sideshow quality of this whole display embarrassed him at all, Winslow wasn't letting on. He ran a hand through his wispy hair, smiling a big, wide, used car salesman's smile. "Next question, anyone?"

Allison Price stood up behind us asking about the pension plan. From his expression it wasn't the question Winslow would have liked but he was wading in, smooth-voiced, like a late night radio disc jockey on the mellow, mellow station: "The Gold Rush offer presents a great value for the current and future prospects of Whytebread. To tie a new owner's hands by committing them to a retirement program such as is no longer seen in this industry or any other limits that value. In addition, with the change to a cash balance plan, Whytebread will be instituting a 401k plan with 3% matching for those not yet drawing retirement."

"Blah, blah, blah, blah," Justin whispered in my ear.

"For those of you vested, your benefits will continue to accrue under the new plan." Wes ended smiling hopefully, but changing the pension now cut off the lucrative tail-end cash in the payout calculation. Whytebread's under-funded pension plan was transformed into a trust that Winslow could reasonably assume he would never have to feed again, but

Price would have to work maybe five or ten years longer to achieve her current benefit.

"So, I'm shit-out-of-luck, huh, Wes." She had her bottom lip pushed out, braying like the rube who has just discovered the milk bottles at the carnival baseball toss are weighted. "SOL. That would be the short answer, huh?"

A troubled expression had driven Winslow's forehead into his receding hairline so he looked like an emotionally wounded Sharpei dog. "I can't see there's any need for profanity, here." He had begun to back pedal masterfully. "Even if you do not perceive these arrangements to be sufficient for your needs, I can at least assure you that these are the best opportunities available."

"Oh, no." Price was shaking her head. "I get it, Wes, SOL."

In the face of this obstinacy, the crease that had come up between Winslow's small, blue eyes grew deeper, relaxing only when Price sat down, freeing Wes to call for friendlier inquires. Conveniently, Cal Fraiser had jumping-jacked his arm up in the air.

"How soon can we get our money out, Wes?"

"Why, almost right away, Cal." With this answer, Winslow had brightened. We all had brightened, recovered from Price's ugly intimation that there was going to be no free lunch.

"That's the beauty of this opportunity. We don't have to hold the Gold Rush stock, of course. All of us here have a great deal of our personal wealth or our retirement savings bound up in the fortunes of this company. I think it's time that we take our own good advice and diversify now that we have the chance." Winslow was showing all his big square teeth, smiling into our great collective lowing, the sound of bankers looking forward to becoming fatter, dumber, and happier, my own voice loud among them.

Just then, The Irishman lifted himself up out of his chair to heckle: "Diversify me out of a job will you, Wes. WHAT

ABOUT THE LIST?" Jon Patel and Hal Hobert were pushing down the center aisle like riot cops before he'd even gotten it out.

Winslow had momentarily paused in his sales patter to stare at Tom along with the rest of us in silent astonishment. Justin rolled his eyes, mouthing a pretty passable Betty Davis. "Fasten your seatbelts —"

"YEAH THE LIST, YOU MOTHERFUCKING FAGGOT BASTARD." The Irishman boomed, but rather than answer the commotion at the back of the room, Wes had decided to press on: "One of the prime comforts you can take in the sale of our company is that now regardless of what happens here at Whytebread in the future, we are financially secure in our retirements." Wes was seemingly unshakable in his mission to do what was best for us. "This sale will create much needed diversity and liquidity in our personal portfolios."

Rows in front of me, Rupert Dean was bouncing his big, dopey jug-head up and down agreeably as if he were one of those Noddy Dogs riding in the rear window of a big American car, but the rest of the room didn't look nearly so sure about the buyout anymore. Winslow hadn't even acknowledged the existence of his Layoff List, the rumors of which hovered at the edges of every conversation lately. At Whytebread rumors were always true.

This one I knew for sure, because Ellen Borgia had The List. She'd showed it to me, or rather a copy of it, four weeks before. Waving me into her office like a car-trunk hustler, and grinning so hard I thought her face might break from the strain. One look at the typewritten page, she'd put between us on the desktop, and I was sure this was the secret List, The List of Winslow's recommendations — who would be kept on at Whytebread after the merger and who would be sacked.

All the names were there. Some names had stars beside them denoting in the footnote that Wes was recommending special incentive option packages. I could only imagine that Starr D'nofio must have contracted a virulent case of disregard for her continued employment if she had leaked this information to anyone — let alone Ellen Borgia — but it was a relief to see that I would still have a job after the merger. Amazingly so would Ellen Borgia. But Zemluski, Allison Price, and Amy Whitacre along with a number of others would not. Even if the stock options, and incentive packages had been reserved for Rupert, Jonathon Krause, Justin Collier and the boys' club, I still felt that odd near-miss-on-the-highway rush of euphoria at the discovery I would be kept on. The strength of the feeling surprised me, the relief wasn't so much at not having to leave — I could go somewhere else, I'd had my offers. Rather it was more that I would not have the arduous undertaking of proving myself all over again at another firm, wouldn't have to jockey for a place in the stack that owing to my racial and gender demographic would not likely be much better than the one I had here. Perhaps it would be less good because at Whytebread I had Justin at least. I sighed heavily before I could stop myself.

"Notice anything else?" The sound of my understandable relief seemed to piss Ellen off. "Why don't you just look at the names again," and I was obliged to give The List a second and even a third read, before I was allowed to give up hunting for the extraordinary.

"White boys rule." I shook my head, but Ellen kept smiling, an almost savage display of teeth and gums.

"What if I told you women make up twelve percent of this firm's professionals and there's not one woman on that list for options. What if I said that 60.23% percent of the people Winslow proposes to cut are female?"

I was starting to understand. For years Ellen's threats and complaints about her unfair treatment had been going nowhere, but with The List, maybe that could change. "You're talking class action?" It was the obvious answer.

"I've got my lawyer working on a letter right now." Ellen threw her stocking feet up over her desk, sounding as if just to say the word *lawyer* made her feel a little breathless. "Did you know, you're a class all by yourself, Virginia. " There was a hole in the heel of her nylons.

I said I heard that all the time.

"No. Seriously," Ellen was insisting, "you're the only Black woman in this firm," as if this were news, as if I were Anastasia, lost heir to the Romanoff dynasty. "You are your very own class."

Not that the thought of suing Whytebread hadn't crossed my mind occasionally over the years. I'd considered it almost seriously for a few weeks after I'd found out that The Irishman had split some unallocated bonus pool money between Rupert Dean and Kevin Cavanaugh.

"Those guys needed the cash," Tom told me, implying, with his June-and-Ward-Cleaver-logic, that I didn't, at least not as much as those pleasant white men with stay-at-home wives and recent, squalling family additions. *From each according to his ability; to each according to his need.* Old news that job performance is like sex, in large part subjectively critiqued — not so much on what you do, but how you do it.

"Look, it's all water over the dam, now." The Irishman met me with the face men reserve for hysterical women. "Just you and your cat; and you're making more money than either of them, Virginia. They've got wives and kids." The Irishman was painting me greedy for wanting, not just the cake, but the icing too.

I was mad for sure. But sue Whytebread and I'd be coloring the gray out of my hair before I got a court date. When I did, gag order or no, news traveled like lightening through the downtown gyms and suburban country clubs. Sue Whytebread and I'd never hawk stocks again in this town or any other.

"How much do you think its worth?" While I was looking at the run in Ellen's nylons, I'd been working the math, independently. Whytebread, unlike its Wall Street counterparts, didn't stipulate binding arbitration for the resolution of employee disputes. At Whytebread you could get a jury and punitive damages, driving the odds of a decent settlement way up.

But of course that begged the question: "How much do you think this is worth?"

She was rolling out the legal litany with a confidence I thought had no basis in reality. "— foregone benefits, and emotional distress, and punitive damages." The only sure thing was what I would have gotten if not for the discrimination against my class. "Punitive damages — that's where the big money is." Rupert's option incentive package was worth about a hundred thousand dollars, even with treble damages it wasn't enough to retire on. "It'll serve those bastards right," Ellen kept babbling along, but I had begun to feel embarrassed for her, like a color blind boyfriend I'd had for a while in high school who went around in clothes that didn't match because his mother had thought it was funny to lie to him about what he had on.

Ellen was promising that Gold Rush's majority shareholder, a big Japanese bank, would want to settle. After the Mitsubishi case, sex discrimination was someplace they didn't want to go. "They'll have to settle if they want to do the deal and they'll have to settle fast."

What if they didn't? I was asking mostly to hold up my end of the conversation; and her face tightened up like a spring — not a pretty thing to watch.

Ellen's fingers had set to curling and uncurling the edge of the paper. "Look, we can't lose even if they won't settle." Her voice had begun to gather volume as if this were a reasonable substitute for persuasion. "How can we lose? I have this List. I have these statistics now. And most important I have the fact that The List is the work of one guy, no committee, just Wesley Winslow and his illegal bigotries. *I know him, Virginia.* When Winslow is deposed, you listen to me, we're going to have our smoking gun."

I'd promised I would give some thought to the suit, both

of us nodding grimly at the seriousness of my deliberation even though it was clear what the answer would be. I had waited a few days before I told Ellen that I needed my job at Whytebread or another one exactly like it even if the Gold Rush deal went through, because after taxes and considering retirement planning, a few million bucks just didn't go as far as it used to.

"WHAT ABOUT THAT SECRET LIST?" The Irishman was growing redder by the second, far redder even than usual, looking, for all the world, like the beginnings of a heart attack. "I WAS WORKING BEFORE YOU WERE THOUGHT OF, BOY. I MADE THIS FIRM." He sounded almost as though his feelings had been hurt. Jon and Hal propelled him steadily towards the doors; and his voice rose and cracked with a hiccupy quality. "You faggoty little PRICK. How much money are YOU getting out of this?"

"Hmmmm." Beside me, Justin crossed and recrossed his legs uncomfortably as Wes's complexion cycled the full range of indignant shades of red. Sure, the sale of Whytebread was going to leave Winslow much richer than the rest of us. He had started out richer, but until now no one had shown the poor manners to point it out.

We were holding our collective breaths waiting to hear what new, career-limiting statement would next issue from The Irishman. He had become a spectacle, that spinout, crash and burn at the speedway you had to watch. Only Herb was left, staring straight at the podium, ghostly gray, as if by ignoring the scene, he could make it go away, but by then, Winslow himself had stopped mid-sentence to listen.

After a few seconds of silence, Wes began his pitch again, this being that the Gold Rush pie was bigger than employment contracts, bigger than retirement annuities, big enough for everyone. "Diversity is the name of the game." Gold Rush was so big that the size of Winslow's personal piece didn't matter. We were all waiting to hear him tell it, like that favorite childhood story where you knew all the words, but you just want it corroborated by an adult. Winslow was getting to the punch line when an uncharacteristic lot of sweat had come up on his forehead. Even as his voice carried on in its regular, measured way; sweat had started running in rivers down his face, wilting the collar of his crisp white shirt. Wet spots were coming up under the arms of his gray suit jacket. I was wondering if anyone else had noticed Winslow's apparent distress, but to look around the room meant to look away from Winslow and I couldn't seem to take my eyes off the man.

He was incongruously divided, the calm slow voice and the wildly sweating face, belonging to two separate people. The sweaty one had taken to wiping himself down every few minutes, swabbing a rapidly waterlogged handkerchief across his forehead. The calm voice kept chanting Winslow's all-purpose capitalist mantra, "Diversity. Liquidity."

Leaned back in the soft lumbar-supportive conference hall chair, I was meditating on the message, investing that buy-out money in the bull market of my fertile imagination. I'd been watching it grow into my future life of early retirement, until somehow the sweat running down Winslow's cheeks didn't seem to matter. I had hypnotized myself with the smell of the future and the sound of his well-modulated voice.

I almost didn't notice when it stopped, Winslow's drone replaced by the disorderly sounds of people scrambling. When I finally registered that something was very wrong, a thin, green film the color of Justin's suit was spilling over the side of the podium and the guys in the front row were swearing as they pulled chunks of half-digested spinach greens out of their hairpieces. Rupert Dean, having rushed the stage at Winslow's early signs of distress, was helping Cal Fraiser to maneuver Wes to the door. Most everybody else seemed to be in complete, collective shock, although Starr D'nofrio had taken this opportunity to finish pushing back her cuticles.

Herb Symon had made an immediate motion for adjournment and no one saw the need to vote.

V

"Forget for a gol-darn minute there are police in the lobby." Now in the lunchroom at the corner of my eye, I could see Herb's lower lip quivering like an angry child's. He snatched at Winslow's obituary from the refrigerator door and crumpled it in his hands. "Can't you just give the man a little respect?"

A piece of broken magnet went skittering along the hard linoleum floor and I couldn't stop turning the Post-it Note over in my head, *I will repay*, both Ellen and me still gaping at the place on the door where the paper had been.

Around the firm, feelings about Winslow were, had been, (I had corrected the tense in my mind), resoundingly mixed. Barring affection, Winslow had commanded at least respect, a grudging admiration for his business machismo and a whole-hearted enthusiasm for the physical vigor he paraded on the "sports wall" in his office.

The wall was a collection of signed photos, various Bulls, Bears and Blackhawks, interspersed with pictures of himself in rugged action poses: Wesley Winslow sailing the Mackinac, running the Chicago Marathon, fly fishing in hip-high waders and a faded khaki sun hat. These provided ready-made topics for ass kissing, Whytebread's coin of the realm. I couldn't have said who might have had the chutzpah to post and *dis* Winslow's death notice. But at least, I was consoling myself, I knew now why The Irishman had been looking for me.

"I will repay?" It was a kind of small talk really. At the news of Winslow's death, I was babbling to fill the space in the room with some sound besides the hoarse little puffing noises coming from Herb. "That's heavy huh?" I said to Ellen, nervously giggling.

"No. That's Roman's." Alcee Couteau, an ancient Black man with skin that shined like worn brown leather had an age-hoarse voice that went with the picture. He scowled, fixing me with sepia, red-rimmed eyes like a Weimeriener dog's, but there was nothing sleepy about the man. Couteau was sharp like his suit and his matching vest. He was carefully presented like the blocked fedora hat that perched on his withered, gray head, a dapper bent that for fifty years had made it seem right to call him *Mister Couteau,* even though he only ran the mailroom.

"Romans." Preaching from the doorway in a bawling tenor, Mister Couteau interjected himself into the room cane first.

"Oh, Jesus," said Herb.

"Romans 12:19. I will repay. Vengeance is mine saith the Lord." Couteau inclined his head sourly in my direction as if this knowledge gap were confirmation of my lack of character. It was not the first time I had disappointed him. Early on in my tenure at Whytebread, Couteau noticed me in the hall, introduced himself and seized upon my professional standing — not a secretary or one of the seemingly legion Filipino research associates. He'd decided I was a fine example of the advancement of our Colored young people, claiming me with a parental familiarity, the way any adult on the block could take me to task when I was a kid, and, in the ways that I didn't fully meet the ideal of The Race, gently improve me with a variety of heckling suggestions posed as friendly observations. *Shouldn't you be getting to school? Such a pretty girl if she'd just stand a little straighter.* Alcee fretted on my unmarried status so relentlessly that I had come to worry he had his son, Ned, in mind for my suitor, a slack, surly Brother, five years my junior, who, after dropping out of University of Illinois–Chicago, had come to work for Couteau in the mailroom, a temporary arrangement that had continued now for over ten years.

Couteau would bawl at me down the hall, "How come you're not married yet? You come on to Sunday meeting with me, girl; and I'll find you a good, Christian man."

I was too young, too smart, too fast to be caught, ready, clever-tongued excuses that were nonetheless warily respectful of my elder. He had read in my carriage somehow, good home training, assuming deference to age without question. He had, of course been right, that my upbringing would make me fear the shadow of my parents in Alcee's disapproval, needing Couteau as their proxy somehow to be unreservedly proud of me.

This precluded my telling him where to get off. Who, I reasoned, was he hurting? Who would it help to disillusion an old man with his social mores still resolutely in 1953? So I had danced around his prying apparently too many times, because after a while even Mister Couteau had cottoned onto my intractable attachment to what he must have imagined was sin, pure Godless wickedness of all varieties — not that it wasn't a relief. But I couldn't help feeling unaccountably embarrassed that his banter had cooled so to polite acknowledgement, his questions replaced by a look like he was closing the door on me.

Mister Couteau had had better luck as the mentor of Camille Gutierrez whom he'd helped to become a committed follower of Jesus. They studied the bible together over lunch nearly every day. When Camille's daughter Elana got a part-time job in the Whytebread library she joined them as well. A pretty enough girl to restore nearly anyone's faith in God, Elana shilled for Alcee's sermons drawing a crowd among the young men from the mailroom — and enticing the occasional junior analyst with her eye candy for Jesus. I'd even seen Rupert Dean and his friends linger through a Couteau monologue if Elana was in the room.

Herb was still making soft puffing noises that sounded a little like a mild asthma attack and Couteau was still preaching not at me especially anymore, but just in general as if he felt it would be instructive to all concerned. "Vengeance is mine —"

"Aw Jesus," Herb apparently had no wish to be instructed, particularly by Couteau whom I'd heard him say on a number of occasions didn't seem to know his place.

Mister Couteau drew himself up, pooling seventy years of bristling dignity. "The Lord says, 'do not seek revenge.' "

"Alcee," Herb said, "can *you* just give it a rest today for Chrissakes."

"And you —" Alcee lifted his cane very slightly, the cane as much of his managed persona as were the three-piece suits. Mister Couteau lifted his cane at Herb so there could be no mistaking his meaning. "And why don't *you* call on somebody you know?"

It was a fine effect, a second grand arch of the rubber-tipped wood, conveying Couteau from the room. I'd see the old man throw that cane, a prop, aside to catch a box that teetered and fell from the top of the mail stack, running at an impressive gallop.

I had the idea that Couteau was the author of the Post-it Note on Winslow's obituary. He had come around unable in his terminal self-righteousness to resist the editorial opportunity. He had done it before. That was part of the rancor between them; before Herb stopped him, there were Post-it Notes turning up all over the firm, office surfaces were thick with Mister Couteau's opinions.

I'd found a note that read: *More precious to me is a sinner who accepts God, than a righteous man.* It was stuck audaciously to the green glass shade of my polished brass banker's lamp. Rupert Dean had received: *Be sure your sin will find you out. The way of transgressors is hard,* was left on the top of the Tupperware container Wesley Winslow used to bring his salad lunch.

Herb made a final indignant sniffle, still working the balled up newspaper in his busy hands and watching in disbelief as Ellen slipped through the empty space Mister Couteau had left in the doorway. I watched as well wondering how no one in fifty years had thought to fire him for that mouth.

No one had even tried. Mister Couteau had been August Madsen's pet, unable to work his way up through night school like The Irishman, but I was thinking perhaps by walking the halls for fifty years pushing a mail cart, dressed like a partner, by simply the constancy of his presence he had made the way for me into a job where such attire was expected.

The refrigerator motor cut in softly as Herb crushed and crushed the paper into a progressively smaller ball. He tossed

it at the trash and missed, standing there for a good while
blinking dimly, before he finally walked over, stooped to pick
it up again, and put the paper in the trash as he left the
lunchroom.

VI

I'd accomplished so little between my arrival and Herb's company meeting later in the morning, that it felt good to leave the few stock reports I had updated in Camille's in-box for proofreading on my way to the 25th floor conference room. The "big conference room" as Herb had called it wasn't really big enough. In the time I had worked there, Whytebread had grown fast from the intimate boys' club its founders had intended into a sprawling conglomeration of folks that Justin Collier, in a way that always slightly rankled me, called "riffraff" — the brown, the female, those others not quite to the manner born.

Whytebread had grown so quickly that all of a sudden there didn't seem to be quite enough room at the table for all the worker bees — not if Justin was a dinner guest, much as he tried to dress it up. In Justin you had one hungry hunter, all of the me-first ruthlessness of Roy Cohn and none of the acne scars, genuinely wondering why he ought to step to the back of the buffet line for seconds just because there were some people who hadn't eaten yet.

By twenty minutes to twelve, Whytebread's great unwashed were spilled out into the entry hall — leaning on the glass walls and sitting on the rosewood credenzas in a disorderly way that you could tell really worked Herb Symon's nerves, despite what I could imagine were Herculean efforts at a sort of open-face friendliness to all on his part. Herb was the kind of guy with a living room full of furniture covered in plastic and he was fairly twitching with annoyance as he directed a steady stream of new arrivals to the huge, pink-cardboard, bakery box balanced across the arms of a high-backed chair, encouraging everyone with put-on graciousness to take a donut.

"That's what they're there for." The sentiment at least was genuine; to look at Herb with his short thick waist, I was confident he was a great friend of the donut.

The donut had many other friends that day. I had squeezed myself into a corner beside Camille Gutierrez who was devouring a large, white cake donut, a light frosting of powdered sugar dusting her lower lip and chin. The departure from Winslow's preferred bran muffins, bagels and fruit tray signaled a change on the horizon. Had Winslow not been dead, that would have killed him.

The man himself, a stern-faced reminder of his culinary predilections, looked out from a stray edition of the past quarter's Whytebread Investor Newsletter that had been left on the credenza. The black and white photo of Wesley Winslow sat above the caption: *Malaysia! Kuala Lumpur has 19 million consumers, the first and second tallest buildings in the world and nowhere to go but up*, eerie in its naturalness. Herb Symon was there on the second page, always number

two, with his little perspective column: *What does it profit.*
Like this one I had been considering, Herb's commentaries
usually started with some lofty quote, a blatant rip-off of
Forbes Magazine's only slightly more pretentious *Thoughts on
the Business of Life.*

"Excuse me," Allison Price reached over me licking at the
dollop of jelly on the side of her hand, and clip-clopping back
lumpishly into the crowd with her cherry Danish.

"Too bad about Wes," Cal Fraiser was saying to Marty
Goodman, "but at least now we can have pastry again."

I was relishing an apple fritter myself as Herb called for
quiet, pushing down the air in front of him with both hands.
"Let's take our seats people. Can I have your attention
please?"

The chatter barely decreased to a low roar until Jon Patel
stood up on his chair and gave a long shrill whistle through
his teeth. Then Herb began: "For those of you who may not
have already heard, Wesley Winslow passed away over the
weekend from a severe case of flu. I'm sure I speak for all of
us when I say he will be deeply missed."

Camille Gutierrez snorted loudly enough that I wondered
if anyone else had heard, but her disdain was lost in a variety
of other disrespectful raspberries from nonspecific areas of the
room directed at Herb or at Wes, who could say?

"Wes," Herb continued either oblivious or unperturbed,
"had only begun to realize his potential as leader of this firm.
He had just begun to make what all of us expected would be
significant contributions to the financial health and prestige
of Whytebread: the inroads he forged in client contacts, the
Gold Rush investments offer, which Wes solicited," and to this
there were vague kind of prayer meeting rumblings from Jon
Patel, Rupert, and others eager to position their lips on
whatever rosy buttocks would succeed Winslow's.

Herb paused extravagantly to let Wes's accomplishments
cast their long shadow, leaving all but the dimmest minds in
attendance to wonder how long he had been rehearsing this

51

particular speech. "Of course," he said, "Wes Winslow's untimely departure creates some challenges for those of us remaining, but I am sure he would have the utmost confidence in our ability to meet them. Until the board names Wes's successor, his uncle and our Chairman, August Madsen, has asked me to take responsibility for the day-to-day operations." Barely able to contain his pleasure, Herb was fairly chortling, "I will make every effort to run Whytebread in a manner which will do justice to Wes's vision for this firm."

The applause was sparse, but he continued: "I will be asking some of you to take on expanded responsibilities in the new organization as well," and with that applause was very much greater. Satisfied, confident looks were beaming on the faces of Herb's old cronies, The Irishman among them. Then Herb said, "In light of our loss, however, the Board has decided to table the vote on the Gold Rush offer until further notice."

From somewhere behind me, The Irishman's whoop was followed by a perfect silence as if all the rest of us had taken a moment to mourn the loss of our fortunes. By canceling the Gold Rush vote, August Madsen had dropped the financial equivalent of a neutron bomb on Whytebread and Greese — the building was standing but the money was gone, the money I and everybody else had already spent in a million ways, and a million times over in our imaginations.

The silence gave way to pandemonium, but Herb Symon had slipped off already, presumably back to Wes's old office where he was no doubt adjusting the executive lumbar support to fit his spineless, pear-shaped ass.

"That's all, folks." Likely in anticipation of his expanded duties as senior lieutenant, Jon Patel was broadly encouraging people back to work, herding us out of the conference room towards the elevators like a sleepy dinner party host expelling his over-staying guests. "Thanks for coming." Jon squeezed my arm with uncharacteristic camaraderie. "Be sure to take a sweet roll back to your desk."

Swept out with the disoriented tumble of my colleagues, I found myself in the hall where The Irishman was holding forth to some juniors a long-winded joke about a Black, a Jew, and a Chinaman. Rather than wait for the punch line I took the stairs back to my office. In the walk, that morning's hangover had returned for an unfortunate curtain call accompanied by a healthy dose of clinical depression. The combination left me so dispirited that I nearly sat down on the note that was taped to the seat of my chair: It said: *Meet me at the Wendy's on the corner of Clark and Madison across from the Bank.*

The note which I presumed was from Cassandra had mentioned no specific time for our meeting but when I arrived, she was waiting with several coffee cups lined up in front of her like an hour and a half's worth of dead soldiers.

"Please sit down." Popping up from her chair, Cassandra took my hand in both of hers across the table, muse-asking "How long has it been?" as if I were a very dear friend unfortunately kept out of touch by unavoidable circumstances.

I shook my head. How long had it been? I couldn't say exactly, although I had considered the question in my walk to Wendy's. Had I been inclined to guess, I would have ventured at least ten years since we had spoken — longer than that since we'd spoken civilly, rather since I'd spoken civilly to her. Leaving me had not really emotionally affected Cassandra.

Not much did. Ten years ago, I had liked her police trainee swagger; it made me feel like I was slumming in a B movie.

I'd liked best that she had been unflappable, matter-of-fact in everything she did, including me. I'd loved that for three whirlwind months, she'd stop by my apartment unpredictably, leave her gun on my dining room table, fuck my brains out, and manage an exit by five-o'clock the next morning. Sometimes she would kiss me before she left. Sometimes she would tell me what she was thinking. Other times she would share little details about her life, which I took to mean in her way that she loved me — loved me specially — which is how I came to mistake our servicing agreement for the intimate relationship I so desperately wanted. Understandably I had been bitter when she dropped me; it made me feel I had been pathetic. And she had ended things unceremoniously, cheating me of closure, a point over which my therapist said I had every right to be angry.

"You prefer tea, right?" Briskly solicitous, Cassandra jerked her head at a lone paper cup set in front of the seat across from hers. Apparently unaware of any issues I might be having regarding her reappearance in my life, there was an economy to her charm I still found charming. So, if it was strange to be catching up there at Wendy's, to have her courting me, that is not to say that the turn of events didn't please me.

"All they had was regular Lipton, but I remembered. No milk or sugar?" The tea was only warm, so apparently she had been waiting for a while. That pleased me as well.

When I'd known her, Cassandra was just starting at the police academy, a career change she had come to in her late twenties after a few years as a grade school teacher. I'd thought police service was more in keeping with her taste for hardball. She was enrolled, now, in night law school at John Marshall, a local institution that routinely flunked out a third of the first year class, but Cassie had never lacked grit or backbone — just the softer parts.

"I didn't think it was smart for us to talk in your office,"

Cassandra put out a business-like tone, but I had already surmised this wasn't exactly a social call.

"Well, no. No, sadly not, I'm afraid." She'd turned up the corners of her mouth with a flat but gracious expression of patience as she told me that Wesley Winslow had been murdered.

That explained why the brakes were on the Gold Rush deal. I was saying, certainly Winslow had not been loved, but I couldn't understand why anyone would want him dead. Allison Price just wanted the windfall of the payout *and* her pension left exactly as it had been. Ellen Borgia wanted to sue. Even The Irishman didn't want the deal stopped; he just wanted to negotiate for a bigger piece of the pie.

"HEY, MILL — IE," I recalled The Irishman had horrified me at lunch the Friday of the shareholders meeting — the day Winslow had collapsed — by throwing up a beefy arm and caterwauling for our waitress. At his summons, she had begun to thread her way through the dining room's maze of tables towards our corner booth, arriving after a short eternity of small mincing steps inhibited by tall, thin heels. She was encased in fashion technology — the control-top nylon of her stockings, the acrylic knit of her dress — all designed to hold a middle-aged body in the general configuration of a twenty-five-year-old.

"I swear you're better looking every year," The Irishman crooned, an apparent regular at the Cock and Bull, the restaurant where he was hosting me and a motley assortment of others he wanted to join him in his plan to hijack the Gold Rush deal from Winslow. The Cock and Bull was a man's place that might best be characterized as a pub with a kitchen. "Yeah, baby," Irishman threatening poor Millie with the prize of himself. "You get me all excited."

I was taking it in, the dark clubby wood walls of the Cock and Bull, the cracking cordovan-colored leather, and the lack of any living flora whatsoever, like eating in the interior of some big, butch luxury car; and more interesting to me than The Irishman's repartee, was the way Ellen Borgia was snuggled into a secluded booth, across the room, opposite Jeremy Bennett, the twenty-something, fuzz-headed ex-Marine who ran Whytebread's local area computer network.

In contrast to his habitual jeans and Nike high-top sneakers, Jeremy was wearing a chestnut brown corduroy suit jacket with professorial suede patches on the elbows, a white shirt, and a harmless-looking blue paisley kind of tie he'd probably ordered from the same catalogue where Winslow got his. At their quiet booth, Ellen Borgia was laughing.

"Aw, these old eyes work just fine." The Irishman was laughing too, patting the black-frame reading glasses in his breast shirt pocket, as my attention returned to our table, waggling his finger at the waitress, and bragging, "My eyes ain't the only things in working order, honey. Now you remember that."

Rupert horse-laughed. Nonplussed, Millie flipped a new page of her order pad, prompting The Irishman to order a round of gin martinis for the table. The tea-tottling Herb had sat scowling until The Irishman added easily, "water too, all around," as if this had been his original intention.

"And ice tea," Herb caught our waitress by the arm. As she left to fetch the drinks, we all looked around at each other like the table of odds and ends at a wedding reception until, thankfully, in their cozy booth Jeremy Bennett told another joke, a point of common interest.

Herb turned and raised his eyes.

"What do they say," Rupert giggled, "— twenty goes into forty a hell of a lot more times than forty goes into twenty."

"The hell you say," said The Irishman, a joke of his own. Herb Symon and I made prudish frowns.

"I'd say when hell freezes over," Justin said and Rupert Dean chuckled maliciously.

It was a context in which I had not considered Ellen

Borgia who seemed to me sexless. But I looked at her, her body attractive, sleek, her bosoms pert and high at certainly over 40. *Well-appointed.* The thought came to me like a glossy description of a luxury car. Even with the age difference, Ellen seemed an undeservedly high-end prize for the likes of Jeremy Bennett, who in the pathetic improvisation of his this-is-my-only-coat-without-a-hood suit jacket, seemed a man lucky to enjoy even basic transportation. For Ellen this seemed the ugly inevitability of settling, like a tired, old house, into the choices of compromised hope which had for its soundtrack my mother's oblique advice on life, offered every time we spoke, "Companionship is important; as you get older, you'll realize that." Only now I thought to consider she might not have been talking about me.

"When hell freezes over." The men around me laughed, except for Herb who didn't, more offended by the dirtiness of the talk, I suspected than the gossip, but he put on a pretty good show of holier than thou.

It had been quite a relief when the drinks arrived, The Irishman bellowing amiably that Millie should, "keep 'em coming." Lubrication assured, he began the personal epic of his career at Whytebread and Greese some thirty years past. "You know, when I was seventeen years old I walked into that old South Monroe Street building . . ." Not that there wasn't one of us who didn't know the story well enough to have performed it as a musical revue, but in the company of a libation The Irishman couldn't resist reprising his role as Horatio Alger.

Armed with his first-generation American ambitions and a high school diploma, The Irishman had stood in the lobby for half an hour reading the names of the businesses, and then, tenaciously presented himself to the receptionists of each one asking for work. He drew this out for dramatic tension, the names of the firms, the rejections. Whytebread had been his thirteenth inquiry. There, August Madsen admitted that Whytebread could indeed use a new boy in the mailroom, looking Zemluski up and down before announcing, "Well, young man, I suppose you'll do."

The table turned as Ellen Borgia's tinkley laughter crossed the dinning room again.

"HE SUPPOSED I'D DO!" The Irishman delighted himself: "There I was in my best church suit, hair cut, shoes shined. Damn fine-looking kid I was in those days too and I'll tell you that old man's voice was withering."

Across from me, Rupert Dean shifted restlessly in the red leather booth as if his butt were itchy, and I was steadily getting drunk, watching Justin studiously eat the ice in his water glass, and finding it all pretty darn interesting, the way he lifted each cube to his mouth with such care, and then crunched down ruthlessly with his back molars.

"WITHERING. Thirty-one years later here I am — a Goddamn senior vice president." The Irishman thumped his chest with pride and wonder at the grand irony of low expectations so completely exceeded. "You tell *me* how well I've done?"

"What would be your point?" Herb Symon's intent was clearly to demonstrate what was meant by *withering*.

Leaning his chest back a little way from the table as Millie laid out his lunch, The Irishman set his jaw and let out a long breath waiting for her to finish. "I was just saying, Herb, I've known this firm, stuck with it here a good, long time. A long time — that should mean something is all I'm saying."

Rupert Dean was enjoying this verbal retreat, brown eyes shining like two angry pennies as seemingly from the heavens another glass of gin and olive appeared at my place to replace the previous one. The Irishman pressed on heedlessly, his words melting if not pleasantly than certainly seamlessly together like the verbal equivalent of a Salvador Dali painting.

"Don't expect those Gold Rush guys to get the heave ho." The Irishman was promising, as Ellen Borgia fed the ex-Marine what looked like veal parmesan from her fork.

"Those Gold Rush guys aren't going anywhere," he said. "My point is, Herb, they're going to fire us. My point is we could pool our voting stock and offer it to Wes in exchange for some assurances."

I was wondering where I fit in all of this. Having seen The List, I knew I wasn't going to get canned. Neither was Herb and certainly Justin wasn't. So, I was nodding politely not out of any special agreement, but more because my head had just gotten started that way. It seemed the easiest thing just to continue along as I was rather than stop it or change its direction.

"He's going to fire us." The Irishman thundered on like a big red-faced freight train. Concurrent with the rise in his voice, I'd elected to sink as low as I could down into my mashed potatoes, hoping this placed me well below the line of fire. We were, all of us juniors, taking the silent prudent posture. At the far edge of my peripheral vision, Jeremy Bennett looked like he just might be getting a foot job under the table and I had to wonder what Ellen Borgia could possibly be thinking. Justin Collier was delicately cutting and chewing little bits of his lamb chop with undisguised rapture, the way his mother no doubt had instructed him, twenty chews a mouthful.

"Things change." Herb's voice was not unsympathetic. I was nodding in accord. Given that much liquor it was hard not to feel somewhat sympathetic to almost anything.

"And besides, Tom," Rupert Dean had decided to speak uninvited, devoid of the good sense God gave stone. "Tom, our Whytebread stock is going to be worth a lot of money," sounding as if he were getting a woody just imagining it. "You could hold onto the Gold Rush stock," Rupert put in more confidently, "if you didn't want to take the cash."

Jon Patel to my right was visibly regretting that he had not had the balls to say as much. Now he rushed to echo. "You could take the cash, Tom."

Across the dining room, Jeremy Bennett called for the

check and my own little mind was wandering back to those hand-signed letters all of the partners had received by Fed Ex at our homes, describing the Gold Rush offer, which Wes had called "exceptionally generous," outlining its terms in detail. Wes and the Madsen/Winslows had emphasized the urgency that we decide upon a course of action. Six weeks from the September 26 date, this Gold Rush money from heaven would evaporate.

Still Rupert had not known when to shut up. "It's a really good offer —"

"That depends on who you are," The Irishman barked back. "You just leave me to do the thinking, boy. I've had a lot more practice."

"Tom, you can't blackmail change." Herb was frowning, perhaps in thought, perhaps in irritation at a meal disturbed. He sent a slow serious look around the table, daring any of us to dispute his right to the last word, and cutting his steak deliberately. "Anyway. There's no point letting good food get cold."

VII

"Winslow's death is suspicious," Cassandra was saying. "Forty-five-year-old health enthusiasts don't usually die from a sudden flu. If Mr. Winslow has been murdered, Mr. Madsen is determined that the killer will gain no benefit from his association with the firm. Although we can't be completely sure," she was bending to open the briefcase on the floor beside her leg, "we suspect Wesley Winslow was de- liberately poisoned."

I had closed my eyes while she was talking, making the desperate wish that when I opened them Cassandra Hope and Wendy's Old Fashioned Hamburgers would be gone.

Instead, there was a legal-sized file folder on the table. It wore Wesley Winslow's name typed on a clean, new adhesive label. Cassandra laid the folder between us. "I can tell you what it says." She was playing her fingers along the edge of the cardboard. Then, she opened the file and began to read what I took for selections; she was giving me the Reader's Digest version of her report, just the highpoints.

"We know that Mr. Symon drove Mr. Winslow home to his city apartment at the Park Shore apartment building on Friday October 2, arriving there at about five-thirty in the evening. Mr. Symon rode up the elevator with Winslow and checked to see that Winslow was going to be okay and then he left, returning to his own home in Wilmette." Cassandra's voice had a perfected quality as if she were reciting something she had studied and knew by heart. "Mr. Symon states that he left about six o'clock that evening and Winslow seemed weak, but recovered. Winslow requested Symon to call his daughter's nanny to let them know he was ill and would be staying in the city that night rather than make the long train ride home. Winslow stated to Symon that he was going to have a bath and go to sleep, planning to return to his residence in Barrington the next day, Saturday." According to the doorman, Winslow enjoyed a steady stream of visitors that evening — Tom Zemluski, Herb Symon, Justin Collier and Rupert Dean who had helped Herb Symon drive Wes home that evening. Everyone had left by 8:00 p.m. on Friday as far as the doorman knew.

When Winslow hadn't come home by Saturday night, the nanny called first the apartment and then the doorman to ask if he would check in on Winslow. The doorman found the body about 5:00 p.m. Saturday. From his report Winslow was all tucked into bed as if he had died in his sleep. The Medical Examiner believed that death occurred between 6:00 and 10:00 p.m. from respiratory failure induced by poisoned mushrooms.

"Toxicology showed Ibotenic acid, Choline, Muscarine," Cassandra was saying. "All natural chemicals found in a mushroom called *Fly Agaric*." Otherwise an examination of the stomach contents such as they were, and a variety of other organs, blood, bile vitreous, muscle tissue, hair and nail cuttings had proved in the coroners' words, *unremarkable,* except for the presence of nicotine residue in Winslow's hair and nails. "We know that Winslow brought a vegetarian lunch everyday and that it was well known at the firm that he kept it in the community refrigerator in the lunchroom. We've looked, but no one can find the container. We think the killer took it."

"You think somebody at Whytebread killed him?" My own voice sounded tiny and unsteady even to myself. I shut my eyes again and tried to get my head around the idea, closing my hands on my paper cup of tea to warm them against the persistent draft from the door. The first hint that fall was headed toward winter, summer slipping away like sand.

Winter was the only reason I could ever think of to leave Chicago, that mid-January hawk blasting supersonically off the lake, the screw-tightening twist of an especially cold snap just before the blessing of a February thaw. Chicago in the winter was all about a wind cold enough to freeze the mucus in your nose, those months when people only left their houses to run their cars once a week so the engine would turn over when it was time to go grocery shopping.

That hibernation had seemed almost nice, when I was with my ex-lover, Emily. The weekends had a lovely quality of enforced intimacy, nesting all day in bed on Sundays with the New York Times, huddled together under three comforters for warmth in my unpredictably heated condo. Spike was usually too far away for the comfort of shared body heat; and Spike, I had discovered early on in our relationship, could never sleep more than three or four hours a night.

Yet another incompatibility: what I called insomnia, she characterized as "the most productive hours of the day," the dozy time between three and seven o'clock in the morning. I would have been content for us to make a pact of disagreement as to the best use of that time, but Spike was determined that we share it, upright, taking walks at dawn, grocery shopping in the conveniently 24-hour Jewel grocery store at four in the morning when there was never any line for a cashier, lying silently together as I pretended to sleep and she staked-out my face for signs of consciousness.

Wes was going to make us rich. "Who do you think did it?"

Cassandra just shook her head. "I'll need to know all the dirt at Whytebread to figure that out." She leaned towards me across the table confidingly. "Someone could have slipped them into his lunch. From all accounts, mushroom hunting wasn't one of Mr. Winslow's hobbies." I thought Wes had been in his way peculiar at least by Whytebread standards. While his pedigree excused his vegetarianism, it had not gone unnoticed among management that Winslow begged off every company business lunch he could, lest he be at the mercy of some Frenchified, animal fat slinging chief, and there was of course his suspicious disdain of pastries.

It wasn't particularly hard for me to imagine Winslow running around his Barrington Estate in his boxer shorts tossing down fruits and berries like *Iron John*.

Still if Cassandra was right it was strangely unsettling to think I'd seen Wes eat his last meal that Friday. He'd brought it with him to my office — a green salad and vegetables — in a Tupperware lunchbox he'd balanced on his knee while we talked about Comstock, my low price to earnings pick. Rather he had asked and I answered, a discussion conducted oral examination style. In his almost legendary knack for efficiency, Winslow used every delay in my response to fill his mouth with greens, squinting critically at the pile of papers that littered my desk as I tried to reel off the minutia that when fully understood by other market participants would drive the price of Comstock Wireless to meteoric heights.

Comstock, I was saying, was a company under-appreciated by nearly every other analyst but me. Winslow chewed. I said that was exactly why my contrarian opinion spelled opportunity, and he kept up shoveling his salad into the yawning cavity of his mouth, stopping only to sniffle occasionally or wipe his slightly runny nose with the handkerchief he was using as a napkin. He had been sick. Even so I'd been able to tell that Wes was interested and engaged in my story: the charm of the eventual takeover angle, the rugged, individualist, Americana wallow of bucking the conventional wisdom. In my only short meeting, I was judging him an intelligent man; and I could tell from the way he had begun to meet my eyes that his fascination with Comstock was growing. In fact, the more I talked, the more I liked Wes Winslow. His sharp angled face, the frankness of his pointing chin and nose, and the rubicund, almost parturient glow of his skin. I liked watching myself grow in his estimation. It gave me a long, giddy, head rush to be, after all these years, on the radar screen of senior management right where I thought I belonged — in the game.

"What did Herb Symon say about all this? Or Zemluski?" Or Justin, I was thinking.

Cassandra shook her head, exasperated. "Nobody's talking here. If they were, I wouldn't need you." That was just like her. I was sure she hadn't meant it as an insult, just a statement of inconvenient fact. So much for the nylons and chocolate.

In her tone there was a flat kind of irritation. "According to Zemluski, he stopped by out of nothing more than friendly concern. Yet, I am told by a more forthcoming colleague that Winslow and Zemluski were not on the best of terms the day he died. I'll have to interview everyone at Whytebread and Greese, of course. Before I do, it would be nice to see where the skeletons are buried — the inside family stuff nobody wants to tell the cops."

"No one but me?" The small affront had returned me, in that moment, to the exact feeling of disappointment I had when she left me years ago, and I was gratified to find that I could still provoke her, even after so long, as if that proved that whatever we had was not simply wasted time. "Are you saying I'm not family?"

"If this is because I haven't called —" she began as if my anger hurt her feelings, "it's not because I haven't thought of you. A lot." My skin felt warm as she squeezed my arm across the table and I would never have it said that I minded a little manipulation when it was done well. I minded not at all that her hand on my wrist could still dial up a ten year-old memory of clothes folded carefully in the wicker chair beside my bed.

"Maybe this will help you decide on which side your bread is buttered," she said, taking stock of me.

On which side. I'd always felt a tingle of superiority at Cassandra's self-conscious compulsion towards perfect grammar, an issue of class. Even as I wanted advancement, I was secure in mine, but I knew from those occasional years-ago, bedtime anecdotes that Cassandra's finger-hold on middle-class respectability and comfort had been so hard-won she worried it could be lost by a careless slip of the tongue.

Leafing through her file, Cassandra removed a single sheet of white paper, and laid it on top of the rest of the report. It was a list. Cassandra carefully smoothed the paper's edges with her palm, as if she expected that at any moment I would recognize and bow down to this delicate artifact.

Cassandra's List was very much like The List Ellen Borgia had shown me, months before, featuring the same two columns with their bold-faced headings: *Retain* and *Terminate*. But now, I was on the Have List along with Allison Price, and Ellen Borgia. The numbers of options beside our names were big. The options awarded to Rupert Dean were mysteriously gone. According to this List, Dean wouldn't even keep his job. Certainly my face must have been a study. I was wondering if Ellen knew that her suit was over because no jury on earth was going to punish Whytebread and Greese for making us rich.

Cassandra was leaned back in her chair, just short of

reclining and smiling now like she could chew me up and not even crack a tooth.

"The Terminations List was supposed to be a secret," I confessed, a little hoarse and breathless in the afterglow. "People said Wes had personally targeted folks to reward and punish." There had been rumors, I said, though I didn't let on I knew they were true; and I couldn't help asking, "Is this for real, the final List?"

Cassandra nodded, now knowing she had me. Explaining, the longer it took to tie up Winslow's murder, the less likely it was that Winslow's List would remain with my piece of the pie untouched, a decision that would be up to August Madsen.

My father had confided to me once in a wonderment that now reminded me of my own, in the kind of intimacy we hadn't shared since he'd stopped taking me and my little sister to *Indian Princess* father-daughter evenings sometime in the early seventies. He'd said, "I never thought I would have this much, ever," speaking of his house, his job, his cars, closing his eyes as if he were remembering a specific day when God had smiled down on his nappy head.

There at Wendy's I was thinking back sheepishly on my scorn for my father's naive gratefulness at the small bit of luck the universe had thrown him, limited by his concept of what could be available to a Black man born in the thirties. *I never thought I would have so much*. It didn't seem quite so pathetic a sentiment anymore. The difference between my father and I was boiling down neatly to a matter of commas. We were both for sale, just a matter of price. Right there at Wendy's, I had nearly swooned.

"Where did you get this?" My fingers grazed The List lightly so as not to damage it in any way.

"From August Madsen — who got it from Wesley Winslow's personal safe. My sources tell me the stock and options could make you a very comfortable young woman." Her voice was grinning. "Are you counting your money?" Cassandra pushed aside the most recent in her line of coffees.

She leaned over close to goad me, catching my wrist tight and twisting almost in an Indian burn. "Well, you'd better not, Virginia. Not until August Madsen is satisfied we've cleared this up."

Like it or not, my bequest on Winslow's List made it *we* now.

"No murderer, no merger, no money." Cassandra ran her tongue across her lips again seductively before she showed me every one of her perfect teeth. "Funny how it seems like we both have the same problem now." Cassandra let go of my arm. While there was still an ache where she had held it, the rest of me was numb. My mind had emptied except for one thought: *Braces.*

When we'd dated, Cassie's incisors turned inward slightly, breaking the monotony of her good looks in a way I could find endearing. She had reinvented herself just as Wesley Winslow had reinvented Starr, down to the smallest details — like Spike/Mary Ellen, with her renaming and her ever-evolving rainbow of temporary hair colors, the piercings that multiplied, it seemed now, monthly. It felt like the world was changing around me and only I remained dependably, sanely the same.

Whatever she had done to her teeth, Cassandra Hope certainly had not neglected her homework. "Tell me what you hear around the firm, Virginia. Tell me what you know, and we can all get paid."

So, I started by telling Cassandra about Winslow's wife. Nervous, neglected and apparently angry, Trisha Winslow had swept into the last Christmas party nine months ago with a host of Whytebread swains from which her husband was conspicuously absent. I'd seen him in a corner, whispering something that looked grave and business-related to Justin, as I found myself saddled with Rupert Dean's debilitatingly gravid spouse. Rupert had left her struggling on a short run of stairs from the lobby in his haste to attend to Mrs. Winslow.

Katherine Dean, Kitty, as I learned she liked to be called,

looked at least eighteen months pregnant with their fourth child. Wearing an outfit that consisted primarily of *Lycra* stretch pants and a tuxedo jacket, she put me in mind of Marlene Dietrich cast as an aerobics instructor with a thyroid condition.

I was none too sure of the stairs myself in my skinny little heels, having fully enjoyed the open bar since about quarter to five, but I took hold of Kitty's elbow as she huffed at me appreciatively, "Wait till you have some of your own," her face exuberantly flushed with the positive brain chemicals of pregnancy. "It's just wonderful how the hormones make you forget everything afterwards."

I was nodding as politely as possible, as we stepped into the ballroom. Even on an Ecstasy drip it would have been hard to forget the horror of those black, Lycra stretch pants. Over Kitty's wide, black, padded shoulder, I caught a glimpse of Maddy Madsen strolling through the crowd, shaking hands as if he were the father of the bride at a big family wedding. Spying an expectant "mommy," he'd changed direction and crossed the room beaming down benediction on Kitty Dean's ponderous stomach.

"Last time," she was telling me, "it was the twins," as if this had been a special blessing.

"Buns in the oven," Madsen observed like something out of Mutual of Omaha's: Wild Kingdom, the oldest male of the pride presiding over the pregnant females as they ensured the perpetuation of the species — in this case scary, yuppie White folk. "Good for you, Kitty," he pronounced while I stood there interminably waiting for my special Christmas hello from the craggy old bastard.

No buns in my oven (thank God). Madsen smiled down at me as an after thought. "Nice piece of work you did on Proctor and Gamble." He clapped a big, God-like hand on my shoulder, squeezing slightly with a well-rehearsed quality of spontaneous personal feeling. "Keep it up. Virginia." He had my name easy enough; I was the Black one, but he'd confused me professionally with Allison Price, another barren spinster, the analyst for non-cyclical consumer products. It would have been both impolitic and impractical to protest the mistake. Before I could speak, Madsen was several people away, on to the next warm-employee-shoulder-clasp.

"What a nice man." Kitty Dean was gazing after him with dimwitted veneration. She turned to me companionably, "Proctor and Gamble. Why that's so exciting. With the twins, now I swear by Tide and Rupert — I don't know what he does after work to get so dirty."

I said I couldn't imagine, looking past her for my method of escape, but in truth, worse conversationalists than old Kitty Dean, who had the appeal of at least being sober, had cornered me at these affairs. She had proved herself astonishingly well versed on obscure medical complications of pregnancy, having suffered from them all when she was carrying the twins. Should anyone ask, I would be able to report that Kitty was pleased to be experiencing none of these reproductive difficulties with her current potential litter.

"So glad to hear that." I meant it quite sincerely, managing to slip away just as she was explaining *Toxemia* to Allison Price who'd had the wretchedly poor judgment to join our conversation some minutes before.

Pleasantly alone I had retired to a quiet spot away from the networking to enjoy a little quality time with my gin and tonic.

"Hey, little sistah, I love your dress." Justin had come from behind, stage whispering in remedial Ebonics. He planted both hands familiarly on either of my hips, a suggestive little move that since he was gay suggested nothing, but surely would be misunderstood and discussed that Monday. I'd had enough of the open bar to imagine that he was asking for a piece of my mind.

"Honey," Justin answered back, critiquing my outfit with

the self-assurance of Mr. Blackwell, "sequins are absolutely you."

He was wearing a red and green Christmas tree cummerbund with matching bow tie and socks, the only man in the room in tuxedo pumps and queer family feeling made me hold my tongue.

He unwrapped our bodies and began pulling me towards the dance floor where I minced out an awkward kind of two-step courtesy of the black, *peu de soi* pumps, an inch too high, and a hair too small across the instep. I'd begged off after one or two turns around the nearly empty dance floor, leaving Justin to Starr who had been swaying to the music conspicuously solo for most of the evening. With a partner, she'd been transformed from wallflower to man-eater, all teeth now, floating to the dance floor with Justin on her arm, in her full length gown — a beaded pink affair with a neckline that headed resolutely towards China and a slit up the side that showcased thigh. I watched from my little table as he swirled her around so athletically that her shimmery dress flew out in circles around her legs.

Like most everyone else, Starr was drunk, so loaded that every so often she would lose her balance and just sit down in the middle of the floor, the beads of her dress clattering like the shake of a shiny, pink abacus. Once down, she would remain there giggling until Justin hoisted her back onto her feet again. The entire party, in fact, had drunk itself into an attitude of Christmastime goodwill and giddiness. The Irishman even came around, booming, "Merry Christmas," at me as if it were a job assignment. He threw a heavy arm around my neck chokehold-style and delivered a slobbery kiss to my cheek. "I've always liked you, kid. You know that, don't you? That's why I've got to be so hard on you." He was kneading my shoulder in a way that I hoped was merely fatherly, wondering where The Irishman's wife might be, but

I didn't expect he would remember our special moment on Monday. The Irishman tousled my hair affectionately before he shambled off towards Rupert Dean, leaving me to discreetly wipe the spit off my face.

While I'd been thus engaged, Wesley Winslow had cut in on Starr and Justin, so they were all dancing together. I didn't know where Winslow's wife had gotten to either. Maybe she was talking to Mrs. Zemluski. In the meantime, Wes was swinging Starr under his arm like something out of a Fred Astair and Ginger Rogers musical number, dipping her so low her head nearly touched the floor while Justin watched his boss's moves, clapping effusively.

After a while they both began to spin her around, passing her back and forth in the silent, serious way two guys on a dark quiet porch will share a bottle. Starr would throw herself carelessly backward shouting "Wheeeee" when one man reached out and caught her so she didn't crack her head on the hard, marble floor.

This little stunt show seemed to interest nobody else but me and my pleasantly bottomless drink in the way that, when you're solidly sauced, even the most banal party silliness can seem like rocket science and that chunky, badly-dressed accountant expounding on the mysteries of currency exchange can seem like the most fascinating woman you have ever met.

Yes, the open bar had created a bonanza of social possibilities. The room was alive with friendly, drunken party shouting, Starr's crazy laughter and the sounds of the five-piece dance band. Then layered even above the crowd's roar, a wailing came up like a note from some shrill, angry instrument far away. It was a sudden interruption. Nobody heard it, then, everyone seemed to turn at once towards its source, Trisha Winslow.

"AAAAAAAAAAAAAAAAH," she was saying.

Distracted by this display, Justin had absently let Starr fall backward with a thud that sounded like it would certainly leave an ugly bruise.

Winslow's wife was facing him in the middle of the dance floor, screaming "AAAAAAAAAAAAAAAAH," and pummeling the frozen, horrified Wes on his chest and face with surprising force. Her bony wrists working like pneumatic tools, Winslow lamely held his hands up as if that might at least blunt the shouting.

"GODDAMN IT WES. YOU PROMISED ME!" As she struck out at Winslow, Justin was trying to catch her arms as best he could, unsuccessfully attempting to redirect the blows.

"OWWW," Starr announced rising stiffly to her feet. Pride among her other bruises, she was rubbing her butt with one hand and the back of her neck with the other.

Justin had gotten hold of one of Mrs. Winslow's forearms to stop her from beating on Wes, but Winslow had lost his hold of her other wrist and her free arm kept wind milling, twisting her off balance like a black tie gyroscope.

"Owww," Starr said again more petulantly, but no one seemed very interested in her welfare.

"You get off of me, bastard." Trisha was still screaming, although more coherently now, at Justin, her demure little dress torn off one shoulder. "You're worse than he is." Twisting, she had managed to connect a fist with Justin's nose and he was holding his face, bent down as some spots of red hit the floor like a slow faucet drip.

You could see it had bled down the front of his fabulous tuxedo shirt. "AW FUCK. YOU BROKE MY NOSE." Justin cried flinging blood from his nose as he straightened up.

"Hey. Hey. " Winslow had pressed in quickly towards Justin, moving Jon Patel forcibly aside.

"YOU CRAZY BITCH."A small nervous crowd was

gathering around in anticipation, not the least nervous it seemed being Winslow as Justin hauled back like he might take a swing at Trisha.

"Hey! That's my wife." Wes positioned himself protectively, if reluctantly, between Mrs. Winslow and Justin's threatening fist. "That's my fucking wife for Godssakes."

"YEAH?" Justin held up a palm full of blood. "SHE BROKE MY FUCKING NOSE." He was, at once shaking his fist, holding his face and roaring, until it seemed inevitable that there would definitely be some hitting done, even if it was unclear exactly in what combinations.

All the while, Trisha Winslow, who seemed to me better able to take care of herself than anyone else there, was gamely kicking with her pointy-toed pumps, past her husband's body at Justin's shins. But, then, instead of punching anyone, Justin had suddenly begun to laugh, heartily at himself, at the absurdity of the tableau. Nose still dripping, he reached an arm over Winslow's shoulder and pulled him into a clubhouse embrace. He let his palm slap, slap, slap companionably on Winslow's back as if an expression of manly solidarity in the face of this hoyden had been his original, unwavering intent.

The gesture seemed to unplug Trisha's rage. Winslow, looking relieved and grateful, offered the white handkerchief from his pants pocket to Justin's bleeding nose.

Mrs. Winslow didn't make any more fuss as Wes quickly hustled her off. And almost as quickly as they left, the crowd, which had surrounded the ruckus, began to disperse. Justin had wiped his hand on his trousers, and gallantly marched himself straight over to help Starr up from the floor where she seemed to have dropped herself again. Never mind the blood on his shirt, Starr was obviously thrilled to have Justin escort her through the dessert buffet. The party started up again as if nothing unusual had ever occurred. Although, for the next few weeks after that you'd catch the references in snatches of conversation: "Yes. Well, you know she drinks."

Months later everybody winkingly agreed Starr's promotion was an incredible jump in prestige for a woman who previously spent half her day working for the likes of me and the other half reading romance novels and buffing her cherry red fingernails into high gloss. Camille Gutierrez, was transferred on an afternoon's notice, traded in, Ellen Borgia had quipped, like an old beater car for a newer, faster model. Camille's high school-aged daughter, Elana, who had been working as an after-school page in the Whytebread company library, vanished from the payroll the following month after a suspicious weight gain I'd chosen not to report just then to Cassandra who was shaking her head with an indulgent smile.

Apparently Trisha Winslow had been out of town for the last two weeks at a rose growing convention in Pasadena. "Think a little harder, Virginia, and call me when you do." Cassandra penciled her number on the back of a business card, a handsome, deeply-embossed piece of heavy stock with a handsome Chicago Police Department crest, carrying her name and star number, a phone and pager, pushing it at me across the table. "This is me at home." When I didn't pick up her card immediately from the table, Cassandra reoffered it, turning it over for me on my palm, and pressing: "If anyone can find out what's going on in that place I'll bet its you. Think about it," the matter was in my sole discretion — all I had to do was want to help her badly enough.

I was nodding blankly; too numbed by this barrage of disturbing revelations to appreciate my newly elevated place in Cassandra's world: first Winslow was dead, then he was dead and murdered; now the Gold Rush deal was maybe on hold, or maybe off, and there remained the tricky issue of Cassandra Hope herself, my new best friend. Of course in one respect, she'd been inarguably right; I was going to think about it. I couldn't help myself.

Slipping the card into the jacket pocket of my suit, I'd belted my trench coat, already having started to catalogue the possibilities: Camille and her pregnant daughter for whom she'd had such high ambitions, The Irishman, Price, Ellen

Borgia. Perhaps Justin was hoping for a more precipitous rise at the firm. Maybe Wes had been in his way. In the glass doors, I could see reflected the furious whirl of concentration in my greedy face, pushing my way into the crush of people on the sidewalk.

"I'll be in touch, soon." I could hear Cassandra calling after me. Promises, promises.

VIII

I'd only just stepped away from the office, but when I'd returned there were already signs of senior management circling the wagons, and sealing off the story from the rest of us. Herb Symon was a blur in the corridors barreling down the hall with uncharacteristic speed, first to one big boy's office, then another. In the lower ranks there was talk too, of the uninformed variety, from all quarters. But for once I thought I knew everything Herb and the big boys knew. For once, I was sure that I knew even more.

"Murder?" Ellen was pushing her tea bag around her mug with her index finger, more incredulous at my gossip than surprised, but it was satisfying enough for once to be able to deliver the news while it was still fresh. Cocking her head at me thoughtfully, Ellen squirted into her tea a few murky drops of the Valarian root she collected and extracted herself for her nerves. I preferred my Valium the old fashion way in the little white pills Naomi's dentist gave her to stop grinding her teeth. "Someday," I told Ellen, "that herbal stuff's going to kill you."

"Maybe so. But not today." My news had made her grumpy and pensive, and Ellen went right over my joke to the subject at hand. "I need to find out what this does to my discrimination suit."

"But it doesn't matter anymore." That was just my point, that Winslow had changed his famous List a week before he died — the freshest news of all and I was squealing it in a kind of teenybopper excitement that Ellen inexplicably didn't seem to share. "We have a lot of stock options." In fact, the color was draining confusingly from her face. "We have stock options." I burbled again in case she had misheard me. "Wes changed The List the week before he died."

Ellen didn't look good, not happy and certainly paler by the second. "I don't believe you." Misunderstanding, it seemed, was not the problem. "I never agreed to the settlement."

"What settlement?" It seemed the misunderstanding was mine since there was no need to sue anymore.

"Justin." Ellen shook her head, hands trembling. She was making waves across her tea. "It had to be Justin — that prick or Starr." But her muttering didn't make any sense. I said again, we had the money now, which really, really pissed her off.

Ellen flipped a hand at me dismissively. "Do you really think money is what I'm after?" Foamy white spittle was coagulating at the sides of her mouth as she gestured away a fortune as if it were the kind of money she tossed off on a soymilk Latte.

I was talking the zeros that made the difference between a new car, early retirement and the gross national product of a small Third World country — an order of magnitude. "We have so many options." I'd tried but I couldn't seem to make myself understood, fairly pleading with her, to entertain some perspective, and alternately wiping at my own lips discreetly, a friendly hint to Ellen that the foam on her mouth was expanding to a kind of nasty colony of spit. Despite my best efforts, she remained unaware that she was frothing, her face was so uncomfortably close to mine that I could smell the Valarian on her breath. "Do you really think this is about those fucking options?"

I'd pushed myself back in my chair, away from the germy spray of air spun saliva. "I was going to put his whole sleazy way of doing business on trial. THAT WAS THE POINT."

She was staring at me. I was staring at her; still intermittently brushing the side of my mouth, hoping she would recognize at least the grooming issue. I took a long breath, a tentative truce of silence in which our relations had time to become auspiciously calmer.

"Is there something wrong with your face?" she asked me finally. "Doesn't anyone have a clue here?"

"No." I said, giving up.

"Sometimes I wonder if I'm the only one around here who isn't a complete idiot. You know, they call me the Popsicle," she'd explained, defeated as if this might well be something not everyone in the firm had heard. "They call me the Popsicle. Do you know why?" I shook my head, but she didn't elaborate. "Wes thought it was funny. At least Maddy Madsen discouraged it. I'm sorry, Virginia," Ellen said, "but how can you expect a little bit of money to make that kind of thing all right?"

It was, in fact, a lot of money, enough money that if she was modest in her lifestyle she might not have to work at a place where they called her the Popsicle anymore. I said that maybe she should just take the money and let it go, but Ellen rolled her eyes back in disgust. "I wonder why I am ever surprised." The color was returning to her neck again. "You think Justin Collier's going to make this place all right for you." She had raised herself from her chair, leaned over the desk and puffed her swamp-water Valarian in my face again in order to call me a toady. "Well, let me give you a little piece of friendly advice about Justin Collier. He and Wesley Winslow are like taking a piss in a blue suit — you can't tell the difference. No additional charge, Justin invented the 'Popsicle' — not Wes."

I sat there mutely trying to figure out exactly what that could mean — why Justin had done it and why Ellen was telling me about it. She gave her tea another healthy squirt of the Valarian.

"Someday that herbal stuff's going to kill you." I made my little joke again. I hoped to remind her that we used to be friends, maybe we still were.

But apparently not today. Ellen stood and walked me around the desk to her office door, which she held open for me to leave. "Do you mind, Virginia? I think I really need some space here."

IX

The Number 156 bus winds up the Chicago lakefront from State Street just in front of Marshall Field's department store to practically Evanston. By five-thirty that evening I was on it and still it felt very late in the day. My stop at the corner of Irving Park and the inner drive, could not have come too soon. From there I walked the few blocks home to my apartment, past the Catholic girl's school, now an Islamic College, and the White Hen Pantry convenience store. In minutes the familiar landmarks had reduced me to one of Pavlov's dogs, my mind filled with nothing but what there was to eat for dinner — not much as my last trip to the Jewel grocery store was a distant memory and the culinary possibilities at my house were neither wide nor particularly appetizing; but just the same I found myself obsessively counting the steps to my third floor flat — my stomach complaining steadily as I mounted the last of them and hustled down the ten feet of maroon carpeted hall that led to my front door.

On a little oak-stained pine table in the entryway, the phone machine flashed three new messages; and just beyond the threshold, in the fringe of my Turkish runner, Sweet Potato had left another hairball *con* cat chow the size of mainland China.

Since Emily had left, my life had fallen into the perfect rhythms of single living: Sweet Potato preening himself on top of the metal radiator cover in the dinning room as I sponged his leavings from the rug, a cloudy jelly glass of red wine and a chocolate Pop-Tart with the sprinkles for dinner. I played back my phone message while I ate: two serial calls from Naomi Wolf, apprising me that, should I care, her death was imminent from nicotine withdrawal; crazy old Spike, apologizing for our tiff at the airport on Monday, *if you're there pick up, pick up,* and Emily Karnowski, my ex-lover and current personal accountant. I called Emily back right away.

"Why don't we talk in the morning? I'm trying to get home." Her voice was punctuated by the rustle of papers in the background, the crisp efficient sounds that I had always associated with her and her preternatural competence. Em's impatience rankled me; trying to get home to what? Since we had broken up, it had been a vague source of comfort to me that Em had not had a life. "So please Virginia, tomorrow." She sighed heavily as if the disorder of my accounts was eviscerating. "Six-thirty p.m. at my office and bring a W-4 withholding form, all right."

"Hey, you called *me*." Habit was making me only too happy to insist, given the provocatively dismissive tone Emily had chosen to take. "So what's with my withholding? Just give me a taste — you know how I worry."

Em groaned. "You have under withheld your taxes again,

Virginia, and you need to make it up before the end of the year or pay a penalty." I was sorry I'd asked.

"We both know how you hate penalties." I was detecting malicious relish. "And so, I'll see you tomorrow," she said again, hanging up without saying goodbye.

Another sortie into the refrigerator revealed rancid pasta salad, old orange juice, lite beer, ice cubes and the tuna salad sandwich I had intended as tomorrow's lunch, so I ate a second Pop-Tart, while I got ready for my run.

Running calmed me almost as much as eating, so I was doing it a lot, hoping to take off the marriage pounds I'd accumulated in my four years with Spike. The good news was I'd lost fifteen without the aid of heroin or diet pills. The bad news was that there was as yet no one to regularly appreciate it. Having Spike as an out-of-town lover mostly meant I worked late, came home to a dinner of Pop-Tarts, which could be conveniently purchased nearly twenty four hours daily at the White Hen Pantry only half a block from my apartment, and ran up my phone bill. Still, I felt my career at Whytebread was starting to reflect the extra time I was spending there. I was ready to believe hard work and demonstrated ability, as opposed to some more cynical equation of race and litigation, had put me on Wes's last minute update to the Have List. Hadn't Justin Collier befriended me last year, hadn't Winslow himself stopped by my office to consult with me the day he died? I was thinking maybe August Madsen would be favorably impressed as well if I helped Cassandra find Winslow's killer.

I was thinking of a lot of things and nothing at all, all at once and jumbled together — the *Choline* in both Cassandra's *Fly Agaric* and Ellen Borgia's Daily Diet tea, an Olivia Cruise, Trisha Winlsow, The Irishman, the tropical island I would visit when the Gold Rush deal came through — running south on Halsted towards the fairly well-lit, well-populated strip of Homo bars and nick-knack shops. The sun had already gone down, when I'd stepped out into the red brick courtyard of my building. These fall evenings it seemed to set in minutes, but I had grown to enjoy the crisp, companionable darkness and the slap of my shoes on the quiet streets. October had broken pleasantly into Indian summer, moist, balmy nights and unseasonably warm days. At the bus stop strangers were turning to each other, remarking about how under-rated Chicago weather was.

Cutting down Waveland Street, I huffed a path to the lakefront past the cheerfully painted row houses in nice, easy strides. The air smelled like those Halloweens when I was a kid, thick with the scent of wet dead leaves and fireplaces, old pieces of telephone pole rolled close to the bonfire for benches and hot-dogs turning black on the end of a straightened wire hanger. So engrossing was the mixture of memories and endorphins sloshing around my brain that I almost failed to notice the lights of a slow-moving car rolling up beside me. And all of a sudden, disturbingly there wasn't a soul on the darkened street, not even another car to flag down in the headlights.

I'd picked up my pace such as it was, but the car stayed next to me. The man inside it was shouting my name through the open window. It was Justin.

"Whoa! Slow down little sistah. I've been following you for a block and a half."

I could see as I got closer to the car that Justin was still in his suit from work. "I was just driving and I saw you there." A lucky coincidence because presented with the alternative of a car I didn't feel like running anymore. "Do you want to go for a ride?" He was telling me as I opened the door that the police were saying that Wes had been murdered.

The idea seemed to have shaken him even more than it had me. Even so, I couldn't help but enjoy the authority I was able to put in my voice as I told him I already knew about Winslow, and the way that my knowledge unbalanced him, making my own little dent on events. It proved I mattered.

"I knew Detective Hope many years ago," I said she didn't find Whytebread management particularly cooperative.

Justin kept nodding and hunched himself moodily in his seat. "What do they want? Wes was a strange guy. It's mushroom season. I've really told the police all I know about that night. Herb didn't like it but I told that detective about Wes's issues with The Irishman. That's all I can do."

I thought it was interesting that Justin had been the one to break rank and talk to the police, instead I said, "You know, Wes changed it at the last minute — his list."

Justin was watching the road and he didn't turn. "Wes changed it last week," Justin said, and I asked why he hadn't told me.

"What would you have done differently, if you'd known?" Justin considered this idea with a speculative sort of amusement as if I had demonstrated some unexpected precociousness.

"It may be nothing," Justin said when we had driven several blocks, "but you might tell your policewoman friend, Tom Zemluski never finished college." He was speaking slowly as if he was just reasoning it out. "It's no big deal to lose a job if you can get another one, but if you can't — that's something else." The Irishman had quit night school ten credits short of a bachelor's degree and had never gone back. "It was the summer his first kid was born, almost twenty-five years ago." His career had taken off with Madsen as his mentor. Time had passed. Justin smiled thinly. "August Madsen always thought it was kind of funny, an oddity, but Wes didn't think that Tom projected the proper image for Whytebread, especially in the future as part of Gold Rush investments."

I said, "So, The Irishman wasn't just losing a job; he was losing a career." That made sense of his anger at the shareholders meeting and at lunch that day; he must have felt like Winslow had sprung a trap on him after all those years.

It would be difficult for another firm to hire The Irishman at his grade and age, without at least a college degree, even if they wanted to. But the buyout money ought to have been plenty to live on even if he couldn't work.

Except Justin explained Tom was getting a divorce. "His wife will take at least half the money and probably his house," but Justin said it was more than that: "Tom felt Winslow had singled him out — engineered the Gold Rush deal and The List to screw him." Herb was supposed to take care of things with Winslow, but last week when The Irishman heard he was still recommended for termination on Wes' new List, he'd lost his patience. "He went ballistic. I don't know," Justin seemed to consider this as if it were a new thought, "maybe Wes did want to screw him."

We had nearly reached my house. I said. "So why is it that Wes had decided to give me and Ellen Borgia options? You were in; we were out." I wanted confirmation, a little afraid that Cassandra had been wrong or lying about my little bequest.

"I don't know. He just did. That's all," Justin brushed off the question as if it confused him.

I said, "Maybe Winslow explained what he was thinking to you. I thought you were friends."

But Justin made a puffing sound through his nose. "Wesley Winslow didn't have any friends — not really. Wes was kind of a dick." He had pulled the car over by the iron gate in front of my building.

We sat talking. Down the street the steam rose out of the manholes like ghosts. Just beyond them there was a small dark-colored car, an Escort maybe, an economy car. It had rolled past us slowly a few minutes before and now it was half a block beyond my building parked on the opposite side of the street, waiting. The yellow street lamp lit a brunette on the driver's side who didn't look particularly familiar.

"Do you know anyone who drives an Escort?" I thought we had an audience.

Justin frowned for a moment, perhaps at the lowbrow make of the car. "One of your old girlfriends, maybe?"

I'd always attracted the crazy ones. Or, perhaps as Naomi asserted, I attracted normal girls, then made them crazy, the bias in any case overwhelmed even the statistical law of large numbers. I thought it certainly wasn't one of his.

"Oh, you never know." Just as he'd spoken, the car took off fast.

Her ears must have been burning.

I said, "You know, Ellen Borgia says I shouldn't trust you an inch. She says it was you who started calling her The Popsicle." I hadn't intended to let him know that she'd told me, but there it was. "What's that about?" I asked.

"Jealousy and spite." I had the feeling he'd given that answer before. "Come on." Justin pulled the car away from the curb. "I want to show you something."

X

We were driving generally west, past the strips and strips of old storefronts and businesses on Irving Park, then, a little north skirting the edge of the city, as Justin executed a series of turns onto short residential streets into a neighborhood of tidy, little identical bungalows. He finally stopped in front of a shallow-roofed house set squarely in the center of a short patch of lawn. Justin pointed, "I grew up over there," a studiously casual indication of origins that, for all his airs, were a good deal more modest than my own, more insular and more myopically insulated. "My father lives here, but I don't come around any more — not since college, but sometimes I drive by the house at night. I like to imagine what he's up to."

Across the street a dim, lonely light came on in the front room of the little bungalow.

"My real name is Jacek," Justin said, "after him — that's the name my parents gave me — Jacek Cholodinski. My mother didn't speak a word of English."

It was a nervous making idea as I had my own collection of ingrained prejudices about these neighborhoods and people — White ethnics, first generation — supported too vividly by the memory of the an uneasy evening I'd spent once integrating a Czech restaurant in Berwyn.

"And Jacek Cholodinski senior," Justin chuckled hard-faced, "he can barely limp along, with just enough words to hold down a job with the city, waiting it out for that pension, content with what little he's got and lazy as hell, trying not to tax himself. Tom Zemluski is just like him. He couldn't understand how I could side with Wes on the buyout. All Tom could see was Wes and those rich, Northshore snobs getting richer. He thought Wes owed it to him — a job for life, and a bonus every March. When I left for college, I left that kind of thinking behind. I changed my name to something a little more pronounceable. I changed everything I could about myself, and so Justin Collier isn't so welcome around here, not in years, not since my mother died."

Justin was watching my face very carefully, so it was convenient that I felt rather bad for him. The light in the window went off. Seconds later it came on in the next room, the adjacent window.

Even after my on-going experience with Spike, it was hard to imagine how you could simply excise the parts of yourself that didn't fit into the promotional brochure. "So, is that what Ellen Borgia was talking about — the secret life of Jacek Cholodinski?" It had included not a mention of Ellen's nickname or Justin's part in it. "That can't be all of it," I said.

Justin sighed in consultation with the dashboard of his car, thinking or perhaps inventing a truth that somehow required reconstruction. "Well, not exactly. But there's another side to that story." There always was, so he started, "A long time ago," the way so many stories start, "I thought if I could just find the right woman everything could be more — normal. I was ambitious." He had settled, after some thought on the proper term with a factual simplicity, which implied that this explained it all. "Ellen Borgia was convenient. Anyway, it was always more serious for her than it was for me. I hadn't realized —" Justin made a helpless whiffing sound, as if even to revisit the idea of the relationship horrified him. "That's when it really hit home — we were dancing at her sister's wedding — and she said that it could be us someday, married. Well, of course, it couldn't, so I told her why."

Ellen hadn't taken it well. She had threatened to expose him at work, a serious threat. His lips were tight with old anger. "I couldn't let her ruin my life."

"Your career."

Justin shrugged away the difference, his face made dark by the shadows that fell across the car. "After all that I had done to better myself, I would have been out of the club, some street worker's faggot son, too sorry even to come crawling home to the Northwest side. So, I told the other guys that our sex was like sleeping with a Popsicle." I remembered how he'd laughed, urbane and ironic, when he'd explained it. *Cold as ice with a stick up her ass,* invoking the law of workplace entanglements. Justin, the man, had fucked her and dumped her; now she was the woman scorned, any assertions of fact discounted to nothing, but The Popsicle was such a clever turn of phase that it got around — and stayed around.

In the shadowy light from the street lamp, Justin raised and dropped his shoulders again. "What could I do?"

It was touchingly sordid but still didn't explain why Ellen would think that she needed to protect me from Justin Collier's catty wit.

"Ellen thinks we're an item — so does Starr." His eyes

slipped away, hands folded in his lap a tableau of penitence. "I told Starr so she would sort of leave me alone. I needed cover; so did you." Justin pushed out a hard breath. "Everybody at Whytebread had you figured for a dyke and frankly, my cache with Ellen was fading. It was hurting us both. I did you a favor."

But it didn't feel very much like a favor. The volume of my voice in the closed dark car surprised me, and seemed to panic Justin a little as if he worried the noise might wake his father's neighbors behind the windows of their manicured bungalows, bring them gawking out onto their lawns.

"It's nothing like you think," he rushed to quiet me. "I just told them we went out. I *meant* to be doing you a favor."

I thought more like doing himself a favor. "Give, give, give."

Justin put up his hands. "Okay. It was a stupid thing."

So, I said, we agreed. It was a stupid thing, confirming: "You're sure that's all Ellen meant to tell me — that you're a lying sleazy dick."

Justin smiled, disarmed, disarming. "What else could she possibly be talking about? Stop at my place? Maybe have a drink? I'm sorry." He offered, lightened as if his little deceit had been weighing on him more than I would have expected. As he drove us back towards the familiar streets of Boys Town the city lights rolled by my window faint from their distance, fuzzy in the warm pleasant glow of other people's lives.

I had chosen to let the surreal quality of that day carry me along throughout the evening; and washing down the Xanax Naomi had stashed in my wallet with the scotch Justin served me there on his couch had certainly helped in that regard. I waited for the buzz, and in a faint, feel good blush the drug had painted over my reality; I let Justin extract me limply from the comfortable sofa cushions. I followed his lead, dancing around the small square area rug in his living room to the music of an oldies station. 70's oldies, and it seemed perfectly in character with events, as strange as anything else that had happened that day for the songs I'd listened to as a teenager now to qualify as quaint and corny, legitimate nostalgia.

We danced a careful box, in the center of the low, wool nap as if a step outside the carpet's confines would be a long fall to earth. Naomi's pill let my head ride like a sleepy balloon, hips swaying a bossa nova rhythm, their motion severed from my trunk, my socks moving liquidly over the rug, taking the hints Justin's hand dispensed to the small of my back. After a little while, even following had become too taxing, and I'd simply put my feet, very small by comparison, on top of his shoes like a little girl dancing with a favorite uncle. *I miss Daniel.* Justin sang Elton John's pop melancholy in my ear as he carried me around, not quite the right lyrics, or exactly in time with the music, but somehow I liked to hear him anyway. *You know, I miss him sooooo much.*

XI

I woke the next morning, stripped-down to my bra and panties in a bed that smelled unpleasantly like a man.

Beside me, Justin was groaning and mumbling, "Ummmm. Honey, honey?" in a disconcertingly needy manner that I hoped had nothing to do with me, and yet I found it weirdly interesting. This idea of particular longing was at odds with the notion I had made of Justin's sexuality, which seemed to revolve around the hard commodity of *dick* — chasing it, getting it, good dick or bad dick — transactions he'd related in a bored, casual tone like magazine restaurant critiques, eating places to which he would not return, places he would go again, and none of them so special that a good opinion could not be irreparably damaged by a bad meal.

"Honey?" Justin was groaning to someone in particular as I gingerly felt around my underwear, the spot on the bed where I was laying, the sheet near me and my thighs, but all were comfortingly free from any stickiness not my own.

"Ummm," he continued moaning volubly in his sleep until I shoved him hard, back into relative silence, and got up to find the rest of my clothes.

Yesterday's sweats were easily discovered, folded neatly on the dining room table, socks on top of shirt on top of the sweats in characteristic Justin Collier neatness, a reassuring omen that last night had not involved any grand spontaneous passion. I carried my things down the hall to the bathroom where I prayed there would be a toothbrush as my mouth felt like the outside of a peach. In the dirty mirror of Justin's medicine cabinet my faced look vaguely like my mouth felt, and bed wrinkled. Still I found it reassuring that my breath was bad enough to compel chastity from nearly anyone.

The two rather used toothbrushes in the holder by the sink were sufficient to explain Justin's sleepy mumblings. But there were no extras though I did take a good hard look in all the vanity drawers.

The contents of Justin's medicine chest was mostly pharmacological, consisting of dental floss and a sizable collection of orange prescription bottles with names like a science fiction movie, *Lamivudine, Indinavir* and *Retrovir. Retrovir, 300 mg, twice daily.* That one I knew by the generic name as well: *AZT.* Among last night's strange revelations, Justin had failed to mention this prescription made out in his name, but it gave me another, better idea of why Ellen might be concerned, safe sex aside, that he and I were romantically involved.

I put the medicine away and when I turned from the cabinet, Justin was there in the doorway. "You were out like a light so I put you to bed." He told me. I couldn't say how long he'd been standing there.

~ ~ ~

Justin only drove me as far as the corner of Irving so he could make the left back to the expressway. I was stepping into the crosswalk at the corner opposite Broadway Video, preparing to walk the few blocks to my house when I noticed a little red car idling across from my building, the same red car from the night before, a brunette with the dark glasses behind the wheel. When the light changed, she jerked forward, accelerating around the corner, the whole chain of events happening so fast that I almost didn't register she was plowing unmistakably for me. I froze in the crosswalk, but the car kept coming, coming, I imagined to bring about my death until a pair of arms shoved me hard towards the sidewalk. As the deadly subcompact sped away, my savior, a filthy Black man of indeterminate age who looked probably older than he was and smelled solidly of cigarettes and malt liquor, helped me to my feet. "You all right, sister?"

On closer inspection, he had crowned himself with a plastic grocery bag tied over a ratty, cast-off lambswool Cossack hat like a Jewel Grocery Bedouin, its handles looped around his ears. His attire for the well-dressed deinstitutionalized street resident was further enhanced by a whimsical ensemble of dirty and disintegrating clothing, which amounted to nearly two of everything a man might normally wear — two shirts, two coats, two pair of pants, one shorter than the other sticking out at his ankles above a bulge of multiple socks.

My new best friend might well have been a little frightening if my capacity for fright hadn't been so completely taken up by the hit and run attempt just seconds before. But the huff of his breath shook me nearly as much as my brush with mortality. "You can call me Elijah." Cossack man's smile showed one faintly brown tooth in the crooked line of merely yellow ones. "Now that you're alive, spare some change for me, sister?"

In my pocket, I found my balled up mad money, a twenty-dollar bill. He was welcome to it. I smoothed it generously on my palm before I held it out.

"Bless you sister." He snapped his hand closed around the bill as if he half expected I would notice my mistake. But as I began to walk away, he fell in beside me with his odd glassy gleam, jabbering like a street-corner missionary. "Hey, hey, sister. Can you tell me, sister, what satisfaction do you get when you pay the White man?" He didn't seem to require a response sliding easily into a canned sounding line of high-speed patter. "The White man wants you to give up your soul, then, he won't let you have nothing for it. No money, no jobs, no women," at this, he offered a confidential leer. We'd gotten as far as the White Hen Pantry before the allure of commerce and the twenty dollars in his pocket proved stronger than his need for a discourse on the threat of the White devil. "You watch the Man, now. He don't mean you any good." My friend peeled off shambling up the handicapped ramp to the convenience store.

At almost nine o'clock in the morning the street was deserted of commuters. Why hurry? I was late to work again.

Inside my apartment, Sweet Potato's food and water dish were empty and dry, respectively. His feelings on that fact were eloquently expressed by a perfectly formed cat turd he'd left on my oriental runner, and the steady, dolorous yowling he affected until I'd filled both his bowls. From his wide back and the jiggle of his low-hanging cat belly, anyone could have seen that Sweet Potato was in little danger of malnutrition. All the same, immediately upon its availability, he buried his fat yellow head in his food; and didn't come up for air until the ceramic bottom was shiny with cat spit. Then, the sated Sweet Potato rolled back and forth on the sunlit rug in front of my living room couch.

"And why shouldn't you be happy?" I told him, "You weren't nearly hit by a car this morning. No one's tried to kill you," except, I thought, by starvation which had hardly been intentional. Sweet Potato continued purring and rolling, which I presumed to mean he had forgiven me.

Since the night before I had three more phone messages, to which I listened over a glass of fizzy spoiling orange juice.

Naomi was saying, "Where are you, call me will you? I'm worried." Which meant that she needed me to process her withdrawal symptoms.

Spike was saying, "Where are you; don't you miss me." Which meant she needed me to process our codependency. There were five additional hang-ups that I was prepared to attribute to Ms. McMann — no calls that needed immediate returning and all of the responses emotionally sticky. So I dug Cassandra's business card out from my wallet and left the business-like message that The Irishman had never finished college, thus making him ineligible for employment outside of Whytebread and Greese should he be fired, hoping that this information might move things along to a future where I could afford to run away from my indescribably overwhelming life. I included the fact that I was beginning to worry this might be related to someone who had been following me and who had tried to run me down. Then I double bolted the door and tried to take a shower, but was interrupted by the phone.

"Someone just tried to kill me," I began to say to the caller I imagined was Cassandra, "some dark-haired woman in a red car."

"Bitch." The voice on the other end of the phone was laughing with unmistakable malice. "You're lucky I don't do worse than that." I hung up before I could identify her voice and well before she could expand on the thought. When the phone rang a few minutes later, I waited for Cassandra to identify herself to my answering machine before I picked it up.

"Someone tried to run me down," I told her, "at the corner just as I was coming home."

"Slow down." Cassandra was telling me except I couldn't help but begin to babble: "That woman tried to kill me and then she called here, just now and threatened to succeed."

There was distracting background noise on her end of the phone. "Who called?" Cassandra said with an irritating calm, uninterested in why I was coming home at nine in the morning or whom I'd been with.

I'd given myself over to an assortment of hair-raising conspiracy theories, but now it occurred to me I wasn't really sure.

Did she say my name on the phone? Did I get a license plate number? Was I sure it was the same car as from last night? Cassandra was posing a series of increasingly reasonable questions to which I could only answer no in a small, silly voice. Was I sure the driver was really going to hit me or did the homeless man just run a gratitude scam for my twenty bucks?

I wasn't sure. Of course I wasn't sure, but I was angry. I said, "If you had even an inkling of who was responsible for Wes's murder I'd feel a whole lot safer." I said I wouldn't have to be sure of whether people were trying to run me down in their cars, because it seemed for all she had poo poo-ed my suspicions about Trisha Winslow, Cassandra had no alternative or competing theories. Every suspect she had was coming from my imagination, with Cassandra administratively logging everything I told her, but doing no discernible detection, having no opinions herself — at least none she would share with me. Even over the phone she was patiently temporizing.

"We have some ideas, yes, but I think they're best kept quiet for now." She said, "Your information about Mr. Zemluski is very helpful, Virginia. Thank you. I'll ask Mr. Madsen about it today. You really shouldn't be worrying about anything. I'll take care of this. Don't worry about the car."

Cassandra went on with a smooth calming affect suitable for children worried about monsters residing in their closets. "And absolutely don't worry about the call. It was a prank."

I didn't know how she could be so sure, but Cassandra had decided everything very neatly for me. "Relax," she said. "Let's see if you get another call."

I thought that was easy for her to say.

XII

Despite my safety concerns, I arrived at work uneventfully enough, the greatest subsequent danger of that morning being the potential avalanche of unread mail in my in-basket. There was a like amount of unseemly clutter on my desk just begging to be filed, but I opted for an Internet search of the mushroom, *Fly Agaric,* and an hour or so in the fast lane of the information highway, yielded a general picture. *Amanita muscaria* (muscaria from the Latin meaning fly) was a lurid, yet implausible-looking bright red piece of flora with white spots and visible warts, the kind of toadstool artists draw in fairytale illustrations. But *The Online Field Guide to Central Illinois Mushrooms,* a botanist's dream of a website, had a good deal more to say:

Amanita species are the most common ringed, white-spore mushrooms in our area. Amanitas are impressive often-showy mushrooms, almost always with a characteristic stem base, which is enlarged possessing a sock-like covering or a rimmed appearance. This is the remainder of the universal veil, which covers emerging Amanita fungi. Many amanitas have patches on their caps like the frequently pictured, storybook mushroom Amanita muscaria, which is bright red with white or yellow patches, but occurs as a white variation in central Illinois. The Destroying Angel, Amanita virosa, the world's most poisonous mushroom, is common to central Illinois from early summer through the fall. Cap: to 4 inches pure white or yellowing with age; Gills: pure white; Stem: to 7 inches terminating in a bulb like sock; Smell: not distinctive, but rather foul as it decays; Spore print: white; Habitat: woods. Comments: Amanita muscaria, variant alba is also white but the cap is covered with white patches and the base is not covered in a sock.

From what I could recall, Winslow's mouth had worked with the discrimination of a steam shovel. It wasn't hard to imagine how he might have ingested anything added to his lunch, warts and all, especially if someone had chopped the local flavor of *Fly Agaric* into bite size pieces that hid the warts. From the sound of the *Online Mushroom Guide,* the killer couldn't have been a mushroom expert, not even a gifted amateur, maybe confusing *Fly Agaric* with the look alike *Destroying Angel.* Or maybe there had been no murder at all. The white variant was missing the distinctive Amanitas sock by which the *Online Mushroom Guide* suggested identification.

I was better informed, but not much more enlightened when I'd returned to the filing, successfully having labeled and filled about five manila folders and two green hanging files before the phone rang, two high sharp shrills in immediate succession, digital code for an outside call.

It was my father, talking loudly; a habit he believed made him sound friendly to children and foreigners. "Hey, kid, I've got a website for you." Just as soon as I'd said hello, he was bellowing, a veritable storm of excitement. "You go to AOL.com and search for food, then it will tell you to try *'everything edible'*."

"Uh-huh." I'd picked up my filing again, tuned out and fallen immediately into active listening. My dad and I had grown so far apart that all we had in common was eating, but my father loved food and he was nattering on with unreserved enthusiasm at the prospect of a fine meal.

"So you click on that *'everything edible'* and you go to a whole food page and there at the bottom will be a little button for *meals.com*. Click on that," he told me. "Now at *'meals on line'* you click *'let's start cooking'* and it's going to tell you that you're entering the site and then you just click on the place where it says *'start here.'* "

"Okay," I had begun sorting again, through the stack of back mail, multi-tasking, nowhere near my mouse, but I pretended cheerfully because barring an ability to provide him with a nice Black son-in-law and a lawn full of grandkids, at least I could please my father in these little ways. "Uh-huh, uh huh." I'd started on the pile of folders at the corner of my desk, while he talked at me, letting my fingers do the walking through my mountainous heap of read and discarded SEC filings.

"There's soup, bread beverage salad, main course, appetizer and desert; and you just click on the one you want." Presumably Dad believed I was clicking along, and the thought of a family activity, albeit virtual, really did seem to gratify him. "So, Gin, say you want a main course, you just click on *'main course'*. Then, you can click a cuisine, say French, and you can click on a meat, say poultry. They have ten thousand recipes." Even at its excitement-elevated decibel levels, my father's voice was pouring out of the phone not unpleasantly, with the soothing quality of a heavy rain on the roof at night, no drop, no single word in particular distinguishable from the rest of the deluge.

"Cool, Dad." As speaker phone seemed a sign of disrespect, I was cradling the receiver between my neck and shoulder, awkwardly stuffing a pile of quarterly earnings reports into the file I'd just made for them when I felt it — something in the pile of remaining loose papers on my desk. I was just sweeping the papers into the trashcan, which I'd positioned just under my desktop for easy disposal and there against the heel of my hand was the longish, flatish Tupperware container.

My dad's voice careened on frenetically, reciting the names of the recipes as if he intended to list all ten thousand, "And there's *Chicken Vegetable Crepes* and *Coq au Vin* and *Chicken Tarragon, Chicken Scaloppini* —"

"Great. Right," I told him as on my desk my fingers had found something quite amazing. I knew the second they grazed the smooth plastic sides, missed in my alcoholic post-lunch fog. The stray papers I'd been working with on Friday had obscured it for days. When I moved them away, the Tupperware container that had held Wesley Winslow's deadly lunch was sitting on my desk.

His pager went off as he was finishing his salad and he'd run. I'd left for lunch with The Irishman shortly after, locking my office door; and so, the container must have been forgotten by both of us in the confusion of that afternoon's shareholders meeting and Winslow subsequent collapse.

"*Chicken Cornmeal Crepes, Chicken Cordon Bleu en Croute,*" my father paused to ask reflectively, "I wonder what that means — *en croute?*" I had no idea.

"Breaded maybe?" he was puzzling. "What do you think, Virginia? You took French." Typically, my father was remembering my sister's studies, but he continued undeterred by the translation issues: "Well, anyway there's *Lattice Crust Turkey Pot Pies, Chicken and Fresh Vegetables Provencal*—" He didn't seem to need to breathe.

Holding the Tupperware up to the light by its day-glow green handle, through the clear plastic sides I could see the foul, black soup of wilted lettuce, limp peppers, and what well could have been shriveled pieces of rotting mushrooms, chopped very small.

"Did I say they have ten thousand recipes?" my dad had acquired a reverent awe. "Well, they do — ten thousand recipes and those are just a few — the ones I read." I considered how he and Spike could find nothing to talk about an absolute wonder, setting the lunch container back down on my desk. I'd opened the top just a hair at the edge, closing it again very quickly against the odor that wafted out. Whatever color the mushrooms had been on Friday, like everything else now, they were black.

There were no surprises about the smell.

"If you wanted beef, along the same lines: there's *Veal Marengo*, *Fillet of Beef with Corichon Tarragon Sauce* and *Goulash* —"

"I've got a meeting in ten," I told my dad, then I made a clear space on my desk for the lunchbox and called Cassandra.

It took her barely an hour and a half to have my office crawling with cops, evidence cops, plain clothes cops and cops in uniform. Cassandra was pacing back and forth in the middle of this vaguely Hollywood crime-drama-looking scene, in and out of various rooms with an officious and deliriously happy air of authority, taking notes and barking orders — in her sin. She might have created this pageant a little faster, but Herb Symon had wanted to make her sign an agreement not to use any confidential investment information the cops might stumble across while they were looking for deadly poison.

Herb finally just settled for her threat to have him imprisoned for obstruction of justice and her solemn word as to the ethics of Chicago law enforcement professionals. Just to be safe, he was standing guard outside my office, wringing his hands and admonishing passersby to get back to work.

Officeless at least for a little while, I'd settled myself at a table in the lunchroom with the 10-Q and annual report of one of my corporate problem children.

"Well, isn't this exciting?" When Ellen came sliding up behind me, it was already eleven o'clock and I was only just finishing up the Chairman's letter at the front of the annual. She'd arrived with a Tupperware container in hand presumably full of tofu scramble on the pretense of an early lunch. "Imagine." She talked with a furtive casualness that made me think her primary aim had been to track me down. News traveled fast. "Imagine you finding the smoking gun, Virginia."

I said it was more like the stinking lunch box.

"HA." Kevin Cavanaugh had been eavesdropping. "That's good."

"All right, so the smoking gun." Ellen Borgia was practically oozing goodwill, all smiley-voiced and recovered from yesterday's outrage over the stock options.

I was steadily turning the pages of my 10-Q, which was laying out, at best, a dodgy business plan that I had somehow failed to scrutinize very heavily when I'd moved the stock to a buy last quarter.

"Well it's all over the firm that you found it." Ellen gushed.

Cavanaugh chuckled companionably, "the stinking lunchbox." I guessed the mid-lunch hour timing of Winlsow's memorial, one-thirty that afternoon would prompt a number of folks to eat early, prophylactically as the trek to Barrington promised a long and, knowing Madsen, potentially foodless afternoon. Peek-opening the plastic top of his Tupperware container as if it were a Christmas present, Kevin had taken his own lunch out of the refrigerator. "It's Chinese." He announced as if this might be something of general interest, carefully unwrapping some little pancakes from wax paper, rearranging them on the counter in a presentation, which involved a prodigious number of paper towels. "Usually she makes me salami." Kevin deposited his plastic container into the microwave and in less than two minutes the whole room smelled like *Mu Shu Pork*.

"Oh, yes indeed." Ellen was gushing, "News travels fast around here — and you seem to be getting it all in previews."

I was nodding only half engaged in whatever it was that Ellen was saying. It was clear as I read that I'd missed a HOLD recommendation by a good three months. In that respect, news didn't seem to be traveling fast enough.

"So," as she talked, Ellen made a secretive glance in the direction of Kevin Cavanaugh who was still completely enmeshed in his lunch. "What exactly did you find?"

My stomach grumbled. At the smell of the Chinese food I remembered I'd eaten nothing but a couple Pop-Tarts, some Xanax, scotch, and a glass of orange juice since lunch the day before.

"She was so sweet to surprise me with the leftovers." Kevin was still babbling dimwittedly, as he assembled his food to take back to his desk. "From her ladies night at China Kitchen. What about that?" This thoughtfulness, was clearly an on-going source of pride.

"I think I'll keep her," Ellen sneered, but Kevin didn't seem to hear. I was thinking how nice it would be for someone to make my lunch occasionally. That's what I wanted: someone to love me enough to sacrifice her leftovers — someone other than Spike. I was thinking how nice it would be to eat something other than the questionable tuna I'd brought from home.

With what I felt was admirable courage I retrieved my sandwich from the refrigerator. It smelled barely the right side of salmonella but I took a bite anyway.

"Listen." After Cavanaugh left, Ellen made another

swivel-necked glance in the direction of the door, and then she scooted a chair up close to mine. "Listen, who do the police think did it?"

I'd been letting my thoughts linger on the last vestiges of that *Mu Shu* smell.

"Who do they think killed Winslow? I know you know." Ellen enunciated her whisper as if she suspected I had momentarily lost my fluency in English. Having bragged to Ellen about my inside line on this whole business, this was my reward. "I know you know." She was insisting. "And someone who misunderstood my nature might take our conversation yesterday the wrong way. If you were for example to repeat what happened with the wrong emphasis, someone could get the idea, mistakenly, of course," Ellen added quickly, "that I hated Wes."

I was chewing my sandwich tentatively prepared at any moment to discover some concrete evidence of botulism; I looked up from the annual, a little confused. Of course, Ellen sort of did hate Wes.

"Well, yes — but not enough to hurt him." She was methodically pulling the dead skin off her bottom lip with her teeth. I was nodding. There did seem to be some subtlety in the point she was making, some definite shades of gray in her possible feelings.

"It was a very limited hate," she'd explained. "Really, it was hardly hate at all, a mild distaste. I could never actually hurt anyone. You aren't going to tell your friend on the Police about our talk. Are you?"

"Why would I?" She seemed happy enough with that, happy enough to give my shoulders an impulsive squeeze. "I never believed what anyone said about you, Virginia."

It was nice for once to have hit upon just the right thing to say. More than that, Kevin Cavanaugh's Chinese food had just given me an idea.

Maybe Winslow's lunch had been packed at home, and

poisoned at home, not at work. Maybe, like Kevin, there was someone not so lovingly packing Winslow's lunch for him — not Mrs. Winslow, but a mistress. Hadn't that been what she was accusing him of at the Christmas party? There had been talk about Starr and Winslow. Before that, there was the scandal of Camille Guiterrez' pretty little teenaged daughter.

"It's a sure sign Winslow's sticking her." I'd overheard Rupert Dean, nature's perfect barometer of sleaze, pontificating by the coffee machine. News that Winslow had gotten Elana a job in the Whytebread library and arranged for a special Whytebread scholarship to pay her tuition and books at the Catholic High school had been grist for the gossip mill. "Sticking her — or going to."

Kevin Cavanaugh's face had twitched with uncontrollable angst at the subject of infidelities with teenage girls.

"Well I wouldn't mind a piece of that myself." Rupert leered. "But I guess rank has to have its privileges."

The talk made me sick, but I was sicker yet when Elana had left her job at Whytebread and left school as well rather suddenly. She wasn't exactly showing yet, but some of the older secretaries said they could always tell. Within a couple months Starr had replaced Camille Gutierrez as Winslow's secretary.

"I can't now." I could see Starr through the Plexiglas window at the top of her cube, her jaw working a wad of gum in profile, as she held the receiver to her ear with her shoulder. She'd spun her chair away from the computer desk towards the back of her cube to keep her conversation private, hunched over the phone. It had just rung when I came up, the shrill single tones of an inside call, a call I'd presumed would be brief and businesslike but which stretched on inconveniently as I'd waited outside her carrel, trying not to listen to what seemed quite personal, and when this failed, trying not to hear. Starr's molars had fallen into a deliberate rhythm, testimony to the recidivism of nervous gum chewers. Winslow's hard work gone for nothing. From the pack of Capris on the desk by her keyboard I could see that she had started smoking again.

As the call went on I could guess not entirely satisfactorily from the occasional catch in Starr's voice, the pausing, the chewing, the playing in the hair. It smelled of romantic trauma, and I took a few steps away from her cube having no interest in Starr's ongoing personal entanglements, which could tell me nothing about Wes's murder. Still I clung to my original thought that Starr would know with whom Winslow was keeping company, the same way she'd known to put Emily Karnowski's calls right through to me in the years we were together, the way she'd quickly figured to inquire after Spike when I returned from a long weekend. If Starr would ever get off the phone I could ask her about Winslow's girlfriends, maneuvering myself conspicuously into the doorway of Starr's carrel not so much to listen, but rather to interrupt.

More than conspicuous, as time wore on I had crossed the line into obnoxious, fidgeting, tapping, shifting my weight from side to side in a manner that could not easily go unnoticed. Even so, Starr was so taken up with her low-voiced conversation that she didn't look my way until another call rang through on the second line. "Look somebody is buzzing me." She turned to the blinking lights on her console, dabbing awkwardly at her eyes with a bit of tissue. When she turned to take the other line, her mascara was smudged in ugly black rays *a la* Tammy Faye Baker.

I saw she saw me there. "Are you all right?" I asked.

"Of course. Why shouldn't I be?" Starr had neither wanted nor expected to see me in the doorway and her eyes flickered over to the telephone as an avenue of escape, but the lines had gone quiet. Starr frowned at the lost call and snatched at another Kleenex from the box on the edge of her desk to blow her nose, then she loaded an envelope into her laser printer.

I'd said I was wondering about the corporate apartment Winslow kept in the city. "How would I know?" Her fingers got busy typing an address into her keyboard. This was said with dim suspicion as I'd started to lie ineffectively. I had a friend, I said, who needed a place and I thought there might be a good deal on the sublease, lying so miserably; I'd even stopped listening to myself. "And I was just thinking if you could tell me if anyone else ever used it, besides Wes." I'd hoped that my nervous friendly giggle would engender generous feelings in return, but it did not. "Because if you had the key I could maybe stop by the apartment to see if it's what she's looking for, you know."

Starr looked as if she expected I'd gone crazy, but at least she wasn't typing any longer. I seemed to have obtained her complete, if somewhat incredulous attention. I kept nodding in a way that I felt conveyed harmless curiosity, prodding gently that if she didn't have the key maybe she could say who did.

"I don't have it, all right?" Her fingers arched high above the keyboard again in an unbroken and professional rhythm. Then, as if she'd just that second grasped the point of my questions, they stopped mid-click. "Who did you say was asking about this?"

"Maybe the police." I was hoping to threaten, but Starr just squinted her eyes back at me into insolent questioning little lines.

"I have work to do, Virginia," she told me not bothering to look up again. "Probably, so do you." I watched while she banged out a few final characters, then mouse clicked her document off to the printer and I went to find Ellen Borgia, who had said that she would give me a ride to Winslow's memorial at one-thirty in Barrington. Attendance was apparently mandatory, as Madsen had chartered a bus for the secretaries.

XIII

There are solemn state funerals, public processionals past the open coffins of some beloved leader. There are lurid private affairs filled with children wailing and huge, broad brush theatrical grief. But Winslow's funeral could best be described as a tasteful pageant of dark suits and tightly composed expressions.

What tears there were fell silently down the stony, white faces of his wife and very close relations. Little more than twelve years old, Wallace, the daughter, and Starr D'nofrio were the most distraught, but surprisingly, Ellen Borgia, had managed enough salt water to exhaust the pack of travel tissues I carried in my purse, explaining puffy-faced, "I talked to my lawyer yesterday. When they put that fucker in the ground they as good as buried most of our claims besides hostile environment." The bad news was the feminist law firm of Owens, Babbitt and Coogan now suggested to Ellen that the settlement looked like a pretty good deal and Ellen was desolate enough that I made a mental note to cross her off Cassandra's suspect list which was the good news I couldn't tell her.

After a mercifully short post-service interval, we'd piled into a long caravan of cars, (the secretarial charter bus, a massive black funeral wreath attached to its front grill bringing up the rear), first to the cemetery, and then back to Winslow's compound for a wake-like bit of ritual milling usually reserved for the family of the deceased.

What I was slowly beginning to understand was how genuinely August Madsen believed we employees were his family, placed somehow in his charge as our great white father, the way God had given Man responsibility over the lower forms of life. However odd or insulting it might have been to realize your employer considered you as very nearly chattel, it was stranger still to imagine the complexity of Madsen's emotions around this little gathering or the firm, retrograde obligations of stewardship and human husbandry that in their undertaking proved he was better than the rest of us — a motley, little rag-tag group to baby-sit, the likes of whom neither he nor Wes ever even wanted to contemplate moving in next door.

Not much chance of that because Barrington was very toney, affectedly rural in its narrow quaint roads with names like Steeplechase Way, and Goose Lake Lane, as rustic as the streets I'd learned to drive on back in Blue River, small town America. In Barrington, though, the smell of manure was expensive, and the country lanes ended in the circular driveways of multi-million-dollar homes.

Winslow had lived down a long, gravel, tree-lined lane, a location particularly hard to find since Ellen and I had ditched the main funeral procession to stop for a post-cemetery cup of tea. By the time we'd arrived at the late Wesley Winslow's impressive double, oaken front doors, Madsen had begun his oratory. The old man, Madsen, even at upwards of seventy years old, was still a formidable presence with a full thick head of white hair and wiry eyebrows. Raising both arms for quiet, then opening them in a great, magnanimous, brave-faced, stationary wave, Madsen announced: "We have lost a member of our Whytebread family, but we must all of us go on to the kind of success that Wesley had envisioned for this company."

You could feel an excited vibration run through the crowd. The collective unspoken hope buried in this benediction was that Madsen, inspired by the turnout at Winslow's funeral, had changed his mind and the Gold Rush deal would somehow continue on track, somehow money would still rain from heaven.

"We will fill the gap of leadership and we will succeed together." Madsen was promising so sincerely that it seemed almost as if applause might have been in order. But then, of course, Wesley Winslow was dead, so perhaps applause was not quite the ticket. Most everybody, on turning over this dilemma of etiquette, decided on a general murmur of respectful assent.

Linda Tibbits, however, took a bold step — the wrong step — and as she began to clap, heads turned, first slowly, then *en mass* at the lonely hollow sound of her solitary *faux pas*.

August Madsen was unmistakably frowning, a great, big, daddy of a frown. We were all, the rest of us, just google-eyed staring. Then, clearly disoriented, maybe by sadness, likely by some unfortunate glitch in their ass-kissing instincts, Rupert Dean and Kyle Petit joined in the ill-fated ovation as if they imagined Linda just wasn't clapping loudly enough to suit the old man's taste. They started in, both of them, heartily as if he had just announced the bonus pool would be double this year, and August Madsen began to frown more deeply until, after a few very long moments, the applause sputtered out to sad intermittent pops.

Recognizing a problem, Rupert's face dropped instantly into a picture which might well have been entitled: *whoops.* Rupert presently transitioned to a more fittingly somber expression of grief, and then, both he and Kyle turned together eyeing each other critically, as if to suggest that the other one had been solely responsible for the gaffe.

"We've lost an important member of our family." Madsen began again, this time in a less stirring tone whose intended effect was unmistakable. "Whytebread will go on without Wesley Winslow, but that does not mean we won't mourn him. We will mourn him and remember him together as a family."

Madsen then turned and opened both doors with a vigorous pull. As we all filed into the house behind him, I noticed Justin's red BMW pull in behind the bus.

From the hall I could see that Madsen had thoughtfully catered a cold cut buffet, which was simply laid out, almost picnic-style, on a table that could have seated twenty in a dining room entirely adequate for a ballroom dance competition. The food stood at the end of the short gauntlet of Winslows and Madsens blocking the table, which we negotiated one by one, shaking Trisha Winslow's hand and saying something unoriginal, but well-considered, to convey how sorry we were for her loss, our loss as we had now been asked by Madsen to regard Winslow's death.

Hands clasped decorously and quietly in front of her body, poised for a hug or to limply press a hand of the next person in line, it seemed since the Christmas party, Mrs. Winslow had acquired a kind of grace.

"Valium," Ellen pronounced less discreetly than I would have liked. But through the long line, as I waited my turn to express condolences, there was time to watch the show of perfect widowhood and to be amazed that Trisha Winslow could graciously accept not just her husband's tearful runny-nosed secretary Starr, but Camille and her daughter, as well, both of them weeping, and Elana looking so pregnant she might have burst. Mrs. Winslow offered her husband's suspected teenaged mistress a warm embrace of presumed absolution.

I wasn't the only one watching. Cassandra Hope was standing unaffected at the edge of this spectacle in a fabulous black crepe pants suit, doggedly taking notes while Trisha Winslow hugged Camille, and Allison Price, Herb Symon, and The Irishman, all of Winslow longtime colleagues, right down the line, calling them each flawlessly by name, the perfect corporate wife.

I could only imagine that in deference to his death she was trying to be what he had wanted. It was the funeral dance, too little too late — August Madsen's speech about his Whytebread family, Trisha Winslow's sudden conversion to silent dignity and composure, Camille Guitierrez's effusive tears for a man who had knocked up her underage daughter and then demoted her for complaining about it. They were the fragile personal lies of revisionist history, vainly rewriting our memories of dead relationships, making them better than they were and us better in them when, conveniently, there is no one to contradict our version.

"Thank you for coming, Virginia," Trisha Winslow's eyes met mine for absolutely the correct number of seconds, and then dropped demurely, overwhelmed by the depth of her sadness. I waited at the sidelines, after she had released me, for Justin to move through the line, watching as Trisha clasped his hands, both of them. For him she had a special half smile of I don't know what, a crack in the near perfect execution of her role.

I would have liked to know Justin's thoughts on all of this, but Starr was on him seconds after he'd delivered his kiss to Trisha Winslow's cheek. Before I could catch them, Starr had steered him over by the shrubbery that lined Winslow's back patio for a little tête-à-tête. As they talked they stood close, but I had the sense as I watched that they were much further apart than the distance between them.

I looked away as Justin was touching her arm in a comforting gesture. Then, I'd gone to fight the buffet line alone, carrying off an enormous sandwich in which I had sampled a little of every kind of meat available plus two kinds of mustard, and retired to a quiet corner of the dining room which even with the milling fifty or so people didn't seem quite full. The back wall of the house opened through a combination of French doors and freshly washed, picture windows onto a huge, gray slate patio and, beyond, to a rose garden.

It was quite a lawn. Not a single weed or blade of grass peeked through the sandy spaces between the patio stones. Invitingly in the distance there was the faint, peaceful blue of a small private lake.

I'd wanted to take my lunch and just wander off — far away from Whytebread and the rest of my life, but there, on the patio, I could see Cassandra Hope was blocking my way. Raising a hand to her ear, she pantomimed the telephone call she would make to me later. Then she was immediately gone, leaving me with Winslow's million dollar view of the lake and the trees. I would have preferred to enjoy it alone, but Ellen Borgia seemed intent on conversation.

"Look at all those rose bushes." She held a glass of red wine, a napkin and sandwich plate balanced God knew how, as she managed to give my elbow a friendly squeeze. "They say she doesn't use manufactured chemicals. Starr said Wes made her hire extra gardeners to paint the rose leaves with nicotine to keep the aphids off — Trisha." The name came out with a quiet reverence, Ellen talking the way people do about Jacqueline Kennedy Onassis, celebrated widowhood having somehow conveyed a certain glamour that simple affluence had not.

I imagined Trisha Winslow would be spraying with Ortho

insecticide now on the formidable rows of roses for aphids, and mildew and black spot.

"There's eight acres or something like that — not of roses, but the whole estate," Ellen told me.

"Quite a place." I struggled, full-mouthed, with enunciation, "a dream house," wiping away a dab of mustard from my upper lip with the back of my hand.

"Do you think so?" Ellen made a jerky gesture with her head towards the widow Winslow. "When we're gone she'll be dancing on the tables. When we're gone the only ones who'll still be crying are the old man and Winslow's dog-faced little girl." It seemed to me an ungraciousness assertion in the face of all that nice free food and I began to ask what she meant by that, but Ellen had walked away, melted into the crowd at the buffet.

Maybe she went straight out to her car. Maybe she went back through Madsen's buffet line for seconds or even thirds, but in any case, Ellen didn't wait around to drive me back to the city. I returned to Whytebread packed onto the secretarial bus where Camille Gutierrez explained at interminable length the parable of the prodigal son, in a way that I could only surmise was an invitation for me to find Jesus. Whatever Camille's intentions, when I got back to my desk there was a completely unambiguous invitation to find Cassandra in the conference room.

XIV

"Just a second, Virginia." Cassandra crossed the legs of her beautiful suit, as I took the seat kitty corner to her place at the head of the table.

I was admiring the blouse and the toned appearance of her forearms; the sleeves on her white silk blouse carefully rolled two turns, when the creak of the closing conference room door revealed the second cop. He was standing quiet as a deer by the console table, a hard-looking young, black man with a haircut that featured his scalp from nearly every angle and an air of frank appraisal that left me to wonder how obviously I had been admiring Cassandra.

For her part, she'd barely raised her eyes. "This is Officer Hamilton, Ms. Kelly." The young cop made a silent noncommittal nod as he took a seat on Cassandra's side of the table. "Well, then," she turned a blank page in her open notebook asking Hamilton to get us some coffee as if we were seated in her offices rather than my own, "and some tea for Ms. Kelly." He had apparently found the lunchroom or maybe Herb had shown them in a sudden fit of hospitality. "We'll start when you come back."

"Yes, ma'am." Officer Hamilton now discovered a voice.

"Would you like that?" She turned to me indulgently, barking at Hamilton as if she liked to lord it over him: "And see if you can't find some herbal tea, will you?" Cassandra rose, pushing closed the conference room door, which he had left ajar.

"So, are you doing all right?" Cassandra asked when we were alone. She had shined on an enigmatic smile like high beams meant to blind and dazzle. Her hand made its way across the table to squeeze my arm, reassuringly. "You're okay, Virginia?"

"You weren't worried about that this morning." I said.

"Relax. If it would make you feel better I'll have a car keep an eye on your place, dear." I thought that it might, and, that matter settled, Cassandra continued to stroke my wrist until young Hamilton returned. Then, somewhere in the serving of, and the thank yous for the tea, her hand made its way appropriately into her lap and Cassandra became all business again. "Can you tell us again how you found the lunchbox for the record?" She switched on a small tape recorder, affirming, as if we'd just become acquainted, that it would be all right to record our conversation.

In addition to the history of the lunchbox, Cassandra had a number of questions. "You said Mr. Winslow was sweating profusely before his collapse. Did Winslow collapse after Tom Zemluski was ejected from the meeting? Was this after Mr. Zemluski had threatened Winslow?" Annoyingly, she seemed not at all interested in the car that had been following me, the idea that Winlsow's lunch had been packed and poisoned by a mistress, or the information that the *Fly Agaric* is not usually fatal which I had unsuccessfully tried to work into the conversation. Just the same, for the better part of an hour, the tape recorder turned steadily on the table in front of me. I watch the box and Cassandra watched me, stopping occasionally to write what I was recounting.

Hamilton was taking notes too, quite faithfully as if he expected later to be tested on the material. I'd left some people I didn't think really mattered out of our discussions, notably Ellen who it seemed to me wanted to sue Winslow more than anything else, and since you couldn't sue a dead man, I couldn't imagine that she'd killed him. I was holding onto Tom in my mind, but tenuously as he didn't seem the poisoning type, more a blunt heavy instrument kind of guy. Just the same, I told Cassandra The Irishman had been lobbying against the merger and that he wanted us to pool our stock so we could blackmail Winslow into giving us some assurances we would all keep our jobs after the sale.

"And what did you say to that?" She glanced up at me when I answered as if she were making a determination on what I was telling her, and nodding noncommittally.

I'd told Tom: no — not in so many words but that had been the gist of it after the lunch bill was paid.

Cassandra kept nodding. "I have Whytebread's phone list here." She slipped a paper from the briefcase, which lay on the chair beside her, a premeditated move requiring not even a glance to locate the right paper, the right folder. "Maybe you could give me a little insight into the personalities involved." Inexplicably I noticed the tape recorder had been switched off. "For example," she posited laying the paper down flat on the table so that I could read it, "does Herb Symon dislike Justin Collier for being a homosexual?" Hitting me again with that challenging smile, the force of which struck me momentarily dumb.

Hamilton had taken up a very serious expression. Head

down, he continued to write, although our conversation had come to a precipitous pause.

"I asked you if you know that Justin Collier is a homosexual?" A confusing question, Cassandra repeated as if I simply had not heard her the first time and I wondered, what did it matter? The room seemed to become even more quiet as I settled on that question for a question.

"What could it possibly matter?"

"Oh, it doesn't," Cassandra folded her hands across the table top, leaning in at me. She was smiling a smug, brutish triumph. "It doesn't matter at all, not in the least, Ms. Kelly."

Despite what I took as his best efforts at decorum Hamilton's face had cracked into a mean little smirk. "I only asked to make a point." Cassandra was grinning bald-faced, "That point being you'll need to report circumstances exactly as you understand them, unfiltered. You'll need to be completely forthcoming with us, even if the circumstances are a little uncomfortable; it's the best thing. Of course you can rest assured that we will keep any unrelated personal information between us." She flattened her palm lightly above her chest, then made a companion gesture towards me. "A man is dead and it's very important, Ms. Kelly, that you be completely candid. Don't we all want the same thing?"

I was beginning to wonder. "You know I don't have to be here." One of the many, hard muscles in Hamilton's jaw began to twitch threateningly as I concluded, "I really don't need this."

"That's right, Ms. Kelly." Cassandra smiled. Hamilton twitched. She said, "Of course you don't have to be here, but for some reason — maybe it's your interest in justice — you *are* here." Sometime in all of this the tape recorder had begun to roll again and Cassandra was dishing it up like soft-serve ice cream. "And now, I'd certainly appreciate any information you could give me about Alcee Couteau."

I said, "Well, he's not a homosexual," but no one laughed;

so, I began grudgingly to recount Mister Couteau's bible study activities along with my suspicion that he had placed the Post-it Notes, a monologue which received a warmer reception. So, the questions went on until Cassandra abruptly clicked the tape recorder off, after memorializing the time of the interview's termination.

"Well, Ms. Kelly, I think that does it." She began to gather up her litter of notes and papers from the table. Squaring their edges neatly against the wood, she slipped them into the front flap of her big, leather briefcase. There was a rattle as she dropped them, from, I surmised, the chain of Winslow's house keys in behind the papers. Cassandra held her own keys in her hand. "I guess you've had a long day. Can we offer you a lift home?"

Across the room, Hamilton was packing up his notebook as well, seemingly oblivious to our discussion.

"Can I offer you a lift?" Cassandra turned the brass button that locked down the flap of her bag.

I can't say why I decided then to let her take me; maybe it was just perverse curiosity or a little case of nerves from the drama of that morning. Whatever the origins of the impulse, I went with it.

Cassandra pushed with her back against the heavy glass door, holding it open for me. "Come on." In the lobby, Pamela was singing "Whytebread, Greese, Winslow and Sloat," into her headset. "How may I direct your call?" repeated, *ad nauseam* with an almost automated brightness; and we had just stepped into the elevator when Hamilton motioned Cassandra back inside the office. She sighed, walking over to meet him in the reception area and I left the elevator to the relief of a number of hurried commuters. Cassandra's sidebar showed no signs of an ending anytime soon. So, I waited by Pamela's desk until after a much longer while Cassandra broke away glancing back, as she talked to me, at Hamilton like a dog owner with an undependably trained animal, down at her watch and then over at the office door where Hamilton had gone. "I'm sorry Virginia," she said, "Can you wait a few minutes?" The bag seemed heavy on her arm.

I'd remembered then, the suggestive rattle of keys in the front flap, a fated opportunity. If I could get into Winslow's apartment I would know if he'd had a girlfriend and maybe even who it was, so I reached for her briefcase. "I can take that."

Cassandra hesitated for just a moment before she gave it over, her eyes flicking back to her bag once more protectively, then she trotted off through the side door to find Hamilton. I'd taken her bag and mine over to the leather guest couches, and set them both on the floor by the thick padded arm. While pretending fascination with Fortune magazine, I maneuvered my free hand over the side of the couch in a long, exaggerated stretch to Cassandra's bag, which was tucked premeditatedly behind my own. After easing open the zipper of my black canvas case, I walked my fingers slowly along until I felt the leather top of Cassandra's bag and found the little brass button that secured its front flap closed. It turned quietly and I fished my hand up under the leather flap and down into the front pockets looking for the straight edges of an envelope and the hard, circular outline of the key ring inside. There were four or five of them, fanned out from the ring: one to Winslow's house in Barrington, one to the lobby door at the Park Shore, one to his personal apartment, and one to his office at Whytebread.

"I'm sorry, he's away from his desk," Pamela was saying. "May I give you voice mail?"

I worried how long before Cassandra would notice the keys were gone. Not long. But continuing in a thirty-three-year history of poor impulse control, I crushed my hand around the envelope, brought it up just high enough to drop it into the open top of my own bag, zipped the top and closed Cassandra's, just as she rushed back into the lobby apologizing with a vague harried gesture.

It was a forty-five minute drive home at rush hour, north up Lakeshore Drive, but that day even at six o'clock, the ride went quickly. I had half expected a continuation of our police interview, but to my relief Cassandra was talking rather incessantly about herself, telling me instead how she had moved to 62nd street, a neighborhood I knew to be middle class and black since the Jewish flight in the fifties. She had bought one of those little brick bungalows, still quite afford-able on a cop's salary, but it seemed to me I said a strange place for dykes.

In Cassandra's relic of a Volvo, the air smelled faintly of oranges and ginger. I thought the old white sedan a charmingly incongruous choice for a woman who cared so much for appearances, a strange practicality.

"Only a strange place for white dykes," she was saying with respect to the Southside, my own Northside condo being really necessary only to my recent succession of white lovers, a point which I now felt reluctant to discuss. She said, "I haven't been up here since you and I were together," and I wanted to imagine a connection between the memory and her sly momentary smile. She said, "So, I guess you're still seeing that girl, Em."

I'd shaken my head, "Not for years now." I'd admitted my girlfriend's name was Mary Ellen, immediately regretting having said even that much, and rushing to legitimize idiosyncrasies of which Cassandra could have no awareness — Spike's multiple piercings, her hair, dyed colors not found in nature. "She's got a restaurant in my home town. We went to high school together." Cassandra raised her eyebrows at the road, still smiling the knowing smile I'd decided now was very sexy. "White?" This was asked with swallowed amusement, the self-congratulatory expectation that I would not surprise her.

I was nodding. She was nodding as if we were together confirming some obvious personal failing.

She said, "Well you've always liked that."

"Liked what?"

I let her say it.

"White women." She palmed the gearshift, a hand brushing lightly my leg. "You know, we could give it another try, Virginia. No obligation." It felt as though the car was a shell, the kind you can hold to your ear and hear the ocean, but what I could hear was my own rather sudden troubling relationship ambivalence.

Cassie was laughing. "Oh come on." Her hand ran a course along my knee up to the inside of my thigh and stayed there until she downshifted again at the bottom of the Irving Park exit ramp. She told me, "It's been such a long time since I've been with someone I really liked."

I couldn't say how I'd managed to get so very easy. It was something I planned to analyze more — but later when I'd been safely in and out of Winslow's apartment. In fact a tryst seemed a not unpleasant way to effect the return of Cassandra's keys, a part of my plan that admittedly was still in embryonic development.

As it was, I made an Oscar-worthy performance of walking innocently through the wrought iron gates and up the few brick steps through the lobby door when she dropped me at my building. I'd hidden in the first floor foyer until I heard her go, and then, after a few minutes more for good measure, hightailing it the three blocks down Irving Park to the rental garage where I kept my car.

XV

It was a happy coincidence that Winslow had lived in the same building that Naomi just moved into, and happier still that for emergencies, Naomi had given me both a lobby key and a key to her apartment. They were still hanging on my key chain intermingled with my own house keys, as I hadn't quite gotten around to labeling them and putting them away. For once my tendency towards procrastination was a benefit. Now, Naomi's keys saved me from having to fumble there at the lobby door conspicuously with Winslow's set in Cassandra's envelope.

"How's it going, Joe." I'd cribbed the security guard's name off his uniform pocket on the way past his desk. His frown at my unfamiliar face relaxed at the sound of his name and my competent entry. Waving back at Joe in a kind of vacant smiling sure-I-belong-in-this-high-security-apartment-building-way, I took the elevator to Naomi's seventeenth floor apartment, and let myself in.

I was still refining the elements of my plan as I opened Naomi's refrigerator to forage for food, which I imaged would serve to sharpen my thinking. I was hoping for leftovers, a little remaining Chinese carryout, some doggy bagged dinner from a nice downtown restaurant as Naomi emphatically did not cook, but there was nothing there but a liter of Fresca, and in the freezer some vodka and one lonely Stouffer's Macaroni and Cheese, so I poured myself some vodka, slid the frozen entree into Naomi's microwave, while I considered my options with regard to Winslow's apartment.

I had Winslow's keys, but I didn't know his apartment number, and if I asked Joe down at the front desk that would certainly arouse suspicion or worse. But as I ate I wrote out a note with the always-available blue felt tip pen hanging on Naomi's refrigerator, and one of the many yellow legal pads she kept around the apartment. With a little luck this would get me into Winslow's place with relative ease. Having scrawled, almost illegibly, with my left hand, I folded the yellow paper over once, stuck some scotch tape on the back, and dialed down to the front desk where I informed Joe the security guard that I'd found a letter stuck to Naomi's door, apartment number 1702. I fibbed, "I came by to water Naomi's plants, while she's out of town," and I crossed my fingers hoping that Naomi would not return from work anytime soon.

There was a long stupid pause until I clarified I was the Black girl who had just come up on the elevator. "Yeah. Okay." Joe warmed, having put me into context, so I went on.

"I'm calling because I just found a note here, taped to the door. It's for someone named Wes — Wesley. I'll drop it off with you." Praying that Joe was just a little lazy, I said, "Maybe you could take it up to the right apartment," and was

encouraged when my gentle speculation that he might render
some service other than sitting behind his desk was greeted
with an interval of silence. After a while I could hear him
paging through the list of tenants puffing slightly at his
inconvenience. "Anybody named Wes in the building?" I held
my breath while I crossed my fingers. Wesley was an unusual
name. There were two of them at the Park Shore.

"But one's dead," The doorman added not seeming to
relish any prospect of a mystery.

"Well," I was offering in the most helpful perky affect I
could muster, "I could drop it off if it's not the dead guy. Why
don't you tell me their apartment numbers," I suggested, my
stroke of genius. "Whoever left the note must have gotten the
number mixed up with Naomi Wolf's 1702, so maybe we can
figure out from the apartment numbers who this note was
meant for."

He made a rather labored breath before he read down the
tenant list again. "Take your pick." There was Wesley
Grumman in 2701 and Wesley Winslow in 2101 and I told him
that it seemed to me Mr. Grumman was the right guy.

"You think so?" Joe, the doorman, sounded truly relieved
that the situation was so easily resolved, "Because if it's for
the dead guy I think the police are going to want to see that
note."

"Sure," I said that whoever had left this note must have
gotten the numbers mixed up in his head. "1702 for 2701.
See?" In this day and age of over-diagnosed learning
disabilities dyslexia was rampant. "What else could it be,
right?"

"You know, I'm not supposed to leave the front," he put
in after apparent deliberation; so, I offered again to drop the
note off at 2701 on my way out and Joe seemed happy enough
not to think about the matter a minute longer than he already
had.

I tossed the forged note into Naomi's kitchen trash and

fairly skipped to apartment 2101 where the first and second keys on the ring turned smoothly in Winslow's double locks. Inside a small, marble-tiled entry way led unremarkably down a long, narrow-feeling hall, all of it painted stark white, the walls, the molding, the ceilings achieving an upscale futuristic sterility that told me nothing about the man; and all those smooth white walls seemed to be bringing on a migraine headache — either that or my tuna sandwich this morning really had been a little off. Following the long institutionally painted hall, Winslow's master bedroom proved no less stark and white — no more instructive.

By all appearances, Winslow's weekday place was just that, genuinely nothing more than a commuting convenience, to which I had stolen keys from a police detective for, it would seem now, absolutely no good reason. This as opposed to my hoped-for, murder solving clandestine love nest. There was no women's clothing — and little more men's in the master bedroom walk-in closet than a set of five nearly identical, conservatively cut, dark suits, and their complement of white and blue shirts, conclusive evidence of nothing other than maybe Winslow was shacked up with his pathologically tidy identical twin. There was no information in the assortment of regimentally striped and unimaginatively paisley ties and the two pairs of wingtip shoes — one black, one brown. Winslow's cedar-lined bureau drawers contained nothing more enlightening than undershirts and skivvies, both boxers and briefs, all of them cotton, none of the carefully folded items made of anything a clothing moth might want to eat. There was oddly not even a pair of running shorts, though I had heard tell that Winslow often ran to work at dawn, showering in his private office bathroom long before my generally mid-morning arrival.

If Winslow's office sports wall of trumpeted physical achievement suggested a rugged outdoorsman, this was an interest he pursued on his weekends that clearly were not spent in his spartan Chicago flat.

The master bath, while more luxurious in its gray marble wainscoting (that was missing from Naomi's apparently lower budget apartment) made no useful statement other than superior maid service. Whoever cleaned Winslow's apartment kept the tub shiny enough to serve soup from even after his final bath.

Perhaps it was Winslow himself. A man of known compulsions, Wes had been fastidious about his personal appearance as well. The flat, mirrored wall chest above the sink contained, along with shaving cream and an antique-looking, silver straight edge, an assortment of face creams and tonics, which had clearly contributed to his fabulous skin. I fingered the potions with my own agenda. The first of them arranged in the cabinet by size was Clinique Turnaround Cream, the hydrating moisturizer I used myself. Winslow had certainly bought it in bulk — an absolute waste of the 32-oz industrial size jar he wouldn't be needing anymore. I found myself unscrewing the thick white cap before I had considered the potential breach of law or etiquette in taking some. The Turnaround cream on my own vanity and all the samples I'd ever tried at the Marshall Field's make-up counter had smelled of potpourri, but that afternoon there was the faint odor of bad fish, an ugly olfactory hallucination courtesy of today's impending migraine.

Still, I spread the thin, light cream lightly over my temples and neck in an upward semi-circular motion exactly as the beauty magazines had taught me — never down. I pressed some cream across my forehead to reverse the faint lines that were beginning there and to help calm the ominous, pre-headache throbbing that had begun to pulse in my left frontal lobe.

My post-beauty regimen examination of the remaining contents of Winslow's medicine cabinet prove uneventful, yielding one of everything you would expect in an apartment for one — not even back-up provisions, the extra toothbrush, an extra razor, the back-up hand cream. Winslow's efficiency had apparently extended to *just in time* purchasing in his personal life. In the refrigerator there had been no leftover mushrooms, no leftover anything — no evidence, no insight, no crime solving theories, which left the fairly daunting problem of how I was going to get Winslow's keys back into Cassandra's bag. It had never occurred to me that taking them wouldn't enable me to solve the crime, thus making their return a kind of non-event in comparison, but the way things were going I would be lucky if I didn't end up in jail.

I'd consoled myself with another little dollop of Winslow's Turnaround Cream as I puzzled out how I was going to avoid a cell in Dwight Women's Prison, rubbing the cool lovely lotion over my wrists, and dabbing it gently under my eyes (because God knew I wouldn't be able to get this high-end stuff in the slam) when my stomach pitched and the room began to move very oddly.

The tuna had almost certainly been rancid because my forehead was pulsing with a disco backbeat and I could hear the opening movement of a monumental headache behind my eyes. As I examined the lines in my hands — a short, deep-looking lifeline, crossed by a worrisome number of creases — my palms had begun to sweat. All of this would have been far more troubling if I could have found the wherewithal to connect it together into a coherent string of thought.

Down the hall there might or might not have been the click of a door and the muffled sound of footsteps on the plush, tight carpet, but within the muddled confines of my brain I thought I could hear my mother calling me as she had when I was a little girl and the days stayed light very late in the summers. The kids were playing kickball in the lot down by the IGA and she was calling, "Ginny, Ginny, time to come home."

I tried to go home, but a wave of nausea bent me over

Wes's marble countered sinks. Pushing my hands under the luke-warm water, I rubbed them first together, then with the dainty little lavender soap from a small stone dish. I splashed the water up at my cheeks and neck rubbing my face with my soapy hands and after a while the contents of my stomach settled down.

It seemed that everything might well be all right after all, as I grabbed around for Wes's guest towel to dry my face, but then there was Cassandra Hope glaring at me as reflected in the vanity mirror.

"Well, hi." I waggled my fingers at her in a dopey way I'd hope that she would think was cute. But it was hard to tell exactly what Cassandra was thinking as she was opening and closing her mouth as if the unbelievability of my presence in Winslow's bathroom was defying her every attempt at speech.

"What exactly are you doing here?" After the wait, I found the plainspoken outrage of the sentence kind of anticlimactic.

"Surprise." The vagueness in my answer was not purely intentional. To tell the truth, I was still feeling pretty thoroughly out of sorts.

"You stole my keys," she said and I was hurt by the not completely fair characterization of my actions, since I had agonized at least a little bit about how I was going to return them to her. It was almost a relief that I could just hand the envelope back now, no harm; no foul. "Let's say I borrowed them. Look," I began to explain, "I had that idea about Wes's mistress —"

I would have finished my thought, but I was confused — more than just about the mushrooms or Winslow's absent lover — and just as I was formulating my crushing summation of fact, the room seemed to bend oddly inward like the corners of a piece of paper folding simultaneously towards the center. The marble floor reached up and tried to slap my face. I pushed it away just in the nick of time — only temporarily though. The floor had proved an insistent suitor. The next thing I knew, I went down.

"Virginia?" Cassandra was kneeling beside me. "Virginia?" The marble and I were cheek to cheek like Hollywood lovers in a 1930s musical. I had gone down almost peacefully; the way they say it feels to drown.

Cassandra's face held me with a reserved concern as if she suspected my collapse was just a clever ploy to garner sympathy. "Are you all right?"

The edges of the room had uncurled just a little. "I'm better than ever." I managed to say, "I'm the new improved model with scrubbing bubbles."

I don't remember getting up or walking, but I must have walked down the champagne carpeted hall, out of Winslow's apartment, down the elevators past good, old Joe from security and out to her car. Whatever questions were asked by security, Cassandra must have answered. She'd driven me home, but all I can reliably recall until the warm lapping water of the bathtub is the pain in my head, which was sharp and the complaints of my gut, which were, unfortunately many.

After my bath, Cassandra had put me gently to bed in a dark quiet room. She was still there with me when I woke up.

"Am I under arrest?" It seemed a reasonable question.

"I don't think so," she said rather kindly. Then, she kissed me and it started up again — Cassandra and me, revisiting the one great over-reaching dilemma of my adult life: Which would you rather have, Order or Craziness? I kept shooting for Order, but it never ever seemed to take.

"What a funny book," she was saying, her face turned away and her brown back stretched out prone, laid sideways. We were kitty corner on my bed and her long, seemingly flawless arm having reached awkwardly behind her head to take the book from a low shelf in the wooden headboard.

"Would you like it if I read to you? You used to like it." She read aloud, *"My face hasn't collapsed as some with fine features have done. It's kept the same contours, but its substance has been laid waste. I have a face laid waste."*

I was almost myself again the next morning, wakened by the sound of the shower running and the smell of coffee somewhere in my apartment. It was nice, if disorienting, as I hadn't remembered buying any coffee since Em left. Shortly after the water stopped, Cassie appeared in the bedroom, damp-skinned, holding in one hand a ceramic mug and a jumbo Styrofoam cup, the apparent source of the coffee smell, in the other.

She settled down beside me on the bed, at home in the tacky geisha-style bathrobe Spike had brought me from San Francisco's Chinatown and which,until now, Spike herself always seemed to get to wear. Somehow the gaudy robe looked better on Cassandra than it ever had on Spike — or me. On Cassandra it looked like it was real.

Sweet Potato had positioned himself in the hammock my legs and bedclothes had made of my lap, and it seemed to me overnight my life had been perfected. When Cassie told me, "See, I remembered you like chamomile in the mornings," I found myself unaccountably pleased, filled up with that dopey coupled satisfaction I was always inclined to ridicule in others.

"Were you worried about me, Sweet Potato?" I was

rubbing the space between his black, saucer eyes, asking Cassandra, "Where'd you get the coffee?"

"White Hen Pantry around the corner." She raised her still-steamy cup. "Hazel nut roast." Apparently even the corner store had moved into the world of designer beans.

"So do you think Winslow had a mistress?"

"It depends," Cassandra had a better question. "Can you tell me why Winslow would have left Elana Guitierrez a quarter of a million dollars in trust?"

"A trust?" I was almost as surprised as when I'd first spotted Elana in the Whytebread library, a job jealously reserved for the walleyed albino children of Whytebread big men. Elana didn't look the part, a brown pretty girl with long shiny black hair and a frightened sort of smile that suggested she might rather jump off the bridge into the cold Chicago River than raise her voice.

That day she was talking though, gushing to Winslow, "I got an A on my Calculus test, and my history teacher says she will recommend me to Wellesley College. Massachusetts is really far away from Joaquin and Momma, but he says I should go."

"Well, that's fine." Wes touched her cheek lightly, listening with uncharacteristic patience to her discussion of Joaquin, a boy in her neighborhood who would go to Loop College in the fall and who was escorting her to the movies that Friday night.

Crouched behind the library shelves, where I had been looking for bond yield data, I was now uncomfortably privy to the tiny touching details of Elana's life that I was certainly never meant to hear, but it seemed far worse to announce myself. So, I'd stayed hidden there, reading the Moody's Reports and developing a terrible crease in my calf muscles until Winslow left, and I could slip away while Elana re-shelved something or another.

A couple of months later when Elana had left Whytebread

rather suddenly before the end of the school year, the buzz on her pregnancy was strong. I told Cassandra from Elana's gravid appearance at Winslow's funeral, it seemed like the rumors were true. Cassandra said the trust was independent of Winslow's will and my only conclusion was that he was providing for his baby.

"You don't think Camille or Elana had anything to do with his death?" As I asked, Cassandra bent down to kiss me.

"Do you know how much I've missed this?" She was licking my ear, I thought conveniently changing the subject.

"What subject was that?" She had pushed me onto my back, then kissed me again harder with an open mouth.

Cassandra never did answer my question about Winslow's mistress, but later we spooned through at least three cycles of the snooze on my alarm. By the fourth one, I was vaguely aware of her sitting on the edge of the bed again, talking quietly into her cellular phone.

"I had a meeting," she was whispering. "It ran late and I stayed at Lonnie's," and then her voice got short. "Well you won't have to wait up tonight."

I didn't move, just watched her because I didn't want to actually catch her at it. I didn't want to know who it was on the phone. So, I closed my eyes and began to stretch my arms, groaning softly as if I had just woken up.

"Look, I have to go." She folded and palmed the small phone almost noiselessly. I wondered if it was possible that Cassandra was talking to her mother, which I thought would make sense of her address at 62nd Street. That made me feel all right again.

When I opened my eyes, her arms were around my waist as if she had been lying that way all the time.

"Do you have a suspect yet?" and Cassie's grip on my waist loosened noticeably. I was saying, "How can I help you if you won't tell me everything?"

"I'll tell you when there's something to tell." Cassandra had begun to untangle herself from my body now with a minimum of unnecessary intimacy.

Sitting up and retrieving her gold bracelet watch from my nightstand, I watched her pause to admire her wrist. It was a beautiful watch, the kind of gift a lover would give, I told myself — perhaps as an anniversary gift. Then I told myself I was being crazy, looking for the complication in a tryst that could remain pleasantly simple if I could only stop myself from ruining it. Cassandra kissed me again lightly and left the room.

She was wearing a pale blue, woolen pants suit I hadn't seen the night before, when she returned, and she ran a hand along my cheek anticipating my question about her change of clothes. "Sometimes I can't get home so I keep some extra things in my car."

Sweet potato arched and stretched and strutted across the bed purring and swinging his big orange tail.

She kissed me again, calling me, "sleepy head — you and your cat." She was petting my face with one cool fingered hand and reaching out to scratch between Sweet Potato's ears with the other. "Nice kitty, kitty, kitty."

He'd let her pat his head for quite a while before he wrapped himself around her wrist, digging into her arm with his sharp back claws. Cassandra shook him off swearing and he landed against the bedroom wall with a dull, ugly thud, although he seemed no worse for wear.

"I'm sorry." I said, "I guess he's jealous." Sweet Potato shook himself lazily and walked over to the middle of the rug to calmly lick his private areas.

Cassandra winced. "Jealous? I guess so." I traced with my fingers the bloody welts that ran from the bend of her elbow along the inside of her arm to the wrist, and dabbed at them with a little Kleenex. The scratches looked worse than they

137

were. Sweet Potato hadn't much liked Spike either, and then I asked her as the thought came suddenly into my mind. "How did you know Justin Collier was gay?"

"August Madsen mentioned it." Cassandra said this offhandedly as I was bending down to kiss her arm, I hoped, all better. "Despite what Mr. Collier believes it's hardly a very big secret." She kissed me back, summarily though, removing my hand from her shoulder, standing, and apparently ready to leave, Cassie's exit scene had an unpleasant déjà vu from years past.

She squinted critically into the mirror, brushing down her manicured hair. The perfect bob had been somewhat disheveled by the night and I could see this put her out. Cassandra gave her whole attention to righting her appearance as she talked to me. "Thanks so much to you and your cat for a lovely evening. If you don't hit it, Virginia, you're going to be late to work." Purring once again, Sweet Potato blinked his narrow cat eyes slowly in my direction.

XVI

I made a resolution that morning to drive to work more often because even with Cassandra dropping me by the Park Shore, I'd ended up at Whytebread a good half an hour earlier than I would have arrived on the bus. Not that I got much face-time credit for it. That morning, like most of them lately, the office was quiet. Most doors were closed, most people shut behind them and only The Irishman had the self-confidence to be loitering in the hall — lounging was more the picture, like he owned the place — not just the hall, the whole universe.

"How are Wes's chosen people this morning?" He fairly shouted at me in a voice of good nature I was not inclined to trust. "Hey. Hey." The Irishman was calling. "Don't get used to it, Virginia." His body seemed to have swollen so that it stoppered the hallway and I couldn't get around him. "Do you hear me? Nothing around here is going to change for you." The Irishman had pushed up very close to me, breath hot and jubilant. "Too bad there isn't going to be any Gold Rush deal."

"Is that what Winslow told you the night he died?" I managed to ask at a prudent number of paces. "Or did you just beg him to let you stay, Tom?"

"Oh, I'm going to stay all right, young lady. Things around here are going to stay just the same as they always were." The Irishman hissed, any pretense of goodwill completely eroded, "You just remember that." Then he stepped aside politely as if he'd been wishing me a good day.

I'd had the strange idea that with Winslow's death life would slow down, but somehow my world kept turning, at least the phone kept ringing. A frantically blinking phone message light greeted me in my office: Two calls from Naomi, a message from my old friend, Sandra Rutherford, for whom I had promised to baby-sit on Friday night, and three messages from Emily Karnowski, my ex-girlfriend and tax accountant, who I realized, just at that second, I'd forgotten to meet the previous night.

Em had called at 6:35, 7:00 and 7:30 the evening before, the night I'd spent reacquainting myself with Cassandra, regarding our appointment to discuss my tax situation. With each message Em sounded progressively more piqued, so the return call required a really good story. In the meantime, I checked my e-mail.

There were twelve electronic messages since yesterday afternoon. Nine of these were client-related. There was one from my dad whose subject line read, *My new cooking class.* There was a message from Starr who'd apparently, had a change of heart, wanted to meet me back at the office at 8:30

tonight, and a long, rambling, indiscreet epistle from Spike. While I was cringing over how I would answer her, Naomi called again.

"I left two messages on your home machine last night." Naomi began to berate me almost immediately, and I thought Cassandra must have turned the ringer off.

"Wesley Winslow, the president of Whytebread was murdered, last weekend," I started to say but Naomi cut me off.

"Yeah, I know, your dead financier and his ultimate exit strategy." She was never one to miss a scandal. Part of the reason Naomi'd been trying to reach me was to dish. "By the way," she asked, "were you in my house yesterday?"

I admitted I'd been doing some investigation. "Winslow lived in your building."

"Uh huh." I could feel her roll her eyes. "Right. You know, you parked in my spot, which meant I had to park outside in the visitor's lot. You left all the lights on including the one in the microwave. FYI, Virginia, when you don't use up all the time you can just press stop. And there was some weird note in my trash." It seemed Naomi had been doing some investigation of her own. Besides, "what am I, only good for my convenient location?" She was complaining fluently, "you know, I'm having a life change here and you've practically abandoned me."

It sounded like Naomi was talking about menopause.

"That's next." Through the phone, I could hear her lighting a cigarette and I said I thought the plan was to quit smoking.

"Of course. I did quit." She snapped at me. "At least four distinct times since Tuesday. I tried to quit. That was just my point. Where were you when I needed support?"

I'd begun recalling for Naomi's benefit the nasty and potentially deadly side effects detailed in the Nicoderm information packet. "So, I took the patch off for a little while." She said. "Okay? All right? Keep your shirt on. There's still stick-um on it; it'll go right back on — well, maybe with a little bit of tape." She was exhaling irritably into the phone at the prospect of such a project. I called you six times so you could talk me down for Godssakes."

"I've been tied up," I said. "I've met someone." It seemed the simplest explanation.

"Young love. Why am I not surprised?" Naomi made her voice a singsong imitation of my own. "Now you've met someone. How could you possibly have met someone, Virginia? There isn't a single new dyke in the world."

"I've recycled an old one," I told her. There was a hopeless smile in my voice. "Someone I used to see before Em, before I knew you, even."

Naomi breathed out in mute annoyance. I could hear the wheels in her head, grinding along, as she hated any of my relationships to predate our own. "Fabulous, who doesn't like leftovers? You know that's the beginning of the end, running out of fresh women. Mark my words," Naomi pronounced with finality, "it's a sign that Chicago is ruined for you."

"She's the cop working Wesley Winslow's murder," I went on.

"Uh-huh." Naomi was apparently interested enough in Winslow's murder to have stopped smoking into the receiver. "Well, whatever. My condolences on bedding the cop. They are the worst." Already relishing my love affair ending badly, she promised, "It'll never last. Look I'm telling you these things because I care about you. Don't you remember that meter maid — the one with the cute little scooter? Haven't you learned anything from my mistakes?" Naomi sighed, my pain was her pain, even if I wasn't feeling it yet.

I thought there were some major differences between meter maids and police officers, but even separated by miles of fiber optics, I could see her dismissively waving off this point of distinction. "We're talking law enforcement. We're talking a type here. Has anyone ever told you, you need to get out more, Virginia? Meet a wider class of people."

142

I was asking if perhaps Naomi knew any single aerobics instructors, but she let the reference pass. "So to summarize then Virginia," Naomi's voice was imperial condescension, "while Ms. CPD is pumping you for the inside dope like a country water faucet, she's just happened to remember how much she adores you. *Quel* surprise. By the way," she hit upon this like a pleasant afterthought, "what's her name anyway? It's a small world. Who knows I might be able to give you a run down of her prior bad acts."

"It's Cassandra Hope," I said. "Detective Sergeant."

Naomi snorted. "Very, very fancy. And you don't think your Detective Hope could possibly have a somewhat different agenda than happily ever after." She had paused for a moment in this diatribe, mumbling absently to herself: "I know I know that name and in a minute I'm going to tell you why."

"Because you know every dyke in Chicago. Talk about a city ruined." I was reporting with what I'm sure was a nearly insufferable gush of self-satisfaction how Cassandra and I had consummated our little affair just this morning following my investigation of Winslow's apartment.

"This would be the investigation where you lied to my doorman about my being out of town and left the microwave on?"

I said, "the only problem is I don't think Sweet Potato really likes Cassandra."

"Honor that," Naomi blew out heavily into the phone. "That cat is a fine intuitive judge of character."

I said Sweet Potato didn't like Naomi either.

"Well, yes, that's exactly what I'm saying." She made another loud sound of exasperation. "Besides, Virginia, what are you going to do about Spike?"

Sweet Potato hated Spike. I was feeling a tiny bit disloyal that in my mind Spike had already passed into the past tense. But matter of fact, Naomi hated Spike as well. "I've been thinking Spike and I need to take a little distance, you know," I told her, "a little space?"

She was chuckling that the space from Chicago to Blue River seemed like distance enough. I said, "Can we get back to Winslow's murder?" hoping that Naomi could offer something as disconcertingly most of my information had come despite Cassandra — not because of her.

Naomi stopped chuckling and had given herself over to out and out laughter. "You mean you can't just ask your new playmate? You're telling me you can't just query your girl cop in the afterglow? Who's zooming whom?" I could hear Naomi smoking again and worrying over the name: "I just wish I could tell you why she sounds so damn familiar. It's making me nuts."

I was considering how to respond to this when my second phone line lit up. Naomi continued to smoke as I put her on hold, after which the receptionist informed me that my incoming call was from Emily Karnowski, CPA.

I had to go. Em's announcement of her professional title had the same significance as when in anger my mother called me by both my given and surnames as a child.

"Yeah sure," said Naomi, "I know where I rate."

As I was retrieving Em from whatever receptionist's digital limbo is described by hold, Camille came in and dropped a stack of mail at the corner of my desk.

It had never once occurred to her to knock, which I supposed I shouldn't have taken so personally as the buzz had been all through the halls that Linda Tibbits had walked in on Rupert Dean masturbating last year without so much as an "excuse me," from either end. She'd just put his mail down and left. Of course the next day she'd requested an immediate transfer.

"Hi there," I said to Em in a way I hoped would sound guiltless and friendly. To Camille, I directed some not-so-subtle eye contact that she should scram, but as usual she seemed in absolutely no hurry to leave, poking around in the vicinity of my out-box with the air of a big, dumb anteater.

When she'd first started working for me, I was sure this

was her cover for eavesdropping on my conversations, imagining her as a spy for The Irishman, imagining that my conversations were worth eavesdropping on. After a while, though, I realized not only my insignificance in the world of Whytebread, but that Camille simply believed she was as invisible to me as she'd been to Wes. He must have conducted whatever business he had, private or personal, as if she were just a piece of furniture in the room, and she expected that I would too.

"Was I supposed to call you or were you supposed to call me?" As I tried to manage Em, Camille unhurriedly placed the typed reports of yesterday on my desk for me to review and then withdrew from my office, closing the door as wordless and quietly as she had entered. Through the glass wall onto the corridor, I watched Camille recede slowly down the hall. She was wearing a loose, shapeless dress with a pastel, floral pattern that made her look like one of the Hawaiian Islands as seen in the distance from a cruise ship, her big flowery dress billowed out around her.

"Was I supposed to call?" I was trying for a stupid yet repentant tone that would let me slide.

"Don't bullshit a bullshitter, Virginia." As usual Em had me cold. "You were supposed to be at my office last night." She'd never been very long on forgiveness and it was so hard to know where the anger came from — what transgression it was, over what period in our relationship, that was currently fueling her.

I picked up an envelope from the pile in my in-box, slit it open with the side of my thumb and lied. "I was in a car accident." That cooled Em's rage, just barely, and in the lull while she was figuring out whether to believe me, I began to skim the letter which was not the usual request for money from my business school. Instead, they were writing to inform me that the letter of recommendation I'd written for a young research associate hadn't yet been received and would need to be received in the next two weeks for it to be considered in her evaluation. I looked at the date on the top of the committee's letter, which read more than ten days ago. It could well have sat in my in-box for the better part of the last week. Most irritatingly, I couldn't remember what I'd originally written about the associate who admittedly was fairly mediocre, if not offensive.

I clearly recalled putting the handwritten draft paper clipped to a blank form on Camille's chair three weeks ago, but I didn't remember getting it back for signature.

"You know my time is valuable," Em was reminding me, a fact of which I'd become acutely aware since she had begun to charge me hourly for consultations after our break-up. In light of my accident, which it was clear she wasn't quite sure whether she should believe, Em was letting me off with a stern lecture. In the end, we agreed I would meet her after work at Chardonnay, an upscale lesbian bar on Montrose and she'd only charge me half her hourly rate for the missed appointment when she did my tax returns next April.

"Don't think I'm going to forget to bill," she promised. But I had already redirected my irritation towards Camille.

Early on in her fairly short tenure with me, I'd asked Camille to keep a chronological file of everything I'd produced. Apparently this had been a problem. Never mind that Starr, an arguably lesser secretary, had performed this modest feat of organization flawlessly. Starr's binder from last year sat on the back of my credenza for easy reference, but I bristled now to have no such document from Camille whose cubicle when I walked over looking for her was empty and her computer screen insolently dark. Considering the state of my filing, I didn't have much faith in the existence of my chron file, as I began to rifle Camille's file drawers, a cabinet of folders with typed labels, color coded by category: Research Reports, Earnings Reports, Industry Reports by analyst, which certainly should have contained my chron file, but didn't. What was there in an unlabeled hanging folder near the back was a savings account passbook from the First Bank of Oak

Park in the name of Elana Gutierrez. It contained $64,000.00 worth of deposits — seven month's worth of entries at $2000.00 which corresponded to the amount of each of the five checks that were neatly folded into the pages, ten thousand dollars. The folds were crisp and the checks looked pristine, virtually un-handled, that mystery immediately explained by their post-dates. The five checks were dated October through February on the 30th of each month. The deposit dates were uniformly early in the month with the exception of the last one for $50,000 which was dated the day before, four days after Winslow died. Who needed a trust fund? It seemed like Elana Gutierrez was rolling in dough.

I'd read the checks with an eye of wonder. They were all to be drawn on the First Chicago Bank account of Rupert Dean. This was no joint account with his ever-expecting wife, Kitty. There was no notation as to what the payments were for, but Rupert Dean, hardly a generous soul in my experience, was now the second man at Whytebread interested in providing Elana Gutierrez with large sums. I folded and tucked the checks back into the passbook, tucked the passbook carefully into my suit jacket pocket, then pushed the file drawer closed just in time.

"Can I help you?" Camille was asking as if she didn't like me in her workspace. I said, "I was looking for the chron file of my correspondence," and I hoped she hadn't been standing behind me long, putting on some supervisory indignation even as I stepped a few paces away from her file drawer. "You were supposed to type a letter of recommendation for me three weeks ago?"

At the mention of the chron file, Camille relaxed. "It is here. Of course." Walking over to the hutch behind her desk, she produced a thick, black three-ring binder with my name typed on a label on the back from beside one with Rupert's name, and another with Kevin Cavenaugh's.

Turning the pages of the loose-leaf binder, the letter was there, just where it should have been — so was my signature even if I hadn't remembered signing. "All right?" Camille asked. I took a copy and had her send another out for overnight delivery.

"All right," I said. "There's just one more thing." I took the passbook out of my suit pocket and laid it down gently on the top of the letter I'd left on her desk. "While I was looking for the chron file in your file cabinet, I found this," I said. The clutch of folded checks showing in between the pages.

Camille looked first down at the checks and the passbook, then up at me, blinking stupidly as if all the air had been sucked out of the room. "You had no right to take that." Her voice came out in an unconvincing squeak.

"I didn't take it. I found it." And I told Camille she could have it back as soon as she explained to me what it meant.

"My son," she began to stammer unsteadily. "My son is at school." Her gaze came to rest on the heavy black institution-style numbers of the big round wall clock. It was barely eleven o'clock in the morning, but apparently the story was a long one. I said I thought we'd be done talking by the time school got out. But Camille stood firm in her parental obligations.

"I have to get my son. I have to pick up him up early. Teacher conferences are today. But I could explain tomorrow," Camille was promising, as if she might have told me anything just to be able to leave. "Those are mine."

Her hand reached out again hopefully for the checks and the red passbook on the desk, but I swept them both up quickly. "You'll get this when we talk, all right?" I had expected that would make her want to talk to me right that minute, but it didn't. She could get at the money without a passbook, I supposed, but I still had ten thousand dollars worth of checks, which surely was worth a conversation. The passbook felt reassuring in my hand. I would talk to Starr tonight and Camille tomorrow.

"Okay?" I said, "you can have your things back when you tell me what's going on."

~ ~ ~

I'd killed most of the remainder of the day over a three hour lunch with Ellen Borgia at the food bar in Marshall Field's where I didn't know it was possible to run up a fifty dollar tab, but I had two beers and Ellen had six. With Winslow's death, the feminist law firm of Owens, Babbitt and Coogan had grown downright bearish on her chances of a successful suit against the Whytebread, and they wanted Ellen to start paying them on an hourly basis rather than contingency. At three o'clock I had poured her drunken clinically depressed remains onto a Number 32 local bus right in front of Fields, then gone back to Whytebread and finished up my day with another Internet search of the *Fly Agaric* mushroom, clicking through the blue highlighted list of related links until this description caught my eye: *fairy tale fungus is always stunning to come across in the field. In some parts of the world it is eaten because it causes hallucinations.* When I broadened my search I was surprised to find a plethora of web pages devoted to the praise and lore of *Fly Agaric*, a common source of Psilocybe.

Two hours later I looked up from my screen to find Justin Collier knocking on the black metal frame of my open door apparently as an after-thought because he was for all intents and purposes already standing my office.

"Quitting time." Justin consulted his watch, which prompted me to check my own wrist the way that yawning is contagious. The day was gone. It was nearly six o'clock, there had been no phone call from Cassandra, no flowers, not even an e-mail card. "Did you drive? Can you drive me home?" Justin was asking. I practically never drove to work due to the frugal allowance Emily Karnowski dispensed, but it was Justin's kind of perfect luck that I'd left my car at the Park Shore after my swoon in Winslow's bathroom and had to pick it up that morning. Which reminded me again there had been not a peep from Cassandra, but I was choosing to believe some acknowledgment of last night might be waiting for me at home. The thought cheered and hurried me on my way. "Time to go," I agreed. There was just enough time to drop Justin at home before I met Emily at Chardonnay.

I was parked in the garage underneath the building. At the lobby, Justin and I merged into a thick stream of our departing colleagues, flowing into the elevator, which then stopped at every other floor as well, filling with more people pressed like sardines back to front. The elevator stopped finally at the lobby and then at each of the two parking levels before we got off at the bottom floor.

When we had a little privacy, I'd shared with Justin my revelations about the *Fly Agaric* and its poisonous cousins, and gave him a sanitized account of my ad hoc investigation of Winslow's apartment.

"But what do the police think?" he asked the several-million-dollar question.

Climbing into the car, I reached over and unlocked the passenger side door. The convertible I bought years ago as a lifestyle statement had seen a few too many Chicago winters despite its rust-proof undercoating administered in the Italian factory where they did not appear to have a very good understanding of either snow or salt. The car was a purchase made in the same spirit that you buy a party dress a tad too small hoping it will inspire you to lose weight. I imagined this fast little open-top in snowy, cold, dogged Chicago would inspire me to be reckless, but in truth, it had never been the same since early on when Naomi had blown out all four tires driving it to the limits of its capability on a test track out in the western suburbs. I was thinking that the buyout money might facilitate the purchase of a more practical car, if not a more practical life. I had high hopes for both if Cassandra would just move her investigation to a conclusion.

"So, what is your police detective friend telling you?" Justin asked again.

I didn't like that Cassandra hadn't told me much more

than I knew on Tuesday, but there it was. What did the police think? I didn't really know.

Justin was stooping to bend himself into the low leather seat. "Well, do they have any suspects?" He reasoned, as if together we would be able to puzzle out the Byzantine workings of Cassandra's mind. "What about The Irishman?" He reached back behind him to stow his briefcase on my tiny ledge of a back seat. I had passed on everything he'd told me about Tom to the police, but I was beginning to hypothesize that Cassandra had someone specific in mind as a suspect — someone she wasn't inclined to tell me about.

Taking my security card from the ashtray, I applied it to the reader, and the garage gate went up with a heavy, metal creaking sound.

"Could Winslow maybe have actually fired The Irishman that night?" I was paying less attention than maybe I should have to rush-hour traffic, wondering aloud, but Justin couldn't say. Winslow had told him that The Irishman came begging but he didn't think Winslow looked like he felt good enough to fire anyone.

"How'd he look?"

"Bad." Justin seemed to consider this for a moment before he elaborated. "Well, sick, but not like he was going to die — just beat. Honestly, Virginia, Wes was up and around when I talked to him. If he'd looked really bad I would have taken him to the hospital. I offered to stay, but he said he was going to take a bath."

I asked if anyone else could have stopped by that night, but the idea seemed to make Justin edgy. "What do you mean?"

I meant girls. Starr had cut me off at the knees when I asked about Winslow's social life. Now, Justin made a wincing face. "Oh come on, Virginia."

I said I thought it seemed naive to imagine a man his co-workers had nicknamed 'the Wolf' didn't have a social life.

"You think he was entertaining women?" The muscles in

151

Justin's cheeks and around his eyes relaxed. "What does it matter?"

"That depends on what women," I'd persisted. "Maybe it was Starr or maybe Elana Gutierrez, of the brand new enormous trust fund?" Justin was considering me incredulously as if I'd just developed a bad case of idiocy. I said, "Did you know he left Elana a trust fund?" It was really beginning to irritate me that I was trying to help the firm by finding the killer, which certainly would help us all but nobody, including Cassandra and now Justin, wanted to help me. "Maybe Starr will know when I talk to her. Tonight, in fact — eight-thirty tonight." I dared him to dismiss my efforts. "Don't you want the Gold Rush money?"

Justin rolled his eyes, "You're fucking that Detective Hope aren't you?" I guess I ought to have been offended that he'd made no efforts at tact, as if this completely explained my tenacity. Maybe it did. Reflected in the side-view mirror, my face wore a ridiculous, shit-eating grin that had hijacked my face at the mention of her name.

"My God, Virginia. That is just pathetic," Justin was saying. "You know she's just using you for what she needs, information," as if this were a subtlety to my relationship with Cassandra that I might, in my mind-boggling naïveté, have missed. But she wasn't *just* using me for information because she didn't have to sleep with me to get that in case Justin had forgotten about the options, the fortune I would make when the deal went through. I said it wasn't like him to lose sight of the money and his face flushed slightly.

"FYI," Justin said, "when your friend Detective Hope called me in for questioning today, she asked if I was gay, which is not something I want advertised in case you've forgotten. Just because she's in your pants, Virginia, doesn't mean I want her in mine."

"News flash," I said Cassandra had gotten his story from

August Madsen so I imagined it was already pretty public knowledge.

"She's lying." His face got redder, but he didn't say anything else.

"I neither confirmed nor denied." It was an expeditious lie, and after the little cover story Justin had put out around the firm about the two of us, I thought we were even. "Look," I was trying to get things back on the subject. "What do you know about Wes's girlfriends? How angry do you think you'd be if your boyfriend had gotten Elana Gutierrez pregnant?"

"Who said he got Elana pregnant?" Justin shook his head, then sighed in a kind of moral defeat, rubbing his forehead with his palms. "The guy's dead. Can't people just give his sex life a rest?"

But Winslow's sex life seemed the key. "Isn't that why Winslow demoted Camille, because Elana was pregnant?" Justin shrugged out the window, shifting in the seat beside me as if his legs were getting stiff. I could see him from the corner of my eye let his shoulders rise and fall lazily having completely lost interest in what I was saying. "I think if you're looking for angry women, Virginia, you should talk to your friend, Ellen Borgia. Ellen's lawyers were advising her to take the settlement for weeks. Against their best advice, she refused."

Remembering that afternoon's drunken lunch at Marshall Field's, that was beginning to make sense. Justin made his voice confidential. "I shouldn't be telling you this, Virginia, but Wes was afraid a law suit would kill the Gold Rush deal even if he could win it. That's why he was bother- ing to talk to Ellen at all. Whytebread's lawyers suggested that he just change The List to look a little more favorably on Ms. Borgia and others that might be part of her class action."

I thought so much for a good job rewarded. "So the new List was a bribe." It upped the ante big time to get Ellen

Borgia to go away. Somehow the whole thing hurt my feelings; if it had been a bribe for her, it was a bribe for me too, something taken undeserved. "Ellen didn't know this was coming?"

Justin face went casually blank as he smoothed down his hair. "Well, she certainly must have expected it."

It had taken more than the normal half an hour to go from Whytebread's offices to Justin's apartment. Now when we got to the end of the zoo, traffic was a ten-minute back up to the underpass. After I dropped him at his door, I'd had to haul it north up Lakeshore Drive as fast as I could. I made Chardonnay shortly after seven, praying that Em had been in the mood to wait. The gravel lot was nearly empty but her Saab convertible was there, parked under a streetlight. Em's little accountancy practice had done very well in the time we'd been apart. The Saab had been the final, nasty parting cut after all those years of criticism she'd leveled at the impracticality of my own convertible car in a cold Chicago winter, the frugality she still imposed on me, but now it seemed, not herself. As I passed her car, I took a mean-spirited pleasure in the thin line of undercarriage rust below the door.

Em herself had held up rather well; she was still the same big blonde girl, who years ago had swept me off my feet, imposing that Teutonic discipline on my life and finances.

"You look fabulous, lost weight?" I was guessing.

"No." It made her smile with a kind of modesty, only half put on. "I've gained actually, ten pounds, but I've lightened my hair again." Em certainly had become preternaturally blond — and with winter coming too, but there was something else.

"Well maybe it's just that I'm in love." She broke into a dopey grin.

She might as well have hit me hard in the stomach and, of course, she knew it. Not that I wanted her back. I just didn't want to be left out. There she was my old girlfriend, grinning foolishly at something that had absolutely nothing to do with me. She had beaten me to the punch — truly moved on.

"Yes, I'm in love," she exuded now a breathless kind of self-satisfaction. "I was wondering if it really showed."

"Sure," I told her it showed. It always did. Of course it hadn't ever showed like that when she was in love with me. She was grinning a grin I'd never seen before. "That must be it," I conceded grudgingly.

The little half-hearted prompting was all it took for Em to begin reciting the gooey history of her new grand passion: how they met (in line at the Joan Armatrading concert); what she was wearing (a black leather jacket, and day-glow pink Skechers, of course); where they first made love (Em's apartment four weeks before, on the couch, the dining room table, the kitchen sink, and the bed). She (her name was Karen) had moved in the following week. "She makes me really happy." Underneath this reported bliss was the implicit dig that I had not.

"Well enough about me," Em announced after the bartender had brought her what was apparently a second or third draft. "We both know your taxes are a wreak, so how's your love life, Virginia?"

It hadn't escaped my notice that since we'd broken up Em had gotten to be a tad competitive that way, daring me to have a better existence than the one she was having, or than the one we had together. Up to now I'd been winning, and I wasn't pleased to have to tell her my relationship with Spike was headed toward catastrophic failure. It had been Em's final prediction when she'd left — that no one could make me happy. "I've met someone else," I admitted not wanting to be completely outdone.

"Really?" Em sipped on her beer, smiling speculatively. The thing about being married, the thing about being with Em was she really knew me. She saw me for the deeply flawed individual I was. "Does Spike know yet?"

It was almost a relief to drop the pretense of decency. I spilled it all to Em, my faithlessness unvarnished and waited for the comfort of her censure. It can feel good to be punished when you've done wrong, a restorative for your belief in the order of the world. I confessed that Spike had no idea. "I feel like shit."

Em was frowning. "Yes. I'm sure you do." Since our split she had perfected the moral high ground. "You always feel like shit, Virginia — just not enough to stop," which wasn't exactly true.

It was just that whatever it was that I was waiting for, the sign that I ought to settle down hadn't happened yet. Now I was worried that it might never happen. Despite Em's needling superiority, it was nice to reveal my innermost fears to someone who held me in minimal regard. Talking to Em was like unloading my myriad sins on some priest who by training anticipates the very worst in human weaknesses. I told her I'd been with Spike for almost four years already and it felt like we'd been married for twenty.

"Oh right, I forgot." Em was shaking her head, as if she expected nothing more evolved. "You were never much good at that." She specified, "Commitment." Ever the account- ant, she had credited my interpersonal deficiencies and with the look on her face, my books were balanced and closed. "You know, I'd like you to meet her — my lover." She squinted at me in a critical afterthought. "You're all right with this aren't you, Gin?" I had the idea it might amuse her if I wasn't, even though it had been years since Em and I had anything other than a slightly cutting accountant-potential tax evader relationship.

"Oh come on," I said. "Of course I am," and she seemed a little put out not to be breaking my heart. But in an apparent second attempt, she took out my last year's tax returns sighing as she hefted an overstuffed, brown briefcase up onto the bar, a bag big enough for the sun and moon. "You know, I do a routine check for all my clients in the fall," she began to explain as if she wanted to be sure I didn't think I was getting any special treatment. "You paid this amount last year and you've only withheld this amount." Em was pointing briskly with a sharp new pencil at an entry on the most recent monthly paycheck from the stubs I sent her so she could keep my bills straight. Apparently the tax law said I had to withhold at least what I withheld last year or pay a penalty for stealing the time value of money from the federal government.

Em replaced her pencil neatly behind her aggressively blond ear. "Bottom line you're going to have to crank up your withholding for the rest of the year to avoid a penalty. I don't suppose you remembered your W-4?"

I hadn't, but ever the Boy Scout, Em was prepared with a fresh form from a pocket in the leather case. Where it said exemptions, she wrote a large, fat zero in pencil and then dug in her case for a pen, which she used to reinforce the character with black ink. "Sign it." She pushed the form and pen at me and I wrote my name with a carefree flourish.

"That was easy." At least I would be able to avoid the penalties.

Em had drained her beer. "You think so?" She was collecting her things from the top of the bar and making to go now that she had someone to hurry home to. "Just wait and see what that does to your take-home pay." She made a nod of her head at her empty glass, and slung her briefcase over her broad shoulder. "You'll get this won't you, Gin?" Em didn't bother to wait for an answer.

After a while the bartendress came around expectantly so I paid her tab and ordered myself another beer for the road, taking the glass to the payphone near the restrooms and digging out Cassandra's number. It was show really, extracting the card from my wallet as I knew the number by heart from the four or five times I had almost called it today, fooling myself that I still had some pride.

"When will I see you?" I had not identified myself, wanting to be the only one who could be calling her asking this. I wanted one of those sweet, stupid phone conversations about nothing but an excuse to call, but Cassandra's voice was off-putting and literal.

"Tonight I have to study. My Torts class is eating me alive." She was laughing dryly. Her voice held an ego deflating lack of regret, an unaccommodating firmness.

"After that?" Even I couldn't fail to notice my tone of wheedling clingyness. "You know, I was wrong about Ellen Borgia's law suit," I began, unashamed to be desperately baiting the hook with gossip. "Ellen's lawyer was pressuring her to settle. Justin claims she must have known that Winslow would give her the options to force a deal."

I could hear Cassandra's second line ringing in the background. "That's me." She seemed to jump at it. "I have to go, but I'll call you soon," a promise that lacked any clear time dimension.

"What about dinner," I said, "tomorrow? I have to watch my friend Sandra's kid, but I could make us something to eat." There was a long, fat pause, the sound, of invented excuses.

"I have class." Somewhere on her end the line was still ringing.

"What about after?" A little more time had passed between us, slowly. "Maybe I'll come over, but now I have to go." She said *I have to get this call.* "What if I come by your place later, about eleven o'clock?"

Just in time for bed. It was important to me that I take on a more explicit importance to her. I said, "You could have been a man," which I meant as a kind of bracing insult, but Cassie seemed to take it no way at all. The phone on her end was ringing persistently. "I'll call you," she promised, "soon," hanging up.

Outside of Chardonnay, I was sure the sunglasses brunette in the red car was stalking me, parked on Montrose, across from the parking lot, but I was far too dejected to care about my personal safety. As I walked towards my car, she pulled off squealing her tires; and of course, I hadn't gotten a license number.

XVII

After hours the parking garage elevators only went as far as the lobby where you had to swipe your key card first through the reader at the security, and then through a reader on the main elevators to go up to the Whytebread offices. Without a card, the night guard had to sign you in and get up from his desk to unlock the elevators. They didn't like to do that and the night security man was letting me know it was a huge imposition as he grudgingly unlocked the elevator with his master card.

I'd sprinted across the spooky deserted garage, forgetting my access card in my car. I hadn't been the only one.

"Busy night," the security guard remarked and I was heartened to think that Starr was eager enough to talk that she'd come early.

Whytebread's 25th floor lobby was dark enough that it took me a minute to adjust when I stepped out of the elevator. I'd blindly pressed the combination into the cipher lock and held onto the doorknob until my eyes had dilated enough to negotiate the almost completely opaque inner hall.

The floor was laid out over a large area in mostly indistinguishable square little offices and cubes, like a maze of boxes, with and without tops, so that light from the workspaces and subsections of the office didn't necessarily illuminate the hall. The lights were on timers set for blocks of offices after 7:00 p.m. and required dialing up the access number and typing in the specific block code, which I knew for my own block on the opposite side of the floor from the entry door, but not any others. So, that night I was forced to travel the twists and turns of the Whytebread corridors to my office by rote.

I was rounding the corner towards Wesley Winslow's old office when I heard a rustling sound followed by the soft click of a door being pulled gently shut.

"Starr, is that you?" I was calling out in that first-unsuspecting-idiot-about-to-die-in-the-slasher-movie voice. "Starr," not bothering to consider how big a problem it would be if the rustling I'd heard didn't happen to be her. This perspective on safety occurred to me much too late to avoid being vivisected by some psychopath wielding a garden machete, but fortunately no one jumped out from behind the copy machine. So I kept walking and calling, wondering hopefully if the security guards actually patrolled the floors like they were supposed to. About halfway down the hall, I saw a light and a tall, thin shadow fall across the window blinds. By its vertical proportions the figure that emerged from Wesley Winslow's office couldn't have been Starr. It was tall enough to be Winslow himself, a good, solid six-footer — a lean man, or one very big girl, the silhouette of the head showed the uneven edges of bushy hair. It slid out of Wes's office, pulling closed the door behind itself and flawlessly circumnavigating the maze of cubicles and bookcases in the unreliably dim light. It was down the hall and gone almost before I consciously registered that anyone had been there. I was stupidly watching the empty space where the figure had been and wondering if I hadn't just hallucinated the moving shadow until a hand caught my shoulder.

"Shit." I might have screamed, but the hand was Ellen's. "What are you doing here?"

She shrugged the question back at me, but I chose to ignore it, asking instead, "Did you see that guy come out of Wes's office?"

She shook her head and asked again what I was doing in the office as if she suspected my prowler story of being a diversionary ploy.

I explained I was picking up some stock sheets and she countered that she had some research to catch up on. "With all that's happened it's been difficult to stay on top of things." Ellen nodded conversationally, but not saying much else. She was walking away when I caught the shadow again at the corner of my eye. He was standing there, across the office, at an opening in the maze of cubicles like a deer at a clearing.

"Hey," I shouted more loudly now that I had my wits and some company, "Hey you!" but the shadow bolted and was gone again. A door slammed in the stair well. "Hey," I shouted again at the back of Ellen's retreating figure. "Did you see him, a tall guy with an afro."

"What afro?" Ellen spun around. "A guy with an afro?"

She was staring at me goofy-faced. "I thought you were talking about someone else. Jeremy's here," she admitted, reluctantly agreeing that we ought to call security about the prowler.

"A little past you're regular hours isn't it?" Ellen had just, in fact, hung up with the front desk when Jeremy appeared. He sounded a little too friendly and casual for my taste, but among the three of us nobody seemed to think much of anyone else's story.

It had taken the guard, an older, roundish, puffy-faced man who seemed to be breaking a pretty good sweat just from the exertion of riding the elevator twenty-five floors a very long ten or fifteen minutes to arrive, which I spent trying to decide how I would explain it when Starr showed up.

I was telling the guard about the man I'd seen and he was dabbing at the sweat on his upper lip with a well-used handkerchief from the back pocket of his uniform. Of the mystery man, I could say with confidence, "He was tall and thin with big curly hair like an afro," but of course that didn't matter because in the time it had taken for this guard to arrive whoever it was could have hightailed it half-way to the airport.

"Black male?" The security guard asked the three of us generally, to which Ellen shook her head vigorously up and down. Jeremy looked blank and I couldn't say. All I'd actually seen was a brief silhouette that was not very racially definitive, a tall lean figure with a bush of hair.

On somewhat more detailed questioning Ellen had been forced to admit sulkily she'd never actually seen the man at all. "Well, Black or White?" the guard asked again, as if without some basic description there was really not much that he could do. We all seemed agreed it was a man — just from the sense of him and armed with this minimalist description, the security guard promised, in a way that failed to inspire much faith, to make a report to the police.

"We'll do our best, Ma'am," he assured to me mildly as we stood outside Winslow's office. The guard tried the door, announcing, "It's locked," and looked at me as if he wondered if I'd seen anything at all. Maybe I was just a lady spooked by a big empty office at night. I was the only one who'd actually seen anything.

"He must have had a key." It sounded lame and implausible even to myself. Jeremy Bennett was smiling at Ellen in a half-witted sort of crush-induced stupor.

"We'll keep you posted." The undertook half-heartedly as he began to walk away.

I waited for another half an hour, but there was still no sign of Starr.

"What are you really doing here?" Ellen asked again as they passed my office and there seemed no use in lying.

"Starr was going to tell me something about Winslow to pass on to the police," I was saying, "but she didn't show." As I talked I began to worry, wishing I knew where she lived so I could at least check on her. Six years Starr had worked for me and I'd never asked her.

Ellen squeezed her boyfriend's shoulder. "Jeremy can tell you." Apparently everything that went into a Whytebread computer, Jeremy Bennett was able to extract: documents, e-mail, phone lists.

At that he'd puffed himself up just a little, rather sweetly and presumably for Ellen's benefit. "All you need is a password. You want to know how to tell who's logged into their computer?" I watched over his shoulder as Jeremy expertly demonstrated the status command after which we had found Starr's phone, looked at everyone's salary and/or bonus information, and read Herb Symon's personal e-mail. Jeremy would likely have been content to have shared computer tricks all night, but there was still the issue of Starr whose phone just rang and rang with an apparently vacant and troubling persistence when we called.

"We need to go over there," Ellen had decided, insistently concerned in a way I wasn't able to understand and of course whatever wanted Ellen, Jeremy Bennett appeared only too happy to accommodate.

There was nothing to do but go along for the ride. I'd intended to merely follow them in my own car, but when I got to the garage someone had put a long ugly slash in the light brown canvas of my convertible top.

"Aw shit." It was the second time that year.

Jeremy was making a sympathetic clucking sound that nonetheless I found unaccountably annoying. "You know you ought to get a hardtop." I'd had that conversation before. I'd had that conversation a lot — with Emily, with Naomi, with my mom and my insurance agent. I was looking ruefully at what I had imagined when I bought it would be a harmlessly frivolous car, which had already cost me double its price in repairs and replacement canvas.

Jeremy ran his hand along the jagged tear in the ragtop and made a low appraising whistle that I found almost as irritating as his clucking. Walking around to the front of the car, he whistled some more, surveying the carnage. "Your front tire's flat too," he observed with a maddingly objective helpfulness. The vandals had thoughtfully left the car door unlocked and there was an empty hole in the dash where my stereo had been. More of a hassle to replace, my office and garage access cards were gone as well.

"Want to call the police from my cellular phone?" Jeremy offered perkily. I had my own, but was unfortunately unable to dissuade he and Ellen that they needn't wait with me for the police.

After I'd made my report we were still all obliged to drive over to Starr's in Jeremy's SUV. I would let AAA wait for the morning. Truth told, I would have been much happier to let my little visit with Starr wait until the morning. It was nearly eleven o'clock, a little late based on my understanding of universally serviceable ideas of etiquette to be calling on anyone you weren't sleeping with. More than that, I would have preferred to hear whatever it was Starr intended to tell me in private, but when we got to Starr's place the police were crawling all over her renovated studio loft. It was the sort of space to which real estate agents affixed attractive adjectives: open spaces, high ceilings. Certainly they would have featured the big airy windows from which Starr had reportedly taken a disastrous, if as Ellen was characterizing tearfully to the policeman that stopped us at the door, perhaps intentional, fall.

XVIII

Starr had left no note to prove or disprove Ellen's worry of suicide, but in searching her house, Cassandra told me later, there had been a number of sundry items that suggested Starr's precarious state of mind — a long, brown-haired wig in her bedroom closet, some black cat-eye sunglasses in a drawer, and an Avis receipt on her dressing table which solved the mystery of who had tried to run me down. Starr's craziness had sent her through the fourth floor window and onto some poor neighbor's parked car, apparently motivated by jealousy over me and Justin. At Wes's funeral they'd been talking intently, and in a way that certainly could have been an argument. So who was to say that our discussion that evening would have held any relation at all to Winslow's death? The way things looked, I was beginning to think that Starr had just wanted to tell me off for monopolizing the object of her affections. Whatever she had to say, I would never know now because the only certain thing was that Starr D'nofrio was dead.

Cassandra and I were chewing this over as she drove me north to my apartment, making a perfunctory apology for her general post-seduction neglect.

"Sorry I couldn't meet you tonight, but I guess we wound up together anyway." Her phrasing rankled me as did her vaguely accusatory tone. "Why didn't you tell me you were talking to Starr?"

"I didn't know." It felt good to lie to her, satisfying in a kind of passive aggressive way. Cassandra's face relaxed. "I didn't know I was meeting her when I talked to you." I said, "you should call more often."

What I wanted to tell her was how hurt I was that there had been no tribute, no intimate phone calls, no cute little cards, or flower deliveries since the night we'd spent together, but Cassandra's demeanor did nothing to invite such confessions. She'd stared mainly at the road in front of her while I'd talked about Starr, turning only occasionally in my direction at points of professional importance, and only with a mild, professional kind of interest that did nothing to *invite* at all, which to my mind was the crux of the problem with the way our relationship was developing. After I had told her everything I knew about Starr and that evening, the conversation had sagged for some time under the weight of my issues, before Cassandra finally thought to ask if there was something wrong.

"Oh, I don't know." She had delivered the question with the same passionate sentiment you'd expect to share with your dry cleaner over a bad ketchup stain. I said, "I thought we were going to see each other," an undertaking to which Cassandra was nodding, encouraging some elaboration as if there might be parts of this proposition she didn't fully understand.

"See each other. You know? Do something together after we spent the night." It seemed that we had completed that strange lesbian mating cycle of delight and dissolution in a fraction of the time it usually took, and I suppose I felt I'd been cheated, out of romance, out of future expectations.

"I had class." Cassandra managed to make this sound as if it were a chronic condition, as if in fact Wednesday was a very long time ago and the other side of the car was very far way. "I have to go to class. What do you want from me?"

I couldn't say exactly, maybe just for her voice to sound a little closer. Certainly I wanted for us to talk about it but I couldn't seem to articulate a more specific request until Cassandra found my hand and squeezed it briefly, a satisfying gesture even if she never even shifted her eyes from the windshield. In the end Cassandra spent that night with me, but in the morning I found I was more relieved than wistful when she'd gone.

After I'd heard the front door locking with a comforting click, I got up and turned the deadbolt behind Cassandra. Then I went back to bed for a couple hours. At ten o'clock, I called in sick, even Pamela sounded somewhat sympathetic and I wasn't the only one. She said Jeremy, Ellen and The Irishman had called in as well. I waited until eleven o'clock and phoned Camille to postpone our talk. Whatever the story with her check was, I didn't think I had the energy to hear it, but Camille wasn't at her desk, so I left a message emphasizing my desire to give her back her money, and hoped she wouldn't be too concerned. Then I took a shower, put my pajamas back on and spent the rest of the day on the couch, crying to Naomi over the phone, watching Oprah and drinking way too early in the day.

Camille never called back, but at about one o'clock Justin knocked on my door, dressed in a faded sweatshirt, his college colors. To see him so informally made me realize the care he usually took with his appearance, the coordination of his work outfits. In those grungy clothes, Justin could have been much younger, his hair ungelled, cow-licked at the crown.

"I heard." He gave me a hug at the door looking like a sad little boy. Then we sat on the couch for a while, and I told him the story, about going to Starr's, and about Ellen Borgia and Jeremy Bennett whose romance I continued to consider enthralling gossip even in the light of everything else that had happened.

"Uh huh," I could see that Justin was barely listening to me. "Do the police believe that Starr killed herself?" He asked almost guilty as if he wanted to say, "Do you think she killed herself over me?"

Justin and I took a walk all the way down Halsted Street and over to Clark past the rows of shops. He was saying, "We should get a drink," when we passed by The Closet, a gay bar with a brazen picture window so anyone passing on the street could see inside. Justin seemed to have acquired a tourist's enthusiasm for Boys Town as if he were sightseeing on vacation.

Justin bought me a beer at the empty bar, and then another, some beer of a brand I can't remember now, designer beer in attractive bottles. I'd had two or three when he said: "Sometimes I go through the day without even once re-membering I'm queer." It was almost bragging, but he didn't seem proud, rather almost like the feelings confused him. "Do you ever forget you're gay?" He was scrutinizing me as if he thought he could see the answer if he only looked hard enough. "You don't ever forget you're Black, do you?"

There were days when I supposed it never really came up, but not many. "That would be a pretty strange thing to forget."

He said, "Sometimes I wonder why I need this sad little subculture, Virginia, when I'm more like Herb Symon than I am like you?"

I don't think he meant that any special way, just a matter of fact. He didn't say it harshly, but it felt like a hard slap, a kind of betrayal, yet I was so oddly numb that it didn't hurt. The comment was just a data point; I was seeing who he was. "You don't need anyone, do you?"

Justin stiffened. "What do you mean by that?" But I had hardly intended an indictment, rather just a simple observation of fact. "Everybody needs something," he said in retort. "Sometimes you just don't know what it is. For instance, I thought I needed a highbrow company." His mouth turned up in a self-deprecating smile and he took in the environs of the bar in a kind of sweep-armed gesture. "Apparently that is not the case. You can look for whatever it is so hard sometimes you don't know when you have it — something pretty good. You can mess it up trying to make it perfect."

"You miss her don't you?" It had struck me he was talking about Starr, somehow he had liked her attention a little bit, not as corporate cover, but genuinely. "You miss her." The thought made me like him a little better.

"Sure." Justin's thoughts must have been very far away. Even as he talked he was looking past me into the mirror over the bar, watching the door, waiting for the next thing.

I followed his eyes from the door to the street while we drank. Justin was still drinking when I left him there and went home to have a nap before my evening babysitting a two-year-old.

Sandra, the two-year-old's mother, was an old high school friend from Blue River — my best high school friend in fact. We had drifted apart after college largely due to my sexual orientation, which Sandra had confided she found a little bit freakish, even if I couldn't help it. I had likewise found Sandra's aspirations to marry her then brand-new, jug—headed, wannabe lawyer boyfriend, Andre Rutherford, to be conclusive evidence of her acute tastelessness, a condition far worse than my homosexuality because, I thought, with just the tiniest bit of rational analysis Sandra could most certainly help it.

There had been a thaw in the ensuing cold war just before my ten-year high school reunion. Sandra's marriage to Andre (Andy as she called him), who I now rather liked despite himself, and her pregnancy with their first child had mellowed her into almost complete apathy as to the particulars of anyone else's life.

Sandra and Andre lived a self-absorbed black, bourgeois existence on Blackhawk Street in a modern row house that had been constructed nearly a decade ago in anticipation of the demolition of the Cabrini Green Housing Projects. It was a long patient bet on gentrification that had finally paid off. Now they were looking to trade up to the suburbs, Beverly on the Southside with big old houses, gracious lawns, and wooded tracts of land surrounding the racially integrated enclave. Until then, they were a ten-minute ride away; and I was the baby-sitter of last resort.

I'd arrived at the Rutherford's early. There was no answer and my cab had already pulled off when I knocked, so after a few minutes on the chilly stoop I'd let myself in with the key Sandra had given me "just in case." The house was dark and quiet except for the faint bass throb of the stereo which I followed to the living room, listening a moment too long before I'd recognized the unmistakable vocalization of Andre and Sandra on their Ethan Allen sofa.

"Oh my God, Virginia, is it eight o'clock already?" They bolted up dazed and chagrined in the glare of the floor lamp, but I was thankful to note, mostly clothed. "We lost track of the time." Sandra managed the obvious rather breathlessly. "My God Andre," she said, "it must be eight." But Andre was consulting his watch rather dubiously.

"Well it's close to eight." I put in my own defense. In fact it was only quarter after seven, but I'd been early hoping to catch a free dinner.

"Well good to see you, anyway," Andre agreed diplomatically as he tucked in his shirt. Sandra was retightening the belt on her bathrobe.

"Brandon's asleep." Sandra made a guilty admission, because both of us knew that if Brandon was asleep right now, there wasn't a hope in heaven that he was going to stay that way for much more of the evening. Whatever respite from young Brandon was available to the adult world had been squan- dered on the couch before my arrival.

"It's just like dogs." Andre was always unaccountably proud of the frenzied kineticism displayed by his son, a perpetual sound and motion which he took for genius but I was more inclined to attribute to hyperactivity. "Smart dogs are harder to train because they're smart, see?"

Brandon must have been a future Nobel Prize winner judging from his astonishing talent at running his mother ragged. The brains hadn't come from Sandra's side because she'd gone right out and done it again. Now she was four and a half months pregnant with his sister: Eliza. The Rutherfords were efficient parents. They knew the gender, the nursery was already painted, the child was already named, and Andre was putting money in trust for medical school. Why wait?

"We had amniocentesis right away," Sandra announced when she'd told me they were expecting, "just to be sure she's healthy." If I found it disturbingly *Brave New World* that Sandra and Andre felt a sense of obligation to produce genetically perfect Negro children, an effort to offset the progeny of the underclass who Andre claimed were ruining the race, I'd kept my distaste to myself for friendship's sake, an agreement to disagree on our respective life choices. The Rutherfords hadn't much approved of Spike, Sandra lowering her voice tactfully, when she told me, "I hope you won't mind but we've asked one of Andre's law partners to be godmother to Liza. Spread the joy."

"We'd better get dressed, honey," she was admonishing Andre who grunted his concurrence. They went off together in the direction of the bedroom holding hands, leaving the couch cushions warm and maybe even a little sweaty when I sat down there in front of the television set.

I couldn't help thinking that Spike and I never held hands anymore — not even at the movies. Halfway through The Simpsons, Sandra and Andre reappeared typically dressed, pressed, and shined. They were a tidy couple, firm in their connection to both inward and outward order, a condition I could not help but envy.

"If he screams just ignore him and he'll go back to sleep after a while."

Andre took his jacket from a hook of the handsome wooden coat tree by the door, failing to elaborate how long a while would be, but no sooner had I listened to their car pull away did Brandon start bawling.

The master race had a fine set of lungs. Defeated after five minutes, I carried him from his crib out to the couch where we sang innumerable verses of *Abba Dabba Honeymoon,* verses I didn't even realize I knew until they came rolling off my tongue.

The good news was the tears subsided. The bad new was despite the musical interlude and a tablespoon of Sierra Nevada Pale Ale, Brandon was still fully conscious, talking a blue streak.

"Flower," he said. "Daddy. Boo boo. Kitty cat," which was no surprise as Andre had proudly reported just last week that the kid had a prodigious vocabulary of over thirty-five distinct words — up by a good five words from the tally of the week before.

"That kid's going to be hell in litigation," Andre had predicted on more than one occasion. By nine o'clock, I thought I'd heard everything in the little monster's repertoire at least a hundred times.

"Biscuit," said Brandon unexpectedly; and excited by the new expression, I went immediately off to the kitchen and got him one, a hard teething cracker from the jar on the counter as kind of a reward. Who knew? I thought positive reinforcement might lead to even more lucidity in his chatter. Better yet, the biscuit had brought about perfect silence.

"MMMMMM. MMMM. mmm." Brandon was happily gumming the cracker beside me on the couch, as apparently this had been a legitimate request rather than just diction practice. Whatever the source of my good fortune, I took advantage of the child's speechlessness to seek out some adult conversation, digging my phone card hungrily out of the stack of plastic in my billfold and dialing up Spike on the cordless phone. Blue River time was an hour ahead of Chicago and so I woke her up.

"Hi," Spike said in a dreamy voice as if she'd already been sleeping for a long time. "I've been missing you," and I realized how much her emotional availability had begun to wear away at my nerves. "Mmmmmm?" she was asking sleepily. "What are you wearing?" This had been one of our favorite phone games.

"Sweat pants." I told her, preferring just then, not to play.

"Uh-huh. Is that all?" Spike sounded vaguely disappointed, but willing to work with whatever was available.

Brandon was chattering again happily beside me on the couch, the remains of the cracker stuck out of the side of his mouth like a fat and oddly-shaped cigar. "Doggie? Biscuit! Perseverate!" It gave me a frightening glimpse of my godson's future adult self, a back room deal making fat cat. Had his father been there to see it, I thought he would have been wild with joy.

"What are you *doing?*" Spike dutifully offered up yet another of our usual games, but I didn't feel much like playing that one either.

"I'm here with Brandon, baby-sitting." Suddenly, I didn't really feel like talking to Spike. The realization swept over me like the acute nausea I had sometimes mid-bite in one-piece-too-many-pieces of pizza as if the grease had backed up from my intestines all the way to my throat. Suddenly I didn't even want to know Spike.

She was cooing absently in a way that grated like a fiberglass rash, "Baby-sitting. That's nice. Get some practice, honey. Someday we might have a little one to raise back here." I was flashing on the horrifying apparition of a two-year-old with a tongue piercing, shuddering at what a compromise sperm donor between Spike and me might look like.

It wasn't really in my vision.

"What do you mean, 'not your vision', Virginia?" The dreaminess had deserted Spike's voice.

What did I mean? It was a question with so many possible answers. Children? Blue River? Us together? None of it was my vision. For a long time now something had been missing in my life and I had the thought that I was putting together my future as a giant jigsaw puzzle, one which, when completed, would feature wealth and happiness and spiritual fulfillment.

Had I known what specifically was wrong, maybe Spike

and I could have stayed together, but as it was all I knew was that something in my life had to change. This relationship with her seemed as good a thing as any.

"What do you mean, Virginia?" Spike was challenging me to clearly specify which part of her picket-fenced fairy story needed an overhaul. "What exactly do you mean is *'not your vision?'* "

"Well, sort of all of the above." I'd been thinking aloud really, but then, it had been said. A long angry sigh came back through the phone, a threat that if I continued in that vein things between us would be irreparable.

Falling out of love is painless, almost numbing, but break-ups are like ripping the scab off a badly skinned knee, leaving the tender pale skin underneath and sometimes a scar.

"Some people have warm eyes," Spike had apprised me years ago.

"Warm eyes like who?" I'd asked, as for me this was hardly an essential point of categorization.

"Like me, like you, like Allison," and I took the naming of another woman, her ex, as a romantic challenge the way men at a carnival arcade will buy three hundred dollars in tickets to throw a ball and win a two dollar stuffed bear. I hadn't really wanted Spike, but there she was like the last piece of pizza left in the box, something that, certainly, someone ought to have wanted — just not me.

"I had a kind of rush with Ally," she'd admitted early on. "I think the reason I haven't seen anyone for so long was I haven't gotten it back — the rush," and she asked me my favorite color as if that might hold some augury.

I said I liked green and apparently that had boded well.

Spike was the kind of woman who in conversation asked questions, I presumed to know me, the better to take care of me. She had *said* that she wanted to take care of me, and in that context, I found her interest in the crevices of my life completely endearing.

"Where is the most unusual place you've ever done it,"

Spike asked in the second conversation of our, then, recently renewed acquaintance, an attitude I might have decided was inappropriately forward if it hadn't afforded me an opportunity to flirt and brag. I'd decided that Spike had a profound, enlightened disregard for the conventions of polite conversation and confessed to her my most unusual place of sexual contact was on a couch with a stranger at a party where'd I'd been drunk.

"So you're an exhibitionist." She'd given a kind of totaling smile, as if she were embarrassed for me or amused that I was not more embarrassed for myself, as if she thought with that she had completely figured out who I was.

"No." I said. "I was just fucked up. So, how about you?"

With her slight, knowing smile she was momentarily lovely. "I'll ask the questions." Weeks later, she'd replayed our conversation back verbatim to prove that it was I who first brought up sex although, before, I could have sworn it was the other way around.

Spike didn't want me, she said. Absolutely, she didn't want anyone at that moment, wanted to be alone for a while. What she'd wanted was sex, no strings and to settle some unfinished business from a long time ago she'd imagined we'd had. I was responsible for tricking her into her current position and here she was. Here we were: in her waterbed, her bathtub; under her kitchen table, partially clothed; pants at her ankles; pants at my ankles; weekend flights to Blue River from Chicago.

It was like all the advertisement for love without the hassles — for a while. Then, it was the relationship we'd both sworn we didn't want. Now, *I* felt tricked. And when she called I felt grudgingly obliged to pick up the phone rather than hiding, as I liked to do, behind my answering machine: *I'm not home right now, but if you'd please leave a message, I'll get right back to you.*

"Pick up." Spike felt it was her inalienable right as my partner to assert, "I *know* you're there," and later when I hadn't answered, she would demand, "Where were you when

I tried to call? You didn't tell me you were planning to go out?"

At eleven o'clock at night, she would call and say, "I miss you; I'm getting on a plane right now." At first this was very exciting before it got to be a terrible inconvenience having to clean up my apartment on such short notice.

Things change. And of course, I've found they nearly always end badly. Somewhere along the line, Spike had decided unilaterally that she wanted to be married. Not necessarily, I don't think, to me. But there I was; and she wanted to be nesting. House buying. Joint checking account opening. Sperm bank shopping.

"What exactly is the problem," she was asking me now, but I was still finding myself.

"But what exactly is wrong?" she said.

But I didn't know. I was unhappy. With my work. With my condo. With my hair cut.

"With me?" she said.

With her? No. Not with her. "Well not exactly."

"Then what exactly is wrong?" She was crying. "Are you interested in someone else?"

"Well, yes," I said. "But that's really not the problem."

"Well, it certainly seems like a pretty irreconcilable difference, to me." She had woken up now enough to be polysyllabic, certainly enough to be pissed off. "I should have seen this coming. It's the money." Spike was gasping, tearfully, "I wish you still needed me," an indictment in short, reproachful sobs. "You used to need me. I guess this is all," she said. There was nothing to say.

We just listened to each other breathing for a while. There was a very soft click from her end of the line, and then the three shrill rising tones the phone company has to remind you that your phone is off the hook.

I dropped it softly back into its cradle and went to the kitchen to get myself another beer. By the time I'd finished it Sandra and Andre were home.

"You didn't have any trouble, did you?" Expectantly, Andre picked up Brandon from the couch where the child had finally passed out courtesy of that second tablespoon of beer. I got up and retrieved my coat from the coat tree and put it on. "Mommy's angel," Sandra pushed her face to her son's and cooed. "Did you have any trouble tonight, Virginia?" she was asking.

"No," I said, "no trouble at all."

I'd been able to hold it together while Sandra and Andre waited with me for my cab. Andre's discussion of the important career-defining partners they had dined with provided a dull sort of background noise that took my attention away from my own domestic drama. My life could have been worse, I thought. It could have been Sandra's.

Or Naomi's. When I'd called her on my cell phone from the cab, it sounded as if she'd been dead asleep only minutes before.

"Virginia, it's twelve-seventeen and about thirty-six seconds," Naomi reminded me of the time like a threat. "If you're not dying it could be arranged because I have no idea how I'm going to get back to bed without a cigarette. What exactly is your problem?"

I told her, "I broke up with Spike," and almost immediately was crying, desperately, the way I used to as a kid having saved all my grief and disconsolation for the presence of my mother's ear. Naomi Wolf was hardly my mother, but in a pinch it seemed she would do. "It just wasn't working, the piercings and all." As I talked I was crying with regret whenever I happened to recall what a heel I'd been and with embarrassment at the relief I felt to be free of Spike. Em had been right — I was sorry I'd been a heel, just not sorry enough to stop being one. "I know you hated her, but I really need you to be nice to me right now."

"I didn't hate her." Naomi had made her voice only minimally more kind than it had been a moment before but I would take what I could get. She said, "I just thought you could do better. You need somebody who's here for you. Look," she asked as if this was just one example of the kind of thing I needed, "do you want to come over here?" I did. Having just broken up with Spike, I found, ironically, I really didn't much want to be alone.

XIX

Naomi's apartment was fifteen minutes by car in the opposite direction than we'd been traveling. But I'd managed though intermittent sniffling to redirect the stoop-shouldered fatherly Flash Cab driver to the Park Shore.

The last time I'd been there was to snoop around Winslow's apartment. I'd been there with Cassandra who had slept with me and now wouldn't call, for whom I had just broken up with a perfectly good if not quite perfect girlfriend who loved me; and I found myself weeping again.

"You all right, miss?" the driver wide-eyed me in the rear view mirror unused to and a little unsettled by the sight of a women falling to pieces in the back of his cab.

So, I told him I just had a cold.

"There's a lot of that going around," the cabby agreed. He was either the nicest, most tactful fellow on the planet or he had clearly missed the high points of my phone conversation, apparently enmeshed in the music of his swing band station, bobbing his head in time. Either way his lack of commentary was working for me. Now that I was off the phone, he turned up the radio volume, companionably sharing the sound until he pulled the cab into the circular drive of the Park Shore, where my old friend, Joe, was behind the security desk in the lobby.

"2702 never did catch up with that friend of his," he commented while buzzing me in to the elevators. "Shit happens." Joe said, and I agreed.

All my misty way to the seventeenth floor I had the elevator and the dim quiet hall that led to Naomi's door thankfully to myself. I'd barely touched the painted black metal door before Naomi opened it.

"So you finally gave old Spike the boot," she observed, I thought more cheerfully than was appropriate given the salt stained smear I'd made of my face.

"Not exactly *the boot*." It wasn't the way I would have preferred to characterize my behavior.

"Right." Naomi handed me a generously filled scotch glass. "Let's retire to the couch," she said, "for debriefing," making my pain feel, as usual, a little like a prime time television drama, her entertainment.

I said I was going through some changes even if I couldn't exactly say what they were but I was sure that I would know when I came out the other side. Although, the way things were going, there seemed to be no telling exactly when that would be, which caused me to cry again with renewed vigor. I was crying, not with any sound that I could notice, but tears were running down my face the way people cry in art films in the wake of great tragedy, like the sweat pouring off of Wes

Winslow's body that afternoon before he died. Calmed voice, he was falling apart in spite of himself. I felt as if I was on the outside watching my seams unravel, like three highballs into the motor control failure of a very bad drunk. My eyes oozed tears, and I took a couple of ineffectual wipes at my nose with the back of my hand, but I couldn't stop the runnyness it seemed now from any orifice. "It's really clean in here." I was hearing myself oddly notice aloud the Pine-Sol smell wafting from Naomi's kitchen and bathroom, which could only indicate a visit from her cleaning lady. The place had been a pit on Wednesday. "When did Maxine come?" Despite the water works, I was asking in a voice so unaffected by anything other than simple curiosity that it startled me.

"Today." Naomi beamed, a great enjoyer of other people's elbow grease. In Naomi's world, housecleaning was a necessity managed by someone else, sometimes for money, sometimes for love as with the litany of marginally-employed, Gen-X girlfriends who preceded Maria Sacchi and followed Naomi's previous long term relationship with the interminably married Louise. I looked around the tidy room, the empty ashtrays recalling that neither Naomi nor Maria could be bothered to pick anything up.

Once Maria's cat had made her a present of a decapitated mouse, delivering it to the living room couch by Naomi's foot. Maria had shrouded it with a tea towel and Naomi had had to call Maxine, an ancient black woman from Woodlawn with dyed red hair, three days earlier than scheduled. A bent-over old lady, who I had presumed took the hour-and-a-half Hyde Park bus ride up Lakeshore Drive to clean Naomi's Northside flat out of some inexplicable nostalgia that Naomi liked to attribute to the fact that Maxine had cleaned for Naomi's mother when they'd lived in South Shore, this long before the neighborhood went from gracious homes to grasping middle class aspirations in the redlining 50's wake of the advancing black belt.

This seemed somehow obscene, as I'd always wondered

how the geriatric Maxine managed even to push the sweeper. Laughing, Naomi had passed me a clean, white business card with tasteful, raised black lettering. The embossed print read: *Maxine's Cleanin' Service, licensed and bonded.*

"I don't get *the* Maxine, you nut; I get *a* Maxine. The way all the Pullman porters used to be called, *George.*" Naomi had told me years ago she had gotten the original because of her mom, "but lately Maxine's franchised, now she lives in Florida."

Spike had wanted to franchise, it seemed to be the way of the new world predictability, quality control, everything I wanted in my life and I couldn't understand how it was eluding me.

"Are you going to be all right? Why don't you tell me about it," Naomi was saying with that maternally sympathetic lilt that I had been hoping for earlier when I called, but there wasn't, I realized, much to tell.

"I called Spike tonight and I broke up." I'd thought it was the best thing considering Cassandra and all.

"Oh right," Naomi picked up the mention of Cassandra as if this were a detail she'd forgotten, "your police detective." With that she rose abruptly from the couch and went into the hall as if expressly to turn off a light that was burning somewhere in the back of the apartment. "Of course, your police detective. Hold that thought."

She had left the room dark except for the light in the ceiling of her foyer and the skyline coming through her open window, a Godsend as my eyes hurt terribly.

Naomi returned to the couch with a fuller, fresher drink and a brighter attitude, which I thought was for my benefit, speaking in the falsely high happy voice people use to cheer a child.

"You know, I may have an interesting tidbit for you on Winslow's poisoning." Naomi was saying that some friend of hers, Solange, in the Medical Examiner's office had told her that *Fly Agaric* wasn't usually fatal. "It's a magic mushroom and reputedly a Biblical aphrodisiac mentioned in the Song of Solomon." Naomi raised her eyes. Her friend Solange was apparently thorough.

"Usually, people just trip. We're talking half a dozen mushrooms potentially the size of dinner plates to induce death in a healthy adult." It seemed more than you could practically sneak into a salad, but Winslow had been sick that day.

Naomi was saying, "So maybe this Winslow meant to take the shrooms and died tripping because he had the flu. Maybe your secretary and/or her kid are being paid off for what she knows about Winslow's proclivities. You said this guy, Rupert, was a favorite of his. Maybe they were into the same thing. All I know is that the ME is ready to call this an accidental drug overdose. Only problem is Winslow's people are important and they're understandably embarrassed."

The no murder explanation was certainly one I would have liked to believe — no murder and the Gold Rush deal would have been back on. Better for me, better for everyone. Except I hadn't seen any evidence of a wild drug-crazed life at Winslow's flat. I hadn't seen evidence of much life at all.

"Whatever," Naomi concluded. "I'm just filling you in because your girlfriend won't. True love is fine; Virginia, but you just need to remember who your friends are. And," Naomi winked, "God, wouldn't it be nice if there was a lesbian on the planet who could just break up without a back-up plan."

She was right. I supposed what was wrong with Spike had been wrong with her well before I'd rediscovered Cassandra.

"What is it you like about your police detective, Virginia?" Naomi's voice held genuine curiosity, as if my answer might explain what Maria Sacchi had liked about the lesbian jeweler she'd dumped Naomi for, but I couldn't really say right off.

Mostly I liked that she wasn't Spike, I guess. "I don't know." I said, "I guess she was just there." Naomi's shadowy head went up and down in the dark, nodding yes, sometimes that was all it took. Then she leaned over and kissed my forehead.

It was nice; the kind of magic kiss you got as a kid when you had a stubbed toe or a scraped knee. It didn't fix things, but somehow it made them better.

"You know what I think the cop thing is? A bad case of seven year itch," Naomi was certifying with her typical self-satisfaction, "the four year psoriasis in your case but then you always were precocious. Just don't let her hurt you — that police detective." Naomi took my hand, and squeezed it.

"Warm hands," I said.

"Cold heart." She gave the top of my hand a few little pats then let my fingers drop unsentimentally.

XX

The weekend was a blur of bad long distance phone calls, from Spike, to Spike. It was forty-eight hours of painfully exhausting rehash, and lesbian blame processing all managed without transportation as I hadn't collected the energy to call AAA about my car, which with my luck I expected to be stripped and torched when I got back to it. If I had known what it was that got me into work on Monday, I would have licensed and bottled it, but beyond arrival, I was patently unprepared for the remaining trials of my day. These began with Camille calling in sick (I thought more than coincidentally), further postponing our discussion of her sixty-odd thousand dollars, ten thousand of which I was still carrying around on my person, a responsibility that was making me increasingly nervous with every passing minute, as if the availability of airline flights from Blue River to Chicago and Spike's current inconsolable state of mind, didn't offer enough to be anxious and nervous about.

My trials continued with the long and complicated search for the right person in the building management office to see about my stolen parking and security cards — the person in the building management office with whom I could agree that solving my parking card problem was part of their job.

In that respect, Camille's absence was almost fortuitous because it put me in just the right mood to talk to the card dispensing man who resided in the bowels of the building and told me stubbornly that a new card would cost me fifty bucks, a dollar amount on which he would not budge, unmoved by any hard luck story. Stolen, lost, mutilated, it was all the same to him — one free card to a customer; for another, pay up.

Fifty dollars lighter, I went to talk to Rupert Dean. His office was four rooms down the hall from mine, and I could see him now through the smoky glass partition of his office wall, typing just as furiously at his computer table, as he had been when I'd come into work that morning. With his back to the door, Rupert hadn't heard the turn of the latch or my push when I'd opened it. He'd been absorbed enough in composing his resume that I was able to read over his shoulder for a good five minutes, learning that Rupert Dean had graduated Bradley University with honors. Surprise. Surprise. I startled him. "I didn't even know you could read."

"What the hell?" Rupert scrambled to cover his work, then he turned from his computer to face me at the desk, and demanded, "Don't you knock?" which is what I imagined he'd said when Linda Tibbits had caught him masturbating.

I asserted the door was open, which we both knew was not quite accurate, but Rupert had declined to debate it.

"Well, now that you're here. What can I do for you?"

189

Switching off the power to his monitor, Rupert crab-walked his rolling chair across the plastic carpet protector, the few short feet from his computer table to a position of puffed-up authority behind his desk. I'd taken the visitor's chair, surveying his office, which I noticed then was bigger than mine and executively free from dust and clutter. The mountains of paper that in my office would have been strewn around haphazardly resided in orderly piles at the far upper corner of his desk. Rupert's further aspirations were revealed by the little copy-cat, wannabe big man sports tribute area of his own he had started on his file credenza, photos from his college baseball days and a recent picture of him, Herb Symon and Jon Patel holding up a big fish on some corporate outing I hadn't been invited to.

Rupert reached across the shiny wooden desk to one of the work piles and rustled some papers loudly, looking rather put out when he saw that the sound hadn't frightened me away.

"Just thought I'd ask how are things going." I had on my friendly voice disguise. "Polishing up the old resume. Never hurts at times like these." Rupert didn't ask me what times I meant; instead he just looked very cross. I was watching him watching me straining to read the papers he'd been working on by the computer. "So how are things?"

"Well, I've been busy," he told me with what I expected he thought was finality. "I still am — very busy."

As if I hadn't caught the hint, I continued to linger, musing on a photo of one of Rupert's many offspring, "Well, he looks like a good strong boy," my butt parked comfortably in his guest chair as if it were my unshakable intention to shoot the breeze with him forever. "And I hear you're expecting another little bundle of happiness. You know, at times like this, people say they don't know where the money goes."

"Would you mind getting to the point," Rupert finally said,

"because like I've told you, I don't have very much time today."

His attitude didn't seem very sociable to me, but if that was how he wanted to be, I told him, I was more than willing in the interest of time to forego the niceties. "I need some information on a special charity you seem to be supporting, specifically on a series of checks you wrote to Camille Gutierrez." Rupert visibly tensed every muscle from his ear to his baby toe as I took out the examples in my possession and laid them on his desk. "These are yours, aren't they?"

We were both staring at the fan of checks I'd made on his desk for a while. Rupert breathed and untensed, then his hand reached over and played with the pull chain on his desk light. "How did you get those?"

"First," I said, "tell me why you wrote them."

Rupert clicked his desk light on and, then, off a few more times, "I asked you first," he said.

I said, "Beggars can't be choosers," and felt a little like I was back in second grade. All the time, Rupert's hand kept working the chain switch and the light clicked on and off, on and off. "So, do you want your checks back?" I asked, "or should I give them to the cops?"

Rupert's fingers moved away from the light chain and came to rest, palm down on his desk where he drummed them, thinking so hard I could almost hear the rusty little wheels and cogs banging away. Every option registered and dismissed in a series of little flashes of micro-excitement and dejection that came up on his face.

"All I want to know is why you're paying Camille. Easy." I picked up a check, and let the paper waggle back and forth in my hand like a worm on a hook, then I put it back on the desk with the others. "Certainly, you can have these back when I know what's going on. It's up to you."

Rupert seemed to be considering his reflection in the glass

wall of his office. Both he and it wore a murderous expression. "All right," he finally agreed, "but it's none of your FUCKING business.

"They're for Elana," Rupert admitted, "Camille's daughter, Elana. When she got pregnant, they shipped her out of the neighborhood to stay with her grandmother in Oak Park. She has a special tutor so she can finish high school while she waits to have her baby. I'm paying for it, that and doctor's bills until they can put it up for adoption."

Rupert huffed as if he'd had nothing to do with his current predicament. "Jesus freaks. They wouldn't even talk about an abortion. You know it wasn't like I was the first guy she'd slept with. She said no, but I knew Winslow had been there. I was just the one to get caught, that's all. She's eighteen. She's legal. They see a young guy with some bucks and they figured they'll burn me." Somehow though I hadn't pegged Rupert Dean for the guilty-conscience club, and there was still the matter of $50,000 extra American dollars, for which Rupert hadn't bothered to account.

"So, you're just a poor guy who made a mistake and wanted to do the right thing? So, you started writing out two thousand dollar checks every month, because you wanted your kid to enjoy pre-natal care, new shoes and piano lessons?" I didn't much try to bridle my sarcasm.

Put this way, even the shameless Rupert couldn't help looking a little shamefaced, but only a little. "All right. The Irishman was making me pay her. Camille told Wes I'd gotten Elana pregnant and she expected Wes to fire me. Hell," Rupert was saying, "so did I. He threatened to, probably because I had gotten some of his little thing, but he doesn't. You know? Time passes. I'm waiting for the shoe to drop, then one day Wes comes by my office and he says it could all be just water under the bridge, that a big shareholder vote might be coming up, of course he can't tell me what it is, and if I promise to vote my shares the way he tells me he might forget about my indiscretion and he'll make sure I have enough money to fulfill my obligations to the girl. What Winslow doesn't want, he tells me, is a scandal." Rupert laughed derisively. "So, I keep my job because with the Gold Rush deal in the offing, Winslow doesn't want to do the paperwork. But Camille thinks all I got was a slap on the hand and she's irate, takes her case to The Irishman. Then, Zemluski says for me to make it right or he'd make sure Camille gets to tell her story to my wife. Look, I've got three kids and another one on the way. I've got a wife who won't stop having kids; and I've got what The Irishman tells me is 'a marriage of long duration' which means if Kitty leaves me, I won't have a dime between the child support and the alimony. Tom claims he knows how it's going to go for me in divorce court and Camille's $2,000 dollars a month for a year or so until they place the baby is a lot cheaper. He made me write out the checks pre-dated because he didn't trust me. So first Tom's all about how I have to do the 'right thing.' Next, it's all about doing whatever he tells me to do for the rest of my miserable life. So suddenly, I was supposed to vote my stock however he told me, because if I don't he says he'll call my wife." Rupert shrugged, opening his hands in a victimized appeal to my sense of fairness. "I kept my bargain. I paid Camille and I've still got to vote the same stock two different ways or I'm screwed."

Somehow I just couldn't manage to feel very sorry for him. "Then Winslow dies and all you have to do is pay for your illegitimate kid. Poor you." I said, "Why did Winslow demote Camille?" I wanted the complete, full-service revelation.

He shrugged again. "Wes didn't like her attitude no matter what I did. She'd made waves with The Irishman. It was unseemly." Rupert made a contemptuous snort. "Big man, huh."

But I didn't think that was quite all. "What about the $50,000," I said and Rupert managed to look more stupid than usual.

"What?" It seemed as if he didn't know.

I told him, "There's sixty-four thousand dollars in the account Camille set up for Elana. You've only told me about fourteen thousand dollars of that money. Someone wrote Camille a check for fifty grand." I said, "I intend to find out who."

"Not me," Rupert had begun to laugh. "Are you crazy? If I had fifty thousand bucks I could give away, do you think I'd be stuck with Kitty and the kids?" Much as I hated to let him off the hook, I thought Rupert made a convincing point. "Fifty thousand dollars." He'd been snorting again in disbelief when his face had suddenly darkened with an ugly epiphany. "That dirty, bitch," Rupert clapped himself hard in the head with both hands. "I'm not the father."

Maybe old Rupert wasn't so stupid after all. "Sharp as a tack," I told him. "Any idea where Camille might be now?" I asked, but he shook his head.

"When I find her though," he promised, "she's giving me my money back or going to jail." Rupert snapped his fingers twice in angry impatience. "I'll take those checks now, Virginia?"

"Where does the grandmother live?" For me there was still the matter of the mysterious fifty thousand. I said, "I know you have the address." I didn't have to see Rupert to feel him sizing me up, wondering if he was fast enough to beat me to the money. He wasn't. "If you try anything, I'll scream," I assured him, pleasantly.

He was looking at me with his checks in my hand for a while rather sullenly. Then he gave up and wrote the address on a Post-it Note, pushing it across the desk at me.

"You know Rupert," I told him, "I think you ought to know Wes changed The List before he died."

He was appraising me like a playground bully. "So?"

"So," I said, "On the new List Wes was recommending that you get fired, sport."

"That prick." Rupert's face just about made my day.

"It takes one to know one," I'd stood up to leave. "Better keep working on that resume."

"You bitch," Rupert worked his way out from behind the desk with surprising speed. "Hey," he was shouting, "what about my money?" But the checks were safely tucked in my suit coat pocket and I was already a few long steps away in his office doorway.

"I think I'll hang on to these a while," I told him as I closed the door.

Downstairs in the garage the AAA man was standing by my car. He had it jacked up and the tire was halfway off. In another five minutes the flat was changed, I'd signed the little authorization paper, thanked him and was on my way to Oak Park on my temporary tire. I thought it was nice sometimes when things worked out.

Elana's grandmother lived in a 70's neo-colonial style apartment complex on the Oak Park/Cicero border, up a set of open metal stairs and down a long concrete gallery full of insubstantial-looking, badly varnished, wooden doors, the hollow core-looking kind you'd expect to find inside the house rather than out. I pounded steadily on Number 1245.

After a few minutes, there was a shuffling sound and then a woman's voice, "Quien es? Un momento." The door opened a crack and two black eyes peered out at me.

"I'm looking for Camille Gutierrez." I said, but my request didn't rate much of a welcome.

"No hablo Ingles," said the old woman inside. "Lo siento." The door was closing, and I tried to stop it in my halting, high school Spanish.

"Puedo hablar con Camille Gutierrez," but no more sound came from behind the tired, old door. "I could get the police out here," I spoke a little more loudly with a recall I owned as absolutely miraculous, "Voy a llamar a un policia." That immediately got the door open about four inches, which was good, as I had nearly exhausted my store of handy phrases.

"Camille is not here."

In light of the woman's substantially improved English, I asked perhaps, with a misplaced confidence, if she could tell me when Camille would be back.

"Lo siento," she said.

"Can you tell her, then, I was here?" I took a card from my purse and added my home number on the back. "She knows what this is about. She should see me, or I will get the police."

"Un momento." The door closed, opening again in a few moments as promised. "Como se llama?"

"Aqui, tiene mi numero de telefono," I said. "If she calls me there will be no need for the police," I held out my card. "Comprende usted, Senora?"

A hand reached out and took the card, then the door snapped shut like those old-time mechanical penny banks. Across the yard some little boys were throwing a football back and forth in the street. I headed back home and waited for my phone to ring.

Camille Gutierrez returned my call at about six-thirty. "What's the big idea," she demanded, "frightening my mother like that?" I told her I knew that Rupert was writing her those checks for Elana.

"You talked to him?" Her voice had become small and even fearful.

I told her, "Yeah, I talked to him, but it's none of my business. I don't blame you."

This was followed by silence from which I was picking up an indefinite, but much improved interpersonal vibe, and then a mumbled prayer on her end that I didn't quite catch.

"Do you want your checks back?"

"Praise the Lord," she'd answered quite distinctly.

I told Camille we could meet that night at Whytebread about eight-thirty. That gave me enough time to scarf down a turkey and tomato sandwich from the White Hen Pantry's deli. I ate my dinner standing up, letting the crumbs fall into the kitchen sink so I didn't have to wash any dishes.

XXI

By quarter to eight, it was dark as midnight. The street was empty of people with only a train of headlights filing onto the Lakeshore Drive expressway.

"How goes it, Harry?" I said to the night garage attendant. He grunted back a marginal greeting, barely looking up to determine that I wasn't a dangerous thug.

As I pulled out onto the street, a red BMW cut me off, putting down what sounded like a good thick layer of rubber as it squealed out of the alley by the White Hen Pantry, and roared into the turn to Inner Lakeshore Drive.

I pulled onto the Drive behind it and fifty minutes later arrived at the garage under Whytebread's offices with my spanking new security card, an unimpressive piece of white plastic with a magnetic credit card strip on the back. I'd made a stop at the late night dry cleaner on my way into the office, so I was a little late for my meeting with Camille, but I figured if she wanted her money back she would wait. I'd just parked my car into a little compact stall close to the elevator, as this time of night Whytebread's garage was already desolate when the red Beamer squealed up again beside me. I'd felt a momentarily glimmer of pleasure to be running into Justin, but Rupert Dean was in the car.

"I want those checks," he was hanging out of his open window, baptizing me with unflattering names. "Bitch." Rupert pushed open the car door looking more capable, bigger, stronger, and nastier in sweat pants and a polo shirt, than when I taunted him that afternoon. Out of a suit and tie he was faster too. I thought if I could just get to the lobby where a security guard could help me, or to the elevator where I could ring the emergency call. But before I could formulate a clear idea of what was happening, Rupert had practically flown around the side of his car and managed to put all hundred and ninety pounds of himself between me and any escape. "Why don't you just give me the money, all right?" The checks were there in my pocket and I was beginning to see Rupert's point when the elevator opened behind him.

"Justin," I was overjoyed to see my protector. "Hold that door; will you?"

Rupert looked from me to Justin, gauging his options for a moment before he let me pass. "I'll see you later," he told me as if he were making a dinner date.

"Not if I see you first," I said as Rupert slunk off to his car.

"Want to tell me what that was about?" Despite the convenient timing of his arrival Justin seemed vaguely un-settled to have met me there.

I said I'd tattled to The Irishman that Rupert had planned

to vote with Wes on the buyout. "Apparently Rupert promised his votes at least twice."

"Lucky for you I had some reports to get out," Justin held the door to the elevator vestibule. "Just on my way up from Parking Level 3."

"Filing," I touched my chest lightly, lying. I thought with all of this cloak and dagger, I was getting pretty good at it. "The cops made such a mess of my office that I can't find a thing. Camille said she'd help me. She really wants the overtime," I'd embellished the story, pleased with my own cleverness at anticipating any bothersome questions Justin might have asked when Camille showed up.

"You must be moving up in the world, Virginia," Justin consulted his watch and raised his eyes. "I don't think she even worked this late for Wes."

The security guard at the desk waved at us like old friends. "Back again?"

"Can't stay away," Justin shook his head. He pulled an access card from his jean pocket and raised it for the guard to see.

"I've left mine in my car," I confessed to the guard and he bent over his clipboard disapprovingly, signing me in as plus one next to Justin's name in the log. Justin swiped his card in the reader to unlock the elevator.

"I just need to knock a few things out," Justin pressed the buttons of the cipher lock on the 25th floor and pushed open the door off the side of the lobby. "Call me when you're ready to leave." He turned off down the maze of half-lit cubes towards his office and I followed the hallway past the lunch-room towards mine.

From my office phone, I called in the security code, pressed #### for the lights and then, looking down the hall towards Wes's area, I could see someone had already hit them; they made an eerie florescent glow in the distant offices.

From the computer status trick that Jeremy Bennett had

taught me, I'd learned that Rupert Dean was logged on, but I couldn't even begin to guess how he had managed to beat Justin and me into the office. We had just left him in the parking garage, he hadn't been in the elevator lobby, and his office, only a few doors from mine, had been dark and empty when I passed.

All I knew was that Rupert would have to be pretty mad to have sprinted up the stairwell, all twenty-six flights from the garage, and I didn't think I wanted to run into him again anytime soon. Still he was somewhere in the office, or at least logged on to his computer along with Justin, The Irishman, and strangely, Starr, who couldn't possibly have been physically present. There was, however, no sign at all of Camille.

"Hey, Justin," I shouted experimentally, just to see if he was within earshot should I need some help. I wasn't quite shouting, but my voice sounded unnaturally loud in the dark quiet office.

He shouted back, "Hey." The sound carried reassuringly.

In my e-mail there were three new messages from that afternoon. The first was a bulletin to the entire firm regarding the refrigerator in the lunchroom. It would be cleaned out on the last Friday of the month and the contents discarded. "PLEASE REMOVE ANYTHING YOU DO NOT WANT TRASHED!!!!NO EXCEPTIONS!!!!"

I could fairly hear Herb Symon banging those four exclamation points into his keyboard as I surfed my mouse down to the second and then the third message, which were both hate mail from Spike. Again there was nothing from Camille and no flashing messages on my phone machine.

"I'm ready to get out of here," Justin called out wearily from the other side of the building and I would be leaving with him.

If Rupert were still lurking, I wouldn't have to walk out alone. Closing in on nine o'clock, Camille had not turned up, nor had she e-mailed or called in her regrets, but I still had her money. To get it, I hadn't any doubt that she would find me eventually. But then, as we were leaving the office, there in the elevator lobby, Justin and I found Camille.

She was flat on her butt having slid down the wall and out the doors when they had opened, legs first and then the rest of her, on the floor of the elevator like an overdressed rag doll. Her legs splayed out between the rubber bumper doors revealing, dark patterned stockings in low lace-up walking shoes.

As the doors tried to close, they bumped her calves and rebounded, bouncing back again and again against her dead legs. The buzzing doors complained of the obstruction. Camille's face looked out with open-eyed surprise at the elevator trying to amputate her feet.

"Shit," said Justin. The cipher lock clicked, and the door handle turned at the side of the receptionist desk. All the time I could barely take my eyes off the elevator doors, opening and then trying to close around Camille's swollen ankles. Ellen Borgia stepped out into the lobby.

"Oh my God," she said, then Ellen fainted.

Downstairs, the security cop had rounded up three well-scrubbed, brown-skinned children and a bewildered looking young Latino man who I presumed was Camille's nephew, Miguel. The security guard had Miguel by the collar, pushing him along against his protests toward the uniform cop. The kids were clinging to his pants legs, bawling. As near as I could tell from the shouts that passed across the lobby between the security guard and the uniform cop, Miguel and the kids had been parked in the loading zone on Michigan Avenue with the engine running in a Subaru station wagon loaded down with luggage.

After the police brought Ellen downstairs it didn't take long to get everyone sorted out, and in a few minutes more

Cassandra Hope had blown in on the faint smell of a swanky cocktail party, demanding a report of events from the uniformed cop.

"So, officer, what happened here?" Cassandra was smartly decked out in a sleek brown suit and suede pumps outfit that suggested she'd had other, more exciting plans for her evening.

I would have liked a report from her, but somehow it didn't seem prudent to inquire.

As I lay in my bed that night, I thought of my interview with Cassandra who had declined rather firmly to accompany me home. I'd wanted comfort more than sex — most of all, I wanted someone to ask how I was doing with all this, but Cassandra only had professional questions.

"Who was there with you?" she'd asked, her tape record rolling impersonally again.

It was me, Justin, and Ellen Borgia; one happy shell-shocked family in the elevator lobby. Although the status report said Justin, Rupert, The Irishman, and unbelievably Starr of all people were logged into their computers, Ellen was not. I'd listed off the names, and Cassandra dutifully wrote them in her notebook while I went on explaining that someone had been logged into Starr's account. She recorded my run in with Rupert.

But the police had been all over our floor, up and down the building and the only other person they'd found was one very confused Polish cleaning lady — Rupert, The Irishman and of course Starr weren't there aside from their cyber presence. The police thought that Camille had been deposited in the elevator at a little after 8:00 p.m. She'd been riding up and down for about an hour before we had found her and the after hour key car log showed only my card and Ellen's.

At one o'clock in the morning I had considered calling

Cassandra on the slim excuse that she might be interested enough to come over and discuss my ruminations in person, but I couldn't even say if she was at home. Where she'd come from and where she was going to so dressed up was a mystery. I was just too tired and broken to let it keep me awake much longer.

XXII

In the days that followed, Whytebread suffered a massive epidemic of the blue flu. I might have called in sick myself if I hadn't been quite so paranoid about my continued employment or if the alternatives to a day at work had been any more attractive than sitting around my house, cleaning up cat puke and feeling like shit, because I couldn't help wondering if Camille and Starr would be dead if they hadn't been talking to me.

Of course none of that unshakable, free-floating guilt made very much sense as the only legitimate threat I'd received had come from Starr herself. Fact was, none of it made much sense; and the more I considered what had gone on, the less sense it made, so there seemed no rational alternative beyond just marching forward day to day, a depressing undertaking that I was managing through continuous phone support from Naomi Wolf. Cassandra might as well have dropped off the face of the earth for all I was seeing of her.

I'd been sitting in my office, perseverating, about a week after Starr had died, with my eyes aimed in a general and unfocused way at the smoky glass wall between my office and the hall when a tall, weedy-looking mailboy rolled his wire pushcart past my field of vision. Mailboy wore a big retro-seventies, white man's afro, and canary yellow, grudge bell bottoms, which prompted a sudden connection of all the little pieces of things that had been floating around in my creaky mind since the night Starr had died. It was a sudden forehead-slapping realization like when your brain stumbles onto the answer to those word and figure puzzles. My grandfather used to make them out of scrap wood for the people in his church, jig-sawed and glued on a little plaque. Look first and there was only a mishmash of random wooden blocks, look harder and you can read the word, *"Jesus."*

I must have been staring purposelessly in his direction for some time, as if goings on outside my office were a show whose action moved past me while I sat still, before I realized that I was looking at the tall, thin, after-hours mystery man. That unmistakable hair had given him away.

"Hey you. Thief." He bolted as I shouted the complaint that seemed most likely to get someone to help me head him off. But I was able to catch up to him half-way down the hall as he tried to vault over the side of the cart and his big high-top tennis shoe caught in the handle, making him stumble and slow just enough for me to push the mail cart hard into the back of his knees. Then he fell.

His foot tangled up in the cart again, Mr. Bushy Hair went down with a gratifying thud on the low nap carpet, looking up at me dizzily and in apparent knee pain as I began to interrogate him. "I know you've been sneaking around here at night, so you'd better tell me why." Even flat on his back he was a big guy, but I rattled the wire cart threateningly enough to intimidate. "I've seen you coming out of Winslow's office at night," I said, "and I'll tell the police."

"Lady, I'm just delivering the mail." Having gotten himself up on all fours, he was trying to stand, so I slammed the cart back into his legs again. He had tried the wrong girl; I was viscious, heartbroken, and tired and unwilling to be toyed with.

"Aw fuck." The mailboy was floundering on a bed of correspondence, his arms and legs inextricably tangled. "All right, lady. What do you want me to say?" He blinked up at me in whimpering defeat.

According to Bushy Hair, Ned Couteau had been running a little side business in stolen office supplies. Clients requested equipment and Ned would arrange for it to disappear from Whytebread. Some of the mailroom clerks took turns sneaking the stuff out of the building. Ned had security paid off, so there was never any problem.

The story was threatening perilously to shatter my august illusions about *Mister* Couteau senior. In my own twisted little way, I had looked up to him and I was resenting the disappointment. "Did Alcee know about this?"

Bushy nodded diffidently. "He didn't help us or nothing, but Mister Couteau, he always looked the other way when Ned was shipping stuff out of the mailroom."

Now that the mailboy seemed to be thoroughly subjugated, I let him pick himself up off the floor and went to go look for Mister Couteau. "Don't go anywhere, young man," I warned. It was peculiar, if effective, to be getting to an age where I could call someone "young man" with conviction. "I know who you are and I can get your name from human resources."

"Yes ma'am," Bushy, the mail punk sang out gratifyingly as I walked away.

I found Alcee Couteau in the mailroom, surveying his workers from his usual seat, a low, wooden stool in the corner. His cane was leaning against the wall beside him and in my second patently nasty act of the day, I took it. Then I stepped back about two feet and swung the cane at the legs of his chair, feeling much less like a playground bully than I would have expected. I was a little worried that some of his minions might try to stop me, but they didn't seem to care how I abused the old man.

"Hey." The clatter of the cane on his chair had woken Alcee from his supervisory reverie. "Give that back." His hand made a grab at the cane, fingers grazing the wood fruitlessly — not fast or strong enough.

I shook my head, stepping maliciously out of reach. "I just wanted to ask you about the little office supply resale business Ned's been running down here. If you don't tell me what's going on," I insisted, "I'm going to get the police in here and then you can talk to them. I think you'd rather talk to me. I can keep you out of it if this little side business doesn't have anything to do with Winslow's murder. Don't let anyone say I don't respect my elders."

With the last little cut I was starting to feel unnecessarily mean, but not enough to stop, especially since Couteau's disapproval didn't seem to suggest any of the appropriate elements of fear.

"Don't do me favors. No need to leave me out of it." He was scowling at me with that same indifferent contempt I should have been used to. "You just go to the police," he was goading me, "and I'll tell 'em Ned didn't have a thing to do with it. But I'll make sure your boss Herb Symon is in up to his ears."

"Herb Symon is stealing office supplies?" I wondered if my face looked as clueless as I sounded.

"Yep. Knock and it shall be opened unto you." Alcee Couteau bobbed his head. "If you want to send the police after me, you'll have to send them after him."

Herb Symon had been supplementing his presumably adequate income for years now, signing requisitions for office equipment that Whytebread didn't need and then having it stolen by Ned's henchmen as soon as it arrived. They were stealing deliveries straight from the mailroom, but Couteau said he'd put a stop to that.

I gave him back his cane, on that note, feeling a little silly. "You wrote those Post-it Notes around the firm and the one on Winslow's obituary didn't you?" I guess I was hoping to be right in at least one allegation.

"Only wrote the last one — Winslow's." Mr. Couteau accepted his cane although he didn't seem to need it really. "Herb Symon did the other ones to make Winslow stop my Bible group and push me out."

"So, all right." I asked him, "vengeance for what?"

"Vengeance is for God." Couteau was eyeing me pityingly, as if the smallness of my understanding saddened and astonished him. "Don't you know anything? It's all right there in Romans 12:19. Why don't you get a Bible, young woman and read it." He raised himself from the stool, found his hat, put it on his small gray head, and walked out to the hall. "Young people today don't read enough."

I was still trying to think of what I ought to have replied to that, when Alcee handed me a small, but very thick hardcover book, *Hally's Bible Handbook.* "Go on." He held it out to me. "Take it. It'll give you an education."

"Hey there." I still had Alcee's Bible book in my hand when I looked into Ellen Borgia's office. She was sitting idly at her desk with an expression as broken down as I felt — maybe (probably) worse as she was older and I'd noticed her face had started to line. "How's it going?" I might have kept walking, but I'd been worried about Ellen. Since Starr had died, she'd been crying, not episodically, but, as a habit.

"How does it look like its going?" She was still loading up her tea with valarian but I thought it was encouraging that Ellen seemed to have found the energy to be testy. "I've already talked to the police about your friend, Justin. So, there's no news for you to carry back. I've told them Justin was sleeping with Starr."

"What?" I was glad I couldn't see my own face.

"That's why she killed herself — over Justin, I'm sure of it. He had to twist her and confuse her and then make her feel like she wasn't desirable as a woman."

Apparently, Ellen didn't know about the HIV. I wondered if Starr did. Then, I wondered about Justin and about the way Starr and Winslow had danced together at the Christmas Party last year.

Ellen admitted, "I don't know what the deal was with Wes. All she'd said was that working for Winslow and hooking up with Justin was her ticket to everything she ever wanted." What I didn't understand was why then had she leaked Winslow's List to Ellen of all people.

"That was Justin." Ellen had a drink of tea in a kind of brittle amusement. "One day, I came back to my office and caught him at my desk. He just handed me the paper. So, I said to him. 'This is The List?' 'Yeah,' he says. I asked why he was giving it to me and he says, 'because it's right.' "

"Did you believe him?"

Ellen stared at me a little bit harder and more doubtfully. "Not for a minute and as it turned out he was setting me up so Wes could make a new List and I could look like I was crazy, even to my own lawyers. So, that's what I was doing those nights you found me here. I've already told all that to your police detective. I was surfing the e-mail system, researching my suit to keep them from screwing me. Since you told me about Winslow's new List I thought there might be documentation on the old one. Or maybe a little e-mail correspondence that would prove they had a reason for buying me off. Justin hated me and I knew it was too good to be true that he would help. You'd be amazed at what people leave on their computers." Ellen smirked, "All you need is a system administrator's password."

It was Ellen who had been logged into Starr's, The Irishman's, and Rupert's accounts the night Camille had been strangled. The mystery of her relationship with Jeremy which I had managed to load with such significance as a parallel to my own confused little love life was apparently solved as well. Ellen sold herself for e-mail access.

"Why not?" Ellen had shrugged placidly into my horror. "There are worse men than Jeremy — and everybody sells themselves for something." I couldn't tell if she meant to sound pointed. "Any other questions burning a hole in your brain, Virginia?"

There was one. "Were you logged into Justin's account as well as Rupert's and The Irishman's?"

Ellen squashed up her face thinking. "No. I couldn't get into Justin's account until just before I left." The thought intrigued her, "He must have been in his account from six thirty or so until just before we found Camille in the elevator."

I thought I was beginning to understand some things. I just needed Justin's help to know for sure, but he wasn't in his office when I checked.

"He's sick." His secretary, Sara, came from behind me, the picture of matronly middle-aged helpfulness and efficiency. "You could probably call him at home."

XXIII

Justin's place was near Fullerton, a half-hour ride for me on the 32 bus, which was not too terribly crowded before rush hour. I had slipped uneventfully into his building on the heels of an unfriendly woman with blue hair and a little yapping dog. The old lady and I both looked studiously straight ahead all the way up the elevator, and the Yorkie growled, fully prepared, by its demeanor to take me apart at the kneecaps.

"Have a nice day," I said as they exited on the twelfth floor. The woman didn't answer but the little dog continued to bark its good-byes.

Justin lived on the twentieth floor. He was home. I could tell from the rustling sounds behind the door.

"Who is it?" he called. But I waited to answer until the door swung inward and I could see his eyes across the chain. "It's me," I said. "You weren't at work and I was worried." Justin's hand raked open the metal security chain, reluctantly letting me in. "Two funerals in two days seemed like more than my share."

I recalled that at Camille's I'd caught a glimpse of Elana, big as a house, her face as swollen as her belly from crying. I'd put the blackmail checks from Rupert in the hand of the preacher after the service and slunk away before he could thank me. I wanted to turn the page on this horrific episode, go home and have a shower, crawl into the sheets and lay there smelling the clean soft skin of my lover. Too bad my house was such a mess and Cassandra had gotten so lax about returning my calls. When I did finally hear from her she seemed more distant than usual, wanting only to tell me she'd confirmed that The Irishman was out on a date with some waitress when Starr and Camille had been killed, and that Rupert Dean had had the temerity to use assaulting me in the parking garage as his alibi.

Justin unfortunately didn't have an alibi, which is what I'd figured out that afternoon. I knew that he'd killed Camille and Starr and I could guess he'd killed Winslow by extrapolation, but I was hoping he would tell me why.

"It had to be you." It was ironically made obvious by how he had saved me from Rupert, coming from the elevator at just the right time.

"I was coming up from parking level 3," Justin google-eyed me as if I had just grown another head. "So what. You should be thankful that I was there, Virginia."

Still, I said, it didn't change the unfortunate fact that really he had been coming down the elevator. I knew because I hadn't pressed the elevator button yet. Rupert was standing between me and the door. I told Justin, "If you had been coming up, the elevator wouldn't have stopped. You had to have pressed the button which could only mean you were coming down from the office where you'd used the key card you'd stolen from my car to get in so that there would be no record you'd been there. That was why the access card log had a record of me when I'd forgotten my card in the car. Remember?" I asked him, but he was blinking at me still so unperturbed that I had to question whether I'd gotten a little confused.

"You know, even if that craziness were true, there's no way you could prove it."

But there was still the security guard who'd greeted him with, "back again?" when we'd signed in. Surely, I told Justin the guard would remember seeing Justin twice that evening if he were asked. "So why'd you do it?

"I guess that depends," Justin sucked the side of his cheek in contemplation. "I killed Wes accidentally with some mushrooms I bought from a guy at a bar. They were only supposed to make him high and a little sick." That made sense given what I'd read about *Fly Agaric*.

"I didn't mean to kill him. I only wanted him to leave his wife." Justin's face broke foolishly as if he might laugh at himself, but he just sounded sad. "He wouldn't divorce Trisha, and I thought if he understood how short life is he would change his mind."

There it was. "You were *friends?*" I found I had hit on exactly the minimalist word my mother used in her discomfort to slight my own same-sex relationships.

"Yeah we were *friends*." There was a bitterness rising in Justin's voice. "Wes told me the week before he died that he was going to work it out with Trisha."

Stranger things had happened. It gave me an odd sense of relief that Winslow's middle-America persona could remain in tact, and an odder embarrassment at my investment in it. I had scripted Wesley Winslow's two-dimensional motivations and I was not completely comfortable imagining him as a man of emotional complexities. "Maybe they loved each other after all."

"Love, Trisha? I don't think so. They hated each other, Virginia," Justin was promising maybe me, maybe himself, clinging perhaps to a script of his own. "That little scene you saw at the Christmas party, that was just a warm up act. You couldn't have stayed in the room to watch the main event. He despised her and she hated everything about him, his vegetarian diet, his weekend marathons, his men. The only things Trisha Winslow ever cared a thing about were her roses and a mixed drink — and Wes even managed to ruin gardening for her."

"Have you ever heard of anyone growing award-winning roses with out any pesticides. Wes thought they were unhealthy for their daughter, Wallace. The aphids had decimated Trisha garden. We used to lie here in my bedroom during the week and laugh about it. She'd tried everything. Last summer she started making this sun tea of cigarette butts, buying cigarettes to make it, steeping it outside, Wes said, until the patio smelled like bad fish. She'd go out and paint every damn leaf and bud of those roses with a pastry brush. Crazy, huh?"

It didn't seem much crazier than poisoning your lover to scare him into more quality time. "You weren't looking for your bagels that morning in the refrigerator were you?" I asked. "You were looking for Wes's lunchbox."

Justin didn't seem to be listening to me. "You know I brought you here that night to see if you could guess that we stayed here together."

So Winslow had kept his things, not at the Park Shore, but at Justin's place, where according to Justin they would spend their idyllic nights fantasizing about going away together when, as a result of the Gold Rush deal, they had all the money they'd ever need. Justin sounded unwaveringly convinced of his story. "That was why Wes pursued the merger in the first place. Then, at the last minute, he told me he couldn't go through with it. Wes didn't love her, Virginia. Sure. He loved his life. His club, his position at Whytebread, none of which he would have if he left his wife for a man. It wasn't that no one had figured him out. I mean Tom did, I suppose because of what he knew about me. I suppose that's why Wes was so determined that he go. Maybe Herb had a clue, but, except for Tom, nobody wanted to know."

I wondered though, "What about the women?"

"What women? Wes didn't have any women. He just let Herb Symon polish that legend for the masses. The same way I let people think you and I were dating."

"You and Starr were really an item, though, weren't you, you slept with her." That was the question that really bothered me.

"Who told you that — Ellen?" Justin shrugged. "I needed to keep her happy so she didn't get any ideas about me and Wes. Wes made a trust fund for Elana to keep Camille's mouth shut and he didn't want to have to buy Starr off as well. It was cheaper for me to date her. So, I brought her to the place at the Park Shore and told her both Wes and I used it for girls. But then she was jealous of you. Because of that night you stayed at my place, she threatened to tell you that I had the only key to Winslow's flat and we all know where that kind of information would go with your police relationships. Starr's death was an accident, though. She rushed at me and I threw her off — harder than I intended, unfortunately. She fell through the window."

He had to be able to tell that I was appalled.

Two deep lines had come up on Justin's forehead. "You don't think I had unsafe sex with her, do you?" He sounded as if he himself were equally horrified.

I shook my head. "What about Camille?"

Justin had crossed his legs, seeming almost comfortable telling this story. "Well Camille, she did a stupid thing," he was practically smiling at the turn of events. "It's farcical almost, I don't think she ever suspected that I'd killed Wes, but she knew the police would suspect me. Camille said she'd make more trouble by telling them about us. So I gave her the fifty thousand dollars she wanted. Then you found her savings account passbook and Starr died. That should have made her nervous, but of course it didn't — just greedier. Camille wanted more money or she would tell you what she knew."

"Camille," Justin said her name with general disdain, "thought she was being smart, setting up our meetings back to back, using the fact that you were coming to squeeze me into a deal. I had to put a stop to that as quickly as possible. I'm pretty strong," he was allowing reflectively, as if he viewed these events as an interested spectator. "I don't think she suffered too much. You know the rest. I came out of the elevators into the garage and there you were."

"You didn't kill me." I realized I meant it as both a statement and a request.

"No. Well, I suppose I'd had enough for a while." If Justin intended a joke of sorts, neither one of us laughed. "So what are you going to do now?"

I didn't really know, mostly I was just hoping Justin was incapable of a second wind. What I thought to say was: "Justin, you know, I'm wearing a wire." Having hit on this serendipity, I went with it whole hog. "Our entire discussion is being recorded," I elaborated. "So it doesn't leave me many choices."

"No. I guess not." He sounded only a little remorseful, but not very surprised. Justin was smiling still, if weakly and a little reproachful at for what he took as my rude premeditation. "I guess you had this all planned out. Did you do it for the money, Virginia? Or did you sell me out for the girl?" It seemed a simple point of curiosity, but it was hard even to know myself.

"Money's more dependable." He still had on that sickly smile. "But that's alright. It doesn't matter. None of this is real, Virginia." Justin had shifted on the couch, pulling from the pocket of his chinos, a small, red camping knife. "Hold still," he was faster than I would have expected, leaning forward, suddenly catching my hand. He twisted my arm so the veins were up and he cut me once across my open wrist. The blade was sharp and I jumped more from surprise than pain at the ease with which he'd slit my skin.

The blood welled when Justin let go my arm as if his hand had been a tourniquet. "Look at that. That's real," he said. His grip had left marks. He took the knife again and cut his own arm, comparing it to mine. "That's the only real thing." With his index finger Justin smeared the blood nonchalantly down his forearm. "That's all there is — living or not living."

My palms were sweating, itchy as a sure sign, my mother would say, that I was coming into money, but I wasn't so sure about the accuracy this time of that old wives tale.

Justin was saying, "I've tried to show you things, you know — things HIV has given me the clarity of vision to recognize. Wes couldn't. I don't know why I should expect you to either."

"Jesus, Justin." My bleeding had stopped but his went on. The blood ran in a trail down his arm and I didn't want to touch his blood.

"Look, it's clear that things just got out of hand," I said, "with all this money we can hire somebody to help you beat this, get you some help." I thought Naomi was sure to know someone good.

"Save your money, Virginia." Justin winked at me with disconcerting cheerfulness. "Save your money, Ginny," he said, "it's all over now." I was a little worried now about what he might do. "You've got your girl and your girl is going to get her man, right? All those bastards at Whytebread are going to get their hearts' desires." Justin stood me up, walked me down the hall to his apartment door and opened it. "Don't you spend your money in one place, girlfriend. Diversify. Now go on, little sistah, get out, all right?"

I did what I was told, but I ran for phone as soon as I hit the hall. I thought if I were fast enough, Justin might not have to die, but I hadn't gone two steps towards the elevator before I heard him fire.

After that, there were suddenly cops everywhere, so many I couldn't figure out where they all had come from so quickly, maybe the woman with the dog in the garage really had thought I looked suspicious. Among all those cops, Cassandra Hope seemed notably absent, so I let a fresh-faced patrolwoman lead me down the elevator. She was taking my statement in the lobby of Justin's apartment building when Cassandra arrived.

"How did you know to be here?" I was admittedly, breathlessly happy to report. "Justin's dead. He killed Wes."

"No, he didn't." Cassandra was smiling in that patient, indulgent way she had as if to imply the whole time she'd always been several giant steps ahead of me. "We've already arrested the person who killed Mr. Winslow." She tapped the junior cop summarily on the shoulder, all business. "Can you drop Miss Kelly at her home, please."

I didn't quite think Cassandra had heard me, particularly if she was sending me home with the junior cop. "Justin and Winslow were lovers, but Wes wanted to go back to his wife. Justin poisoned Wes's salad to make him sick enough to realize what a stupid thing he was doing."

I kept trying to tell her what I had found out, but all the time, Cassandra had a guiding hand at the small of my back, hustling me out towards the street. I meant to say something or ask something — I couldn't say what, but she was already talking intently with someone else. On to the next thing, which was expressly not me. I'd been shuttled off to the girl cop, my designated handler, who, in turn, placed her hand where Cassandra's had been and guided me firmly into a blue and white patrol car.

I'd only sat there for a few minutes when two other cops came out of the front of Justin's apartment building leading him in handcuffs. "The mushrooms didn't kill Winslow," I'd shouted through the open patrol car window. I thought it would help him to know. It helped me. Justin turned towards my voice in absolute bewilderment.

"You didn't kill Winslow," I called out again. Although I, now, hadn't the slightest idea of who had, I thought the news would make him happy. I couldn't stop myself from following on: "I thought you were dead."

He shouted back, "I changed my mind." That seemed rather like him — survival. And I wondered what he would have done if I hadn't said we were being taped. The thought made me glad to be sitting down. All that for nothing.

The police were still pushing Justin forward a little roughly towards the car that would take him away; and he looked like someone stepping out of a dark room into a bright unbalancing light.

"Are you all right," the girl cop seemed quite genuinely concerned.

That night I dreamed about rows and rows of violet roses waving on a broad expanse of suburban yard like the field of poppies in *The Wizard of Oz*. When I fell down into their smell, the thorns cut my wrists and I bled — enough blood to sweep me out into the circular driveway of Winslow's big suburban house and down the lovely wide, tree-lined street.

I'd woken and wandered, dry mouthed and a bit disoriented down the hall to the bathroom for some water. As I drank from the vanity faucet in handfuls, my head turned sideways towards the florescent ceiling light that strobed itself uncertainly into operation. There was a distracting movement at the corner of my eye. The overhead light had seemed to fill with shadows sort of writhing under the plastic cover, not the predictable static bug corpses, but a good number of them ten, fifteen, half-inch long, mobile cylindrical shadows. Crawling in miraculously ordered concentric circles around the inside of the fixture were maggots, and I screamed with a left over squeamishness from girlhood.

The maggots kept moving round and round, their peristaltic path both strange and calming, mesmerizing, like some living, lava lamp. How they had gotten into my florescent bathroom light, I couldn't fathom.

Perhaps in the warmth of my light, flies had mated and died, their larva incubated, hatched and fed on their parent's bodies. Or, more horribly, a mouse may have died in the ceiling. It was as if they had materialized from nowhere, were going to nowhere in their circular march, until the heat slow cooked their soft white bodies. I could already see spots where they had burned and stuck to the plastic dome. I considered getting the step ladder so I could flush them down the toilet, but instead I opted to call Naomi who picked up her phone only after an uncountable number of rings, complaining that anything I might have to say to her could certainly have waited until the morning.

I was trying to explain with the best level of mature calm I could maintain that Naomi did not have a bathroom light full of maggots. Distressingly, even as I said this, some were finding their way out of the fixture, onto the floor, where they inched their nasty, white maggot bodies towards the darkness under the tub and clothes hamper with an astonish- ing speed that made me worry how many had preceded this current wave. I was never going to be able to sleep knowing that they were loose.

"And I'll never be able to get back to sleep without a cigarette." Naomi was advising me to turn the light back off and maybe they would stay put until tomorrow. "I'll try to come in the morning," she said in a way that made it clear she thought that this concession was very generous. "Maggots are light negative."

"What?" I'd begun the stopgap measure of collecting the stray fly larva from the floor in toilet tissue and flushing them piecemeal as she talked. With my hand buffered by about a half a roll of paper I was finding that the job was not as terrible as I had imagined. I was beginning to believe I might just have the emotional wherewithal to clean out the light all by myself.

"They're light hating, like cockroaches." Naomi was going on in her know-it-all kind of perpetual impatience, "God, I could use a cigarette."

Then as a kind of psychic bonus for my bravery, I suddenly knew who had killed Wesley Winslow, the crime solved neatly in my very own bathroom.

"Look," she was perhaps rethinking her own feeling about my infested light, "I didn't say I was coming over there, for sure."

But now that was all fine. The cordless phone crooked between my chin and shoulder, I had suited up to my elbows in yellow latex dishwashing gloves. "No need," I was saying, "you've helped me enough already." I would rinse my nasty maggot friends down the toilet with a pitcher of water and flush them away. All I'd needed was someone to talk it through with. "I've got it figured out now." I was sure I had — all of it.

"You know, Virginia," Naomi said, "you're a funny girl."

I certainly was a funny girl. Somewhere during Naomi's seemingly endless withdrawal complaints, I had remembered the Nicoderm patch instructions: *"Signs of an overdose include bad headaches, dizziness, drooling, vomiting, weakness, cold sweats.* " I'd experienced the dizziness and nausea first hand that afternoon in Winslow's apartment, which left me pretty sure that Trisha Winslow had murdered her husband with an overdose of nicotine. It was chilling to think that little tainted Turnaround Cream under the eyes might have been enough to take me out if I hadn't washed it off my face so quickly.

I'd given the toilet several additional maggot disposal flushes for good measure, and washed my hands about a million more times before I got around to calling Cassandra Hope at home. She had said, after all, to call her anytime. That was one reason — the other was just for spite.

Cassandra admitted sleepily that she'd known about the nicotine overdose since the day after I'd gotten sick at Winslow's apartment, which really mitigated any guilt I might have felt about waking her up. It had been my sudden incapacitation, in fact, that had prompted Cassandra to send the open jar of Turnaround Cream off to the police lab for analysis. Trisha Winslow had likely been experimenting a long time, testing the strength of the pesticide on the aphids in her rose garden — or perhaps on Winslow himself given the traces of nicotine in his hair.

The nicotine had dissipated from Winslow's skin too rapidly to appear in the autopsy, and of course he'd had a belly full of poisonous mushrooms to divert suspicion from the real cause of death. After a long bath hot and a trying day, Wes must have spread that moisturizer all over his face and body. With his pores completely open from the hot water, the poison could be quickly absorbed, and so he'd died there in an apartment to which everyone would agree Trisha Winslow had no access, and while she was traveling far away.

From Justin, though, I was telling Cassandra what she had missed in her description of the crime was Trisha's perfect element of timing. The Irishman was always carping on timing and circumstance when I recommended a stock. Money was made not just by what you bought, but when you bought it. Now I thought after all these years of resentment, The Irishman might have been trying to teach me something after all. More than just the luck of an out of town gardening conference, Trisha Winslow had perfected her murder in the fact that only a week before, Winslow had elected to stay with her instead of running off with Justin. That made her plan flawless, because all of a sudden she had no apparent motive to kill the man (except, of course, that she hated him for her years of humiliation). And there was Justin, a perfect scapegoat as the lover scorned.

I guessed, "It wasn't August Madsen, but Trisha Winslow who really told you Justin was gay." That closed the loop.

"Very good, Virginia." Cassandra said that the police might have arrested Trisha earlier, but Madsen feared the scandal she would make about Wes's lifestyle if there were a trial. To prosecute Trisha Winslow quietly had taken careful arrangements. "I wasn't able to share them with you, you understand." Had I thought that Cassandra was sorry, it might have sounded like an apology. She was explaining, "then, in the interim Starr was killed and then Camille. I didn't think Trisha Winslow was responsible, but I didn't know and you seemed to have developed a knack for putting yourself inconveniently in the middle of things." Cassandra had gotten nervous when I'd turned up at Starr's the night she was murdered.

"So you had me followed?" I concluded.

"Yes, Virginia." Her voice was attractively hoarse and I could hear in the background above her whisper, the faint rustling of her sheets. "I had you followed. For your own protection, since it had become very clear you weren't telling me everything." I could hear the rustling again, as another body stretched and rolled and sought the heat of her skin in the bed, that unmistakable sound of intimate company.

"Cassie?" He asked sleepily, "who're you talking to?"

"No one." There was the soft muffling, I thought, of her palm closing over the phone. "It's work." She told him. Her hand made more static against the mouthpiece, but I could still hear them until I hung up.

XXIV

I'd asked Naomi to wait outside in the car while I made my way along the tidy concrete walk, up few the stairs to the porch, and knocked on the door of Cassandra's Southside bungalow. I would have like to assign the tall, rather pretty black man who answered to another category in Cassandra's life, brother, cousin, friend, but I knew who he was. He sized me up with the same kind of recognition, turning curtly to call Cassandra before I could ask for her.

They passed each other in the hall as he walked off towards the back of the house and I could hear him whisper fiercely, "What the hell?" The familiar refrain to an old married couple's betrayal song. "You promised."

"This is business," she was still promising against his last hard look in my direction.

"So, what do you want?" Cassandra said as if I'd no right to come there. Maybe I didn't. I could see that I had made trouble for her.

"I wanted you," I said, "I thought you cared about me."

"Did I say that?" She made it sound like the idea surprised her.

She had made me think it, but Cassandra was staring at me with a kind of horrified curiosity as if at the boundless depth of my misunderstanding. Justin was right, I'd done Cassandra's snooping for Cassandra's approbation. The money was secondary to the seduction of belonging — to someone, to something. It was suddenly not so difficult at all to understand how Wesley Winslow had come to be dead for trifling with his wife's affections.

"Did I ever say that I loved you?"

And I could feel the muscles in my throat get tight, cinching down at my neck until I wasn't sure that I could answer, even if I could have thought of what to say. "It was what you wanted me to think."

"What could you have expected?" Cassandra still seemed completely appalled. "I'm not gay," and I was wondering aloud when this convenient orientation change had come about.

Most certainly she had been gay when she'd told me how Spike was no good for me, the implicit message behind such advice was that she would be. She'd been gay enough the times that we had been together, recently and years ago.

"You may choose to be gay," she was explaining, "but I don't."

"Maybe or maybe not." I could barely squeeze the sound out, but it seemed to me and perhaps to her angry boyfriend back in the house that she wasn't so straight either. I didn't bother to wait for her rebuttal. I just walked back out to the car.

"Look, I'm sorry." Naomi showed uncharacteristic

sympathy. But, of course, it wasn't her fault. I'd stepped into that mess all by myself.

"Well, not exactly," Naomi said she had known Cassandra was living with Luther Payton. "I made some inquires and put it together. I'm sorry Virginia," she said again, "for anything I had to do with it. I was kind of hoping for a happy ending."

"Yeah?" I told her, "so was I."

So is everybody.

In the end, I got my money, only it wasn't enough — it wasn't even half of what I thought it would be. The Whytebread/Gold Rush merger proceeded smoothly, greased by three dead bodies. Gold Rush came in and after about a week on tenterhooks the head guy called the old Whytebread people into his office one by one for an evaluation of our future prospects. When my turn came, he said if I kept up my work there would certainly always be a place for me at Gold Rush-Whytebread, which should have been more of a relief than it was.

Ellen Borgia secured an apparently well-deserved promotion to division head and Rupert Dean got canned. So did Herb Symon, courtesy of an anonymous letter detailing his office equipment theft ring. Gold Rush transferred Allison Price to Kansas City where she had heard the golf was fabulous, The Irishman announced he was retiring at the end of the year, and Alcee Couteau agreed to stay on indefinitely with the inexplicable title of Mail Room Director.

Life went on. Then, one Saturday just after the new year, I got an advice of deposit in the mail, made out in my full name with my middle initial, so there could be no mistakes. It was a very big check with zeros that seemed to stretch for a long way after the first few numbers, more zeros than I'd ever seen before in connection with my own accounts. The markets had dropped so precipitously in the intervening months that Gold Rush only ended up yielding about half the money I had originally expected, but even so the first time I read the amount, I found I couldn't make a sound.

I just poured myself a drink, put my feet up on the couch, and consulted *Hally's Bible Study* which had been picking up dust on my long undusted glass coffee table. It seemed the thing to do as somehow, I'd not yet found the time or inclination to research the meaning of Alcee's Post-it Note bible quote. Now I would have lots of time.

Vengeance is mine, said the Lord. Do not seek revenge, but leave a place for divine retribution. Hally's, a marvel of indexing, led me painlessly through a discussion of the Chapter and Verse, which amounted anticlimactically to a fancy rendering of "what comes around goes around," in the vernacular. It pretty much closed the book for me — on Alcee Couteau, Wesley Winslow, Justin.

I'd counted the zeros on my buyout check another couple more times, trying to read the number with the excitement I thought such a princely sum ought to have inspired. But of course it seemed to me that what the old man was saying had been absolutely flawless in its applicability. What comes around, goes around. So, I phoned The Irishman at home and quit.

About the Author

Nikki Baker lives in San Francisco, California. She is the author of three other novels.

Publications from
BELLA BOOKS, INC.
The best in contemporary lesbian fiction

P.O. Box 201007   Ferndale, MI 48220
Phone: 800-729-4992
www.bellabooks.com

MIRRORS by Marianne K. Martin. 208 pp. Jean Carson and
Shayna Bradley fight for a future together.   ISBN 1-931513-02-3 $11.95

THE ULTIMATE EXIT STRATEGY: A Virginia Kelly Mystery.
240 pp. The long-awaited return of the wickedly observant
Virginia Kelly.   ISBN 1-931513-03-1 $11.95

FOREVER AND THE NIGHT by Laura DeHart Young. 224 pp.
Desire and passion ignite the frozen Arctic in this exciting sequel
to the classic romantic adventure *Love on the Line.*
    ISBN 0-931513-00-7 $11.95

WINGED ISIS by Jean Stewart. 240 pp. The long-awaited sequel
to *Warriors of Isis* and the fourth in the exciting Isis series.
    ISBN 1-931513-01-5 $11.95

ROOM FOR LOVE by Frankie J. Jones. 192 pp. Jo and Beth must
overcome the past in order to have a future together.
    ISBN 0-9677753-9-6 $11.95

THE QUESTION OF SABOTAGE by Bonnie J. Morris. 144 pp. A
charming, sexy tale of romance, intrigue, and coming of age.
    ISBN 0-9677753-8-8 $11.95

SLEIGHT OF HAND by Karin Kallmaker writing as Laura Adams.
256 pp. A journey of passion, heartbreak and triumph that reunites
two women for a final chance at their destiny.   ISBN 0-9677753-7-X $11.95

MOVING TARGETS: A Helen Black Mystery by Pat Welch.
240 pp. Helen must decide if getting to the bottom of a mystery
is worth hitting bottom.   ISBN 0-9677753-6-1 $11.95

CALM BEFORE THE STORM by Peggy J. Herring. 208 pp. Colonel
Robicheaux retires from the military and comes out of the closet.
    ISBN 0-9677753-1-0 $11.95

OFF SEASON by Jackie Calhoun. 208 pp. Pam threatens Jenny
and Rita's fledgling relationship.   ISBN 0-9677753-0-2 $11.95

WHEN EVIL CHANGES FACE: A Motor City Thriller by Therese
Szymanski. 240 pp. Brett Higgins is back in another heart-pounding
thriller.   ISBN 0-9677753-3-7 $11.95

BOLD COAST LOVE by Diana Tremain Braund. 208 pp. Jackie
Claymont fights for her reputation and the right to love the woman
she chooses.   ISBN 0-9677753-2-9 $11.95

THE WILD ONE by Lyn Denison. 176 pp. Rachel never expected
that Quinn's wild yearnings would change her life forever.
                                                ISBN 0-9677753-4-5 $11.95

SWEET FIRE by Saxon Bennett. 224 pp. Welcome to Heroy — the
town with the most lesbians per capita than any other place on the
planet!   ISBN 0-9677753-5-3 $11.95

Visit
Bella Books
at

www.bellabooks.com